More praise for the novels of Carol Snow

"Snow's humoro   ce with a bit of social commenta   d the benefits of maturity in a youth- and romance-obsessed society."

—*Publishers Weekly*

"[A] witty, entertaining read."—Kim Alexander, XM Satellite Radio

"Often hilarious, frequently poignant . . . This is a wonderful book, with well-developed characters and interesting plot twists that make it a joy to read."

—*Romantic Times*

"*Been There, Done That* is a totally unique story with heartbreak, a look at what your college student is really doing, and how friendships and relationships change before our eyes. A book that will make you think, *Been There, Done That* will introduce you to a different sort of romance."

—*Romance Reviews Today*

"Using humor as a delightful way to lampoon contemporary life, Carol Snow provides . . . a terrific investigative tale filled with pleasant but surprising twists."

—*The Best Reviews*

"Carol Snow dares to explore some 'what ifs' of college life in a novel full of zany adventures, reflecting the wisdom of an adult revisiting the past and trying not to make the same mistakes. The author's subtle digs at ethics in journalism are right on target for her character's development, but this story has plenty of surprises. *Been There, Done That* is insightful and fun, with a hint of mystery and romance."

—*Fresh Fiction*

Getting Warmer

"With its entertaining combination of a realistically flawed heroine, sharp writing, and tart humor, *Getting Warmer* is absolutely delightful."
—*Booklist*

"[Snow] cleverly combines wit and drama in a page-turning novel. Readers will be drawn to the primary characters with their effortless charm and unique ability to reinvent themselves when meeting new people. Snow's charismatic writing style is superb, making this a true winner."
—*Romantic Times*

"Another great read exploring the lives and loves of likable emerging young women. This refreshingly honest story reveals some funny, sexy and meaningful moments, and that's no lie!"
—*Fresh Fiction*

"A fast-paced story and interesting people."
—*Romance Reviews Today*

"*Getting Warmer* is a terrific look at relationships . . . The support cast, mostly those connected to the school, her family, or his stalker, enhance the prime romance while two other love stories also provide depth."
—*The Best Reviews*

"Carol Snow does a wonderful job creating realistic, likable characters. Natalie is genuinely flawed, and readers can't help but like her for it . . . I'll be waiting on pins and needles for her next release."
—*Curled Up with a Good Book*

Here Today,
Gone to Maui

Carol Snow

B
BERKLEY BOOKS, NEW YORK

THE BERKLEY PUBLISHING GROUP
Published by the Penguin Group
Penguin Group (USA) Inc.
375 Hudson Street, New York, New York 10014, USA
Penguin Group (Canada), 90 Eglinton Avenue East, Suite 700, Toronto, Ontario M4P 2Y3, Canada
(a division of Pearson Penguin Canada Inc.)
Penguin Books Ltd., 80 Strand, London WC2R 0RL, England
Penguin Group Ireland, 25 St. Stephen's Green, Dublin 2, Ireland (a division of Penguin Books Ltd.)
Penguin Group (Australia), 250 Camberwell Road, Camberwell, Victoria 3124, Australia
(a division of Pearson Australia Group Pty. Ltd.)
Penguin Books India Pvt. Ltd., 11 Community Centre, Panchsheel Park, New Delhi—110 017, India
Penguin Group (NZ), 67 Apollo Drive, Rosedale, North Shore, 0632, New Zealand
(a division of Pearson New Zealand Ltd.)
Penguin Books (South Africa) (Pty.) Ltd., 24 Sturdee Avenue, Rosebank, Johannesburg 2196,
South Africa

Penguin Books Ltd., Registered Offices: 80 Strand, London WC2R 0RL, England

HERE TODAY, GONE TO MAUI

This is a work of fiction. Names, characters, places, and incidents either are the product of the author's imagination or are used fictitiously, and any resemblance to actual persons, living or dead, business establishments, events, or locales, is entirely coincidental. The publisher does not have any control over and does not assume any responsibility for author or third-party websites or their content.

Copyright © 2009 by Carol Snow
Cover design by Annette Fiore DeFex
Book design by Laura K. Corless

PRINTING HISTORY
Berkley trade paperback edition: January 2009

Berkley trade paperback ISBN: 978-0-425-22563-9

PRINTED IN THE UNITED STATES OF AMERICA

10 9 8 7 6 5 4 3 2 1

For Andrew

Acknowledgments

I couldn't have written this book without a lot of help (and my husband's frequent-flier miles).

For sharing their expertise, I'd like to thank divers Kris Billeter and Rebecca Topping; human resource maven Rita Mould; and Sergeant Jamie Becraft of the Maui Police Department. Any inaccuracies in this book are entirely my own fault, and I look forward to hearing about them in Amazon reviews and anonymous email messages.

Thank you, as always, to Cindy Hwang, Leis Pederson, Stephanie Kip Rostan, Monika Verma, and all of the other talented people at Berkley Books and the Levine Greenberg Literary Agency.

Thanks to my parents, Tom and Peggy Snow, for their vacation wisdom; Jeff and Diane Palumbo for the tour of Wailea; and Mel and Marilyn Rueben for their terrible taste in T-shirts.

And, finally, to the people of Maui: *Mahalo* for sharing your beautiful land.

Chapter 1

In the weeks leading up to my Maui vacation with Jimmy, I considered all of the things that could go wrong.

Illness ranked pretty high. I could catch a cold, which in turn could mutate into a sinus infection—hardly a rarity in this dirty Southern Californian air, and notoriously resistant to antibiotics. I could contract food poisoning or one of those nasty tummy bugs that my coworkers occasionally import from their kids. I could get the flu (some odd and potentially lethal strain not included in my annual shot), conjunctivitis, or shingles (which are reputed to be extremely painful, despite the comical name).

As our travel date approached without a cough, itch, or looming workplace epidemic, I turned my attention to traffic. Jimmy and I live at opposite ends of Orange County—he on the fashionable end (Laguna Beach) and I in the not-so-fashionable, forty-minutes-inland town of Brea, which is the Spanish word for "tar." Actually, Brea is a nice, unpretentious, wholesome kind of town—just the kind of place where you'd like to raise your kids, if you have them.

I don't.

Jimmy offered to drive to the airport because my car was nicer and more apt to be stolen. Without traffic, Jimmy could make it from Laguna Beach to Brea to LAX in an hour and a half. But since we weren't planning to drive at three o'clock in the morning on a Sunday, we could assume there would be traffic. With traffic, the trip could take three hours. Or five.

There are some things you just can't control.

Like flight delays. Or cancellations.

The odds of weather problems between Los Angeles and Maui were slim (though not impossible), but the flight originated in Atlanta and had to cross the entire country before embarking on the final tropical leg. After ten years here, I'd practically forgotten about weather, which Californians define as anything over a hundred degrees or under sixty, but I knew it was out there. I watched the Weather Channel. At least, I had ever since Jimmy asked me to spend a week with him in Maui.

There was an inch of snow in Denver. It was ten below in Chicago. In Brisbane, Australia, the month was the driest on record. (There's only so much they can say about local conditions on the Weather Channel, and I found the international segments oddly compelling.) But as for the weather between Atlanta and Los Angeles, and Los Angeles and Maui? The skies were clear.

It wasn't until Jimmy showed up at my condo on the day of our flight that I realized what all of my worrying had been about. He was an hour early—a relationship first. When I saw him standing in my doorway in a pale blue polo shirt, his sunglasses hanging from a cord around his neck, I burst into giddy laughter, equal parts joy and relief.

I had never really been concerned about sinus infections, I realized. About traffic or flight delays. All of that was just a diversion, a way to avoid thinking about the worst possibility of all.

I was afraid that Jimmy wouldn't show up.

I didn't think he'd stand me up or anything—he wasn't that unreliable. But he had a way of calling at the last minute, as I was applying my mascara or turning off the Weather Channel. Stuck in a meeting, he'd say. Buried with work. He'd make it up to me, he'd promise. Cross his heart and hope to die.

And today he'd come through. If a trip to Maui wasn't making it up to me, what was?

I never once worried about what would happen once we landed in Maui, after we'd gathered our luggage and set off for the resort.

As long as Jimmy showed up, the week would be perfect.

Chapter 2

"I gave myself an extra hour for traffic," he said as I put my arms around him.

"So you're on time."

"No, I'm an hour early." He kissed the top of my head and strode into my condo. "Something smells good."

"I made walnut bread this morning." He was in the kitchen now, nosing around. "It's on the counter."

He was already opening the fridge to get butter. Slicing the homemade bread, he made what I called his Hungry Jimmy noise: *Mmmmmmm.* He sounded like an airplane. In our first month or so together, Jimmy made that noise whenever he saw me coming out of the shower. Now, five months later, he made it when I baked. I take my baking very seriously, so I wasn't as offended as you might imagine.

He took a big bite. "I luff yer walnut bread."

"I know you do." I gazed at him for a moment and resisted the urge to say, *And I love you.*

It still shocked me, sometimes, to be going out with a guy as good-looking as Jimmy. I'm no troll, but Jimmy—blond, tanned, sculpted—had that kind of freak-of-nature beauty that makes people stare.

"Doesn't it bother you?" my sister, Beth, asked last fall, after I'd e-mailed a photo. "I mean, dating a guy who's prettier than you are?" (Rude, yes, but Beth is my only sibling, so she gets away with it.)

"You haven't seen me in a while," I told her. (Beth lives in New Jersey.) "I got my hair layered, and I've lost three pounds. Plus, I've started wearing this new mineral-based makeup. It's supposed to make your skin look airbrushed."

"I'm sure you look great," she said in a tone generally reserved for the stupid and infirm. "But this guy looks like a model." She said it like that was a bad thing. "He must have girls throwing themselves at him."

"He's given me no reason to doubt him," I said, suddenly wondering when he would.

Ten years earlier, I had moved to California on a whim. It was the first and seemingly the last spontaneous thing I ever did. I had just graduated from college in Boston, and one of my roommates, having received a job offer in Los Angeles, asked me to join her for the three-thousand-mile car ride. I said yes immediately, images of a new life already forming in my mind.

In California, I would live in the moment. I would take foggy-morning strolls on the beach; at night, I would fall asleep to the rhythm of the waves. I'd learn to surf, maybe even scuba dive. Surely California would make me a different person: freer, wilder. I pictured myself sporting a year-round tan and wearing colorful sarongs over my bikinis. (I never did master the sarong thing. It always looks like I've knotted a tablecloth around my waist.)

When we arrived in L.A. my friend spent two tearful hours on the phone with her Boston boyfriend before announcing that she was going home to marry him. (I missed the wedding. I missed the divorce, too.)

But I stayed. My first year was spent in a cramped, shared rental in Hermosa Beach, two miles from the Pacific. I could smell the ocean but I couldn't hear it. Mostly I heard traffic, sirens, and my roommates having sex with an assortment of boys, most of whom seemed to be named Jason.

A temp agency found me a clerical job with a company that made cement fiber roofing. They were so impressed with my collating and copying skills that they hired me to work full-time in their personnel department, first as an assistant, then as a benefits administrator. After a couple of years I outgrew that job and moved to my current employer, starting once again as an assistant in their human resources department (which sounds so much more interesting than "personnel") and eventually working my way up to department head. Career opportunities abound for anyone skilled at living by a daily planner.

I moved beyond that cramped rental in Hermosa Beach, too. After a year of parking tickets and an hour-long commute, I moved inland: first to Fountain Valley and then, later, to Brea, putting more and more distance between me and the Pacific. Now I live ten minutes from work, in a one-bedroom condo for which I secured a fifteen-year, fixed-rate mortgage. There's a Wal-Mart nearby, a Linens 'n Things, a T.J.Maxx. I cannot smell the ocean; I've almost forgotten that it's there. If not for the mild weather, I could be anywhere.

* * *

"When we get to the airport, if we have time, we can go over the week's itinerary," I said, giving my kitchen a quick wipe with the counter sponge (I use a different one for the dishes).

"What itinerary?"

"I've written up a tentative schedule of day-by-day activities. So we don't get to the end of the week and get really bummed because we forgot to go, say, parasailing." I rinsed the sponge and put it back in its stainless-steel holder.

Jimmy grinned. "That would totally ruin the vacation." He cut himself another hunk of bread and took it into the living room. I tried not to notice the crumbs tumbling onto my freshly vacuumed carpet. He clicked on the television and settled onto my couch. To encourage him to spend more time at my condo, I'd TiVoed all of Jimmy's favorite shows: the *CSI*'s, the *Law & Order*s, *Without a Trace*.

My condo is the first home I've ever bought. The day I closed on it (two years earlier, a month before my thirtieth birthday), I hauled in a sleeping bag to spend the night, too excited to wait for the movers. I've always disliked clutter, so I furnished it simply but warmly: beige carpet, toasty walls, sage furniture, and cranberry accents. At first, I accessorized with large bowls of fresh fruit and vases stuffed with fresh-cut flowers. I can only eat so much fruit on my own, though, so the oranges on the bottom of the bowls were always molding, emitting a biting, sour smell, while the apples turned mealy and brown, and the pears rotted and ran. As for the flowers, buying armfuls of tulips seemed homey at first, like giving myself a nice little treat. But after a while, the effort began to feel sad.

By the time Jimmy entered my life, the fruit bowls had been

stacked in cabinets, the vases shoved far back on the upper shelves. But still. I was proud of my little condo, with its granite-tile countertops, its double sink in the bathroom. I liked my gleaming cherry bed, my tidy kitchen table.

"Nice place," Jimmy said, the first time he saw my condo, a couple of nights after we met. "You know what it reminds me of?"

"What?" I said, thinking: *Decorating magazine?*

"A hotel room."

I'd added some more throw pillows since then, a few more prints on the wall. But Jimmy was right: my condo looked like a place where no one lived. Perhaps a few crumbs on the floor weren't so terrible.

"I think I'm ready," I said, consulting a list. "I've emptied the dishwasher, left a light on, locked my windows. I put vacation holds on my mail and the newspaper."

The list seemed too short. How could a life be so easy to leave, if only for a week? I didn't even have any pets to feed or plants to water.

"You shouldn't have put the hold on your newspaper," Jimmy said, flicking through the stations as if he were playing a video game.

"Why?" I pulled my black suitcase across the room to the door. I'd tied a yellow ribbon on the handle to make it easy to spot on the baggage carousel.

"You never want people to know you're not home. Someone who works for the newspaper could break in, or they could tip someone off."

"You don't honestly believe that," I said.

"You can't be too trusting."

* * *

We arrived at LAX three hours before our flight. "You win," I said after we'd checked in.

"What?" Jimmy asked, all innocence.

"We didn't have to be this early."

He stroked my brown hair. "Yes, we did. If we'd been merely on time, you would have worried."

"I just want things to be perfect," I said.

"I just want you to be happy."

We passed the time buying trashy magazines at a newsstand and drinking icy piña coladas at a surfer-themed lounge (surfboard-shaped tables, surfboards over the bar: you get the picture). We hadn't even boarded the plane, yet I already felt like I was on vacation. As I sucked out the bottom of my drink, Jimmy caught the bartender's eye and held up two fingers.

"As long as we've got a minute, we should go over the schedule," I said, reaching into my carry-on bag for my planner (at least I hadn't typed the list; that would have been really anal). Jimmy traveled to Maui on business at least once a month, but the trips were so packed with meetings that he never got to do any of the tourist things.

"I made up a schedule, too," Jimmy said.

"Really?" I was touched. Jimmy knew how much I liked to plan ahead.

He leaned back in his chair and crossed his tanned, toned arms behind his head. "Tonight? I'm thinking we arrive late and have sex."

"Okay . . ."

"Then tomorrow morning, we have sex and then go to the beach. Or maybe we should go to the beach and then have sex. It could go either way." He paused as if considering. "Day after that,

I'm thinking, beach, sex, and then the day after that, maybe we go to the pool for a change of pace. And then have sex."

I tried to look amused. And in a way, I was. Four weeks earlier, when Jimmy announced that his business was good, his frequent-flier balance was high, and he was taking me to Maui, I thought we were taking a step forward in our relationship. Instead, he'd almost immediately started pulling away from me. Some days he forgot to call. And more than once when he'd spent the night, he'd said, "I'm really tired. Okay if we just go to sleep?" I was starting to worry that he no longer found me attractive.

He leaned across the surfboard-shaped table and took my hand. "It doesn't matter what we do. I'm just pumped to be spending a whole week with you." He held my eyes until I smiled. "So, what's the plan?"

Still holding his hand, I looked at the list. "Tomorrow, Friday, I figure we'll explore the Hyatt and hang out by the pool, maybe walk down to Whaler's Village for dinner." I checked his eyes. He nodded.

"Saturday, I've penciled in sunrise at Haleakala—you know, the volcano—and a driving tour of the up-country. Sunday, diving and snorkeling in the morning, a walking tour of downtown Lahaina in the afternoon. Monday, the road to Hana—that'll take all day. Tuesday, parasailing off of Kaanapali Beach, and then a luau for dinner." I paused to check his reaction. "Too cheesy?"

"Nah, it sounds fun."

Back to the list. "Wednesday, we can drive to the town of Wailea. I know you've been there for work, but there's a lava field, a red sand beach—lots to explore. Thursday we're taking the red-eye out, so I'm thinking we take it easy, maybe hang by the pool."

"Wow," he said. "We're gonna need a vacation from our vacation."

I looked up from the list. "Is it too much? Because we can change things as we go along—you know, play it by ear. I just thought it would be helpful to have something to refer to."

He brushed my cheek with his fingers. "You're crazy, you know that? And I mean that in a good way."

"I'd better check in with work," I said, digging my cell phone out of my tropical-print tote bag. "Work" meant Wills Rubber Company, manufacturer of premium playground mats. I was the human resources manager.

Lena, the receptionist, put me on hold for about three minutes before finally answering. "Jane! Omigod, I'm so glad you called!"

"What's wrong?" I ran through my various to-do lists in my head without coming up with anything left undone.

"Tomorrow's Friday!" she said.

"I know," I said, thinking: *Friday, Friday—what was I supposed to do on Friday?* The monthly newsletter had been distributed, I'd given new-employee information to the payroll clerk, and I'd returned all of my messages and e-mails. A customer-service representative with a fondness for micro-miniskirts had received my standard "appropriate office attire" speech, while a receiving clerk had been put on notice about his chronic tardiness.

"Who's going to bring in muffins?" Lena demanded.

A piña colada appeared in front of me. I don't normally drink this much—or anything—during the day. Jimmy held his glass up in a toast. I winked.

"You always make muffins on Friday," Lena said. "You probably don't know how much that means to people, but honest to God, I've had at least five people say to me, 'If Jane's not here, who's going to bring the muffins?'"

Jimmy took a long drink of his piña colada. Then he looked at my breasts and licked his lips.

"You can always buy muffins," I told Lena.

"It's not the same," she said. "Everyone counts on you. It's like you're the company mom."

"I'm the *company mom*?" I said.

Jimmy threw back his head and laughed. A small white scar ran along his jawline. I loved that scar: everybody needs an imperfection.

"Try Costco," I told Lena. "You can get a dozen muffins for something like eight bucks."

After that, I turned off my cell phone. "Where were we?" I asked, picking up my drink.

"On our way to Maui," Jimmy said.

There was no question that Jimmy had changed my attitude toward work. Before we started dating, I arrived at the office early and left late—usually with my arms full of paperwork. My work was my life for the simple reason that I *had* no other life.

Ironically, the shift in attention had been good for my career. A month into the relationship, my boss called me into his office. Bob Wills had started Wills Rubber Company thirty-five years earlier. Mr. Wills was sixty-four years old, married with five grown children. He spoke softly and carried a big stick up his ass.

"Jane." He paused. "It has come to my attention."

He cleared his throat. He hummed. He always hummed when he had trouble finding the right words.

He took a deep breath and soldiered on. "What I mean is, here at Wills Rubber Company, we value your contributions." He turned red.

I had no idea what he was getting at.

Finally, he shoved a piece of paper at me.

MEMO
To: Jane Shea
From: Bob Wills
Re: Your future at Wills Rubber Company
Dear Jane:

It is my hope that you understand how much we value your contributions at Wills Rubber Company. Your work in Human Resources
has been superlative. Beyond that, your participation in the management team has helped form our vision for the future.

However, I cannot help but notice a change in you over the last
month. Your attire appears to be more studied, while you have
been spending more time away from the office.

I can only conclude that you have been interviewing for another job. If you are dissatisfied with your position or prospects at
Wills Rubber, please let me know. We are prepared to take whatever steps are necessary to retain you.

I read the memo twice. And then I squinted at Bob Wills, who
appeared to be on the verge of hyperventilation.

"You think I'm looking for another job?" I asked.

He nodded nervously and began to hum.

"But, why? Just because I've left early a few times?" There really
wasn't anything to say about my "studied attire." I had worn dresses
a couple of times, it's true, but today I was dressed as usual, in a
pair of pressed Ann Taylor slacks and a crisp blue blouse.

"You seem—different," he said. "I can't explain it."

I said, "I'm just trying to find a better balance between my job
and the rest of my life."

I glanced back at the memo. "What steps, exactly, would you
take to retain me?"

"Salary reviews are in April," he told me. "You can expect good things."

Lena, the receptionist, didn't think I was looking for another job. When I'd been dating Jimmy for just over a week, she looked me up and down and said, "You're getting laid, aren't you?"

When I didn't answer—just turned bright red—she said, "It's about damn time."

* * *

Two hours later, Jimmy and I settled into our (first class!) seats as mournful Hawaiian music played over the speakers. Since Jimmy traveled so much for business, he'd cashed in his frequent-flier miles to cover the plane ride and his American Express miles for the hotel.

A plump, gray-haired couple took the seats behind us. She had elaborately curled hair and parrot earrings. He, like about a third of the men on the flight, wore a Hawaiian shirt.

After fastening my seat belt, I checked my watch, pleased to see that the flight was on time, and did a quick check for cell-phone messages. I was relieved to see there were none, though a little perturbed to realize I was not indispensable.

"Are you going to call your office?" I asked Jimmy. Jimmy owned a designer wetsuit business, "Jimmies." They specialized in the dive market, though a lot of surfers were starting to wear their suits as well.

"Nah," he said. "They're fine without me."

"You won't be able to use your phone for the next five hours."

I sounded like a mom, I realized with dismay. Jimmy was always talking about growing his business, how he wanted to be a major player in the wetsuit market. But while he did travel a lot, he seemed to forget about work the moment he was away from it.

Also, the company budget was so tight that he'd been forced to wait tables on the side. If I hadn't been so eager for this vacation, I would have suggested that he save his frequent-flier miles for business use.

I admired Jimmy's live-in-the-moment attitude, but I couldn't stop thinking about tomorrow. Rather, I couldn't stop thinking about the rest of my life. Jimmy had said several times—oh, so casually—that he couldn't even consider settling down until his business became more established. He was thirty-four years old, and I was thirty-two; surely he wouldn't make me wait forever.

Jimmy pulled the airline magazine from the pocket in front of him. "I've built an amazing team. They can handle anything that happens. Scott can deal with any customer issues, and Ana's on top of the logistics."

At Ana's name, I felt a pang of jealousy. Ana was the office manager who, according to Jimmy, was incredibly smart and a top-notch diver, a committed environmentalist and adventurer. She was also twenty-five years old and single. I once asked, as casually as I could manage, why Jimmy had never introduced me to her or Scott, the sales manager. Or any of the other employees whose names he dropped into conversation. Jimmy shrugged and said, "When I get together with them outside of the office, it's to dive. And you don't dive."

One day, when Jimmy canceled our plans at the last minute, saying he had an unexpected business trip, I called his office. He'd never given me the number, but it was listed on his Web site (which was perpetually under construction). To be honest, I half expected the number to be no longer in service or nonexistent, the entire business an elaborate hoax.

But a woman answered: "Hey, this is Ana." Her voice was low

and smooth—not sexy, exactly, but cool. This was a woman who could slip fifty feet under the ocean's surface while looking hot in a wetsuit.

"Is this, um—a business?" I asked, thinking I'd gotten the wrong number.

"Yeah, it's Jimmies, Inc.," she said. "We do wetsuits." In the background, I could hear the kind of rap music that would have sent Mr. Wills running to his computer to compose a memo.

"I'm looking for Mr. James," I said formally, as if I didn't know him. His first name was actually Michael, but since his father was Michael, too, he'd gone by Jimmy since he was a little kid.

"Not here," she said. "You want his cell?"

"That's okay. I'll try him some other time."

I hung up feeling immensely relieved, ashamed of myself for doubting him. I trusted him wholeheartedly . . . until the next time he canceled at the last minute.

I'd Googled him, of course, right at the beginning.

The world was full of men named Michael James. In Wichita, a science teacher named Michael James posted his homework assignments online (his class was studying cell division); in British Columbia, ninth-grade Michael James had an odd fixation on Japanese comic books; and across the pond in England, a Michael James posted a daily blog about gardening, much of which revolved around snail eradication. And those were just some of the live ones. There were loads of dead Michael Jameses, too.

When I checked *Michael James* and *scuba*, though, I got a hit on his company, Jimmies, Incorporated (It should be "Jimmy's," I thought immediately). Two clicks got me to their Web site, which had a catchy logo, the *J* shaped like a wave, and an intro blurb:

Jimmies, Inc.
Artistic Wetsuits
Dive and Surf with Style
Laguna Beach, California
Michael James, Founder and Owner

The page had a menu bar (History, People, Job Opportunities, Order) and a phone number, but a line at the bottom of the page announced, "We are currently updating our site to better serve our customers. For more information, please call our customer-service line."

"You should get your Web site running," I told Jimmy.

He shrugged. "People call us. It's no big deal."

"You spelled *Jimmies* wrong," I blurted, another day.

He shook his head, confused. "What do you mean?"

"Your company name. There should be an apostrophe."

He rolled his eyes at the absurdity. "Nobody likes apostrophes," he said.

*   *   *

Now, on the jumbo airliner, he flipped open his in-flight magazine. "Check it out—kayaking!" He flipped the page. "Or—wait. We could ride mountain bikes down a volcano. Some of my customers on the island have told me about that—they say it's a real rush."

I pulled out my planner and flipped to the itinerary. "We could do that . . . Sunday. After watching the sunrise. There's a company that drives you up with the bikes, then you ride down the volcano. I saw it in my guidebook." I made a note in my planner. "I can't wait to see the Hyatt."

"You're going to love it." He gazed out at the tarmac. "It's my favorite place to stay."

Every guidebook I'd read (and believe me, I'd read a lot) said the Hyatt was one of the nicest resorts on Maui. I'd spent hours perusing their Web site, blinking in wonder at their list of amenities: enormous rock pool, white sand beach, full-service spa, tennis courts, shopping arcade. There were penguins, parrots, flamingos, and swans. Best of all, Jimmy had cashed in extra Amex points to reserve an ocean-view room. Perhaps I should amend my itinerary. Would we even want to leave the grounds?

I put away the planner and got myself into vacation mode by pulling out a trashy magazine. The cover showed a beautiful, smiling celebrity couple with the headline OUR SECRETS TO A HAPPY MARRIAGE.

I held the cover up to Jimmy. "Look at this. You can pretty much guarantee that a year from now they'll be back on the cover, only this time it will say, 'What Went Wrong.'" I don't read these kinds of magazines much, just at the hairdresser and on airplanes, but I secretly love them because they make me feel superior.

The plane pulled away from the gate and taxied down the runway. When it finally accelerated with stomach-dropping speed, I looked out the window and saw the gray tarmac fall away below me. We soared over the Pacific Ocean, a thick layer of brown air hugging the horizon.

The plane hit an air pocket and dipped suddenly. I sucked in my breath. Throughout the cabin, passengers yelped in alarm. Soon, though, we eased into smoother air.

The older woman behind us sighed. "If we're gonna die in a plane crash, I sure hope it's on the way *home* from Hawaii."

I smiled in agreement. Whether or not Jimmy and I wound up together, this was a week I didn't want to miss.

Chapter 3

I'm a big believer in the power of worrying, but even though I forgot to worry about losing my bag, it slid down onto the carousel without a hitch, the yellow ribbon still tied to the handle. Jimmy's blue duffel followed shortly after, as did his beat-up black diving bag.

"I think I'm getting a hangover," I moaned, pulling my wheeled bag to the curb. The first-class flight attendants had plied us with wine during the flight. "And it's only . . ." I checked my watch. "Ten o'clock?"

The evening sky was pink around the edges: it couldn't possibly be that late. "Oh—I forgot about the time change." I giggled. In my whole life, I had never once forgotten to change my watch when crossing time zones—but then, I had never drunk wine for three thousand miles, either.

"How's this?" Jimmy said. "You wait here with the bags, and

I'll go get the rental car. That way we don't have to haul everything on the shuttle."

"Great idea." I sat down on a concrete block and inhaled the scent of tropical flowers.

He leaned over and kissed me. "Back before you know it."

But he wasn't. After half an hour, the concrete block felt really hard under my butt. Near me, a man sucked on a cigarette next to a "No Smoking" sign. I pulled a sweater out of my tote bag. The winter in California had been unusually warm; here it felt chilly.

A white sedan pulled up to the curb. I popped off my block, squinting at the man inside. He opened the door: not Jimmy. An SUV glided to a stop. Two more white sedans. People and luggage piled inside. These were the smart travelers, the ones who'd thought to send someone on to the car-rental agencies the instant the plane landed.

When Jimmy had been gone forty minutes, I dug out my cell phone. The call went straight through to voice mail; he mustn't have turned his phone on yet.

A silver minivan stopped, and a mother and her four children (three of whom were crying) jammed inside. It suddenly seemed too quiet around me, with the sounds of cars and planes but no people.

A crazy idea flashed through my head: what if Jimmy had forgotten about me? He wouldn't, of course. And yet: what if?

The rental car was red and sporty. I sighed with relief and exhaustion when the driver's-side door opened and Jimmy got out. "I was afraid you'd forgotten me," I joked. But when I realized how needy that sounded, I said, "I thought I'd have to find another sugar daddy to put me up for the week."

As he grabbed the bags and started hoisting them in the trunk, he smiled, but something in his face made me nervous. He didn't hold my eyes long enough.

I got in the car and buckled my seat belt. The seats were so low to the ground it felt like I was sitting in a hole. Jimmy put his hand on my leg. "Long line at the car rental," he said.

"No worries," I said, just glad to be on our way.

He took his hand off of my leg and shifted into gear. "I have to tell you something," he said, his eyes straight ahead, his jaw tense.

Oh. My. God. He is going to dump me. He has taken me three thousand miles just to set me loose.

"What?" I asked, keeping my voice steady.

"When I was picking up the car, I called the hotel—you know, to confirm." He shot me a sideways glance and returned his eyes to the road.

"And?"

He sighed. "They lost our reservation. Or something. The reservations person at the Hyatt said the American Express points never transferred."

"Did you call American Express?"

He nodded. "They were really apologetic, said they'd award me some bonus points to make up for it, but there's nothing they can do."

"Did the Hyatt have any more rooms available?" I knew the answer already.

He shook his head. "Completely sold out. February's the busiest month. I called all the other hotels on Kaanapali—the Sheraton, the Westin, the Marriott . . ." He moaned and gave me a pained look. "Oh, baby, I am so, so sorry."

"It's okay!" I said, feeling weirdly relieved. So we might be sleeping on the beach: at least he hadn't dumped me. "So, are we—um, that is . . ."

"I called in a favor," he said. "Got us a studio condo. Really nice place—it's a garden-view unit, but the complex is right on the beach. The view won't be as good as at the Hyatt, but it'll be more private, and we'll have a lot more space. But there's no room service or anything, and no pool boys to bring you drinks."

A condo sounded nice: comfortable and relaxing. "You can be my pool boy," I said.

"I'd love to be your pool boy." He reached over and squeezed my knee. "Thanks for being so understanding. I really love that about you."

*   *   *

The complex was not on the beach. It was on the water, true, but there was no sand, just a seawall that fell right down to some perilous-looking waves. And our condo was not garden view; it was parking-lot view.

"Hey, this is nice!" Jimmy chirped, dumping his duffel bag in the middle of the living-room floor. In the middle of the bedroom floor. In the middle of the floor.

"Mm," I said.

"Check it out—there's a kitchen!" he said. "Which is totally awesome since you like cooking so much."

It did not have a kitchen. It had a couple of hazardous-looking burners, a grotty toaster oven, a dinky sink, a minifridge, and a few brown cabinets that were supposed to look like wood but were obviously brown plastic with some sad attempts at wood-grain designs. The room stank of lemon disinfectant.

"I don't usually cook on vacation," I said—a true statement, since I rarely go on vacation.

"You're mad at me," Jimmy said huskily.

"No!" I said, thinking: *Yes!*

"I'll make it up to you," he murmured, stepping closer.

"How?" I am nothing if not forgiving.

He ran his hands down my arms. He had this way of looking at me, with his chin tucked down and his blue eyes holding my gaze. It was like he was shooting love lasers straight at me. And, understand: I am not the kind of person who normally uses words like *love lasers*.

"How do you want me to make it up to you?" he asked.

I buried my face in his shoulder. "I'm open to suggestions."

"What kind of suggestions?"

"Um, suggestive suggestions?"

I know. Pathetic. But I have fully embraced and accepted my inhibitions.

"Are you hungry?" he murmured.

"Starving," I said, surprised to realize it was true.

He gave my arms a quick squeeze and strode over to the mini-fridge. It was empty. Obviously.

"Hmm," he said. "You got any snacks left over from the plane?"

"Let's go out," I said. "There are a whole bunch of places along Kaanapali Beach. I circled a couple in the guidebook." I reached into my tote bag and pulled out the book. "There's public parking at, let's see . . . Whaler's Village. And then maybe we can walk down to—"

"I don't want to go to Kaanapali," he interrupted.

"What? Why?"

He ran a long-fingered hand through his thick blond hair. "I spent so much time on the phone tonight. You know, calling all those hotels. It was just so fucking frustrating. All I could think about was how you've been looking forward to this week—I mean, you've got that big schedule and all . . ."

"It's okay," I said. "We're here. And it's—nice. So, let's just have fun. We'll head over to Kaanapali and—"

"Kaanapali will just remind me of how I fucked up."

I stared. He was supposed to be the laid-back one.

"We could just, you know, get takeout," he said. "Aren't you tired? We have all week to explore."

"Fine," I said, clenching my jaw and shooting something other than love lasers his way. "Let's just eat peanuts. And maybe watch TV. That'll be fun."

He put his arms around me. "Baby, I'm sorry. You're right. This is supposed to be your vacation. Let's go out to dinner—someplace nice. I just want you to be happy."

That was all he had to say. "You're right," I said. "We've got the whole week ahead of us. Let's just go pick up some food, maybe eat it outside."

*   *   *

Funny thing about Taco Bell: it tastes better in Maui, especially if you're looking at the ocean. Within the hour, we were out on the lounge chairs, eating grilled stuffed chicken burritos and sipping Diet Cokes.

When I finished my food, I set the take-out bag on the grass and leaned back against my lounge chair. "Mm," I said. "We're finally here."

"Do you think a week will be long enough?" he asked, sounding wistful.

"No way. I could stay here forever."

The air was misty damp but not really cold, and my jeans and sweatshirt kept me warm. Guitar notes trickled out from a condo behind us as gentle waves glowed silver underneath a full moon rimmed with clouds. Stars appeared in patches, but I forgot to make a wish.

The misty dampness turned to a light rain.

"You want to go in?" Jimmy asked.

I shook my head. "It's too perfect here. And I haven't finished my soda." I closed my eyes and felt the warm dampness on my face.

"Look!" Jimmy grabbed my arm. "A moon-bow!"

"Huh?" I opened my eyes and there it was: a ghostly rainbow arching over the ocean. "But it's night!" I blinked, half expecting it to disappear, but it only grew brighter.

"It happens sometimes when the moon is bright and it starts to rain. I think it's supposed to be good luck. Or bad luck. Some kind of luck."

"Where's the pot of gold?" I asked. "Under the waves?"

"At the bottom of the sea," he suggested. "Buried treasure."

"Guess the leprechauns will go scuba diving tonight." I turned to Jimmy. He looked so handsome in the moonlight, his streaky hair curling at wild angles, his blue eyes wide with wonder. I put my hand on his face and leaned over to kiss him. After a few minutes, we pulled apart. I looked back at the sky, but the moon-bow had gone.

Suddenly, strangely, I wondered whether the leprechauns had drowned.

Chapter 4

Here's what happens when you travel west: the first morning, you wake up with the sunrise. Sometimes you wake up before the sunrise. You peek out the window and think, *Yippee! I've got this whole great day ahead of me!*

And then it hits you: nobody else is up. Nothing is open. You might as well just go back to sleep.

I woke up a few minutes before five. The room was completely dark, so I turned on the bathroom light and left the door open a crack. Jimmy was out cold, breathing slowly. He was lying on his back, one arm over his head, his mouth open slightly. He'd pushed the white sheets down to his waist, revealing the edge of his blue boxer shorts. His chest was bare. I liked to look at Jimmy when he slept because I could really stare at him. If I looked at him like that when he was awake, he might think my feelings for him ran too deep—deeper than his feelings for me, at any rate. And I didn't want him to think that.

Once I finished ogling him, I crept over to the window and peeked around the curtains. The sky was still murky. I crawled back into bed and slid right next to Jimmy, hoping he'd sense me and wake up. He didn't. I closed my eyes—just for a minute, I told myself.

When I woke up again, he was gone. I pulled on shorts and a T-shirt and pushed open the heavy curtains. The parking lot was looking lovely today. Happily, the previous inhabitants had left half a package of ground Kona coffee, along with filters and some sugar. I started a pot of coffee. Later I'd buy milk.

While the coffee gurgled I set about unpacking, having fought the urge to do so the night before. "Stop acting so anal-retentive around Jimmy" had topped my New Year's resolutions. But now, alone, I pulled out my packing list and checked off each item as I placed it in a drawer. I'd check everything off again when I left. That way, I could make sure I didn't leave anything behind.

Once I'd tucked away my final items (1 pair gym shorts; 3 pairs gym socks; 1 silk nightgown), I poured myself a cup of coffee and settled on the rattan sofa.

The room had looked shabby last night; in daylight it was borderline decrepit. The industrial carpeting was six shades of brown, at least four shades of which were unintentional. The rattan furniture had lost its sheen; several pieces looked ready to collapse, and the edges were splintery. As for the sofa and chairs, the cushions were of two mismatched patterns: one a green tropical print, the other an orange tropical print. The green cushions were in slightly better shape. Slightly.

I stuck the room key, my cell phone, and a packet of airplane crackers in my pocket and took my bittersweet coffee outside. A stocky man with enormous shoulders was pulling a big white laundry cart through the parking lot and whistling. When he saw me, he smiled and said, "Aloha."

"Hi," I said. I scanned the lot; Jimmy's red rental car was gone. Maybe he was getting milk for my coffee? And a muffin, perhaps?

In the daylight, I could really see the condo complex. That was not a good thing. The cinder-block building was long and rectangular, three stories high, painted the peachy-beige color that small children use when drawing pictures of people. Out front, a brown sign with swirly white letters said, MAUI HI VILLAS. There were some palm trees by the edge of the road, some out-of-control salmon bougainvilleas.

The condos looked far better from the other side—the ocean side. The building was pretty much the same, but the Pacific was magnificent. The lightest breeze tickled my skin. The waves were small, their sound soothing, like a tuneless stringed instrument.

Our lounge chairs from last night were free. Actually, all of the lounges were free since it was still pretty early, about eight o'clock. I settled myself down, the rubber kissing my bare legs, and sipped my lukewarm coffee. The air smelled of salt and flowers. I gazed out at the island of Molokai, which rose from the blue water like an apparition. At my side, a tiny brown bird hopped around on the grass, looking up in expectation of a crumb. I opened the packet of crackers from the plane and tossed a piece. Ten or more birds appeared almost immediately, chirping and hopping and knocking into one another. They were sort of cute, sort of creepy: Hitchcock in Hawaii.

In the distance, I saw one splash, and then another. "A whale!" I blurted. The birds were unimpressed. I wished Jimmy had been there to see it.

Once I'd polished off the crackers and coffee, I pulled out my cell phone. I hit Jimmy's number but hung up before it connected. I scrolled down my address list until I found *Mom*, and hit the button.

After four rings, her answering machine picked up. "Hi, Mom, it's me. Jane. I've been meaning to call you. I guess I should have told you earlier, but I'm in Maui right now. With Jimmy. We're here for the week, flying back next Thursday. I'll call you when I get home."

When I hung up, I exhaled. I felt relieved that I hadn't had to talk to my mother. And then, immediately, I felt guilty about feeling relieved.

*   *   *

Let's just get the unhappy-childhood crap out of the way so we can get back to the story. Some recent studies have concluded that many children of divorce have a difficult time forming lasting relationships as adults. To those researchers, I say: "Duh. How much time and money did you spend on this research?"

My parents started dating during their junior year of college and got married a month after graduation. My father became an accountant. My mother became pregnant. Everything went according to plan—until the day my father walked out.

According to my mother, my father once promised to stick around "until the children left home." Presumably, before that, he promised to stick around, you know, forever, but my mother doesn't seem to care about that. He half kept his half-assed promise, leaving the week after my sister left for nursing school. I was fourteen.

My mother never expressed anger at the fact of his leaving; it was the timing that pissed her off. "Four more years," she'd hiss, as if he were a slacker politician who had chosen not to run for reelection. "Couldn't he have given us four more years?"

They sold our pretty white Colonial house (four bedrooms, roomy backyard, on a leafy cul-de-sac) and split the proceeds. My father, in a fit of what he termed generosity but what I saw as making a clean break, let my mother keep all of the furniture. It made his moving easier. Two months after walking out, he found a "great job opportunity" in Florida. The great job opportunity was named Elise. They're still together.

My mother, in what she termed sentimentality but what I deemed a refusal to face reality, insisted on shoving every bed, dresser, table, plate, picture, vase, and candlestick into a cramped two-bedroom town house. Let's just say that no one has ever said that my mother's town house looks like a hotel. Since she had no real work experience, she wound up taking a job at Home Depot. She's been with the store almost as long as my father has been with Elise. I'll say this for my mother: she knows a lot more about drywall grades and plumbing hardware than the average middle-aged woman.

My mother didn't unload any of the furniture the following year when my sister, Beth, dropped out of nursing school to marry her high school boyfriend, a concrete contractor named Sal Piccolo. They're still married and living in New Jersey. I have learned not to make Mafia jokes.

Beth and Sal have five girls (Samantha, Savannah, Stacey, Sierra, and—though it pains me to write it—Sindy), but they're not done. As Sal says, "We'll keep trying till we get a boy." He says this in front of the girls. Beth just smiles. Beth lets Sal do pretty much whatever he wants. Most of the things Sal wants involve really big televisions and overstuffed recliners with drink holders. If Beth ever read about the divorce studies—which is to say, if she ever found time to sit down, much less read a magazine—she'd puff herself up and say that the researchers were wrong: obviously, she'd mastered the secret to a happy marriage.

And who knows? Maybe she is happy. Sal hasn't left her, at least not yet. Among us Shea woman, that counts as success.

* * *

I hung around with my empty coffee cup and the birds for about a half hour longer than I really wanted to. I liked the idea of Jimmy coming back to an empty condo and maybe even missing me for a minute or two.

Instead, one look at the parking lot told me that Jimmy was still out, so I wasn't surprised to find the condo exactly as I had left it. After a brief, familiar pang—one part panic to two parts sadness with a dash of resignation—I relaxed.

At home I worried that every time I saw Jimmy might be the last. It's not anything he did or said. On the contrary, he usually left me with a kiss and a casual "I'll call you later." That's assuming he was awake. With our different work schedules, I often left him sleeping. ("I'm the boss," he said. "I can be late if I want to.") At first, I'd searched for a note when I got home. Now I knew that Jimmy does not leave notes.

But here in Hawaii, I reminded myself, I had nothing to worry about. Jimmy would not disappear. Where could he possibly go?

It was almost lunchtime in California. I sat on the rumpled bed and called my office.

"Jane!" Lena said. "Shouldn't you be on the beach or something?"

"It's early here," I said.

"Oh, yeah, that's right! So, you and Jimmy should be getting all hot and sweaty right about now."

"We've got to come up for air sometime." I forced a laugh. "Did anyone buy muffins?" I asked, changing the subject.

"Oh, no—ya know what we did? Manny—he's in production? He lives in LaHabra, and he stopped off at Boston Donuts on his way to work. That's down on Imperial. I had a jelly-filled one. You ever try one of those?"

"Yes," I said.

"Manny got all kinds—jelly-filled, cream-filled, chocolate, glazed. Everybody was like, 'Oh, cool—donuts!' So, no offense, everyone really likes your muffins and all, but people are really liking the donuts, and Manny said he can pick them up every Friday, as long as he can get money from petty cash to pay for them."

"So, you don't . . . people don't want my muffins?"

"It's not that! People love your muffins, your muffins are awesome. It's just that people are really liking the donuts. But you can still bring in muffins, if you want. Maybe we could have both. I just thought it might be nice for you to have a break, is all. I know you're, like, really busy with Jimmy, and all."

"Oh, yeah." I looked around the empty room. "Jimmy keeps me busy, all right. Speaking of which, I'd better go soon. Can you put me through to Mr. Wills?"

"Morning, Jane," he said. "We sure missed your muffins today." Since Mr. Wills suffered from high cholesterol, I always offered low-fat alternatives. He was especially fond of my apple-oatmeal scones. "Are you having a nice vacation?" he asked.

"Oh, it's great," I said. "Just thought I should check in."

He made his little humming noise. "I wouldn't want to interrupt your vacation," he said finally. "But I just put together some target numbers for the sales force, and I'd love to get your input. Does your hotel have a business center? I could e-mail you . . ."

"Sure," I said. "I'll get it back to you by tomorrow." Maui Hi didn't have hair dryers, much less a business center, but there had to be an Internet café around here someplace.

*   *   *

Jimmy came in just as I finished making the bed (which meant straightening the blankets and sheets; the beige coverlet looked and smelled so suspicious, I'd folded it up and shoved it in the closet).

"Hi," I said, stopping myself before I could ask, *Where were you?*

"Hey, baby—you miss me?" he asked, dropping his key and a white plastic bag on the table.

"Of course," I said, with just enough of a smirk to make him wonder.

He was wearing faded yellow board shorts, a sleeveless white T-shirt, and a shark-tooth necklace. His hair, which was slightly shaggier than usual and a little damp, was pushed behind his ears. He looked really, really cute.

"I had to make some business calls, and I didn't want to wake you. So I drove out to a beach and called from there. When I was done, I jumped in the water—felt great."

I was a little hurt that he'd gone swimming without me, but I was happy about the business calls. Every step toward a more solid business meant a step toward a more solid relationship. Right?

"I've been on the phone to my office, too," I said. (Translation: I have not just been sitting around waiting for you to return.) "I figured I'd catch people before they went to lunch. Who were you talking to?"

"People around here, mostly," he said. "Trying to set up some meetings."

I glanced at the clock. "You left pretty early. Did you wake anyone up?"

"Nah—divers get up with the sun."

"I called my mom, too," I said. "She wasn't home, but I left a message. Did you tell your parents we were coming here?"

He shrugged. "They don't care what I do. I travel so much, it would be hard to keep up with my schedule." Jimmy had grown up in Lancaster, a desert town about a hundred miles inland from Los Angeles, but his parents had moved to Arizona shortly after he graduated from high school. He'd said, "We're just not very close—nobody's fault really, we're just totally different people," but I always got the sense that he was hurt by their semiabandonment.

"I'd like to meet them sometime," I said casually (and not for the first time).

"Sure," he said (as he always did). "Next time they're in town." He fingered his shark-tooth necklace.

"New jewelry?"

He glaced down at the neckace. "I thought a shark tooth was more manly than a lei. I bought you something." He reached inside the white plastic bag that said ABC STORES in blue lettering.

"This is for you." He handed me a string of white shells on a cardboard backing.

I smiled. "A bracelet?" Jimmy had never given me something "just because."

"An anklet," he said.

"Really?" The happy feeling spread through my chest. "I've never owned an anklet before."

"I kind of figured." He dug into the bag again and pulled out a plastic-wrapped muffin. "I thought you'd be hungry."

"I am."

"I had one, too," he said. "It's not very good. I think your muffins have ruined me for anyone else's."

"I think you've ruined me for anyone else," I purred, slinking toward him. He circled me and held me tight.

"I have to leave you," he muttered.

"What?" I said, too sharply, stepping back and looking him in the face.

"I have a meeting today. Well, two meetings, actually. One in"—he checked the digital clock by the bed—"forty-five minutes. And the other one for lunch." He bit his lip. "I'm sorry, baby."

"Oh," I said, stepping back. "It's no big deal. I'll just—swim. And explore. And read. I brought a whole stack of books."

"You're the best," he said, kissing my forehead before heading to the shower.

* * *

As disappointed as I was, there was no point letting the morning go to waste. I could settle in and do some necessary errands.

A quick check of the brown plastic cabinets revealed salt, pepper, rice-wine vinegar, soy sauce ("please refrigerate after opening"), and curry powder. Far in the back was a tin of baking powder, probably left over from the last millennium and presumably inactive. An exploration of the lower cabinets turned up a rusted cake tin and two warped cookie sheets that just might fit in the toaster oven. And, oh—two fondue pots. Because no Hawaiian vacation would be complete without fondue.

The condo office was three doors down from our studio. Jimmy had left me in the car when he'd checked in the night before, so I hadn't seen it yet. I expected something dark and shabby, and I wasn't disappointed. The room was deep and narrow, with only one parking-lot-view window to let in light. Hula music gurgled from two wall-mounted speakers, only partially masking the buzzing from the fluorescent lights overhead. Bamboo-print wallpaper covered the walls, while framed posters advertised catamaran rides, snorkel trips, and luaus. In the middle of the room, a bunch of rattan chairs circled a glass coffee table. A long counter overlooked it all from the back wall.

The woman behind the counter had a wide, calm face with perfectly square teeth. Her skin was mocha-colored, her shiny black hair pulled back into a braid. She could have been twenty-five or forty-five. Her blue polyester muumuu was at least two sizes too big. Her name tag said MARY.

"Aloha," she said when I walked in the door.

Lacking the Hawaiian words for "this place sucks," I said "aloha" back and wandered to the counter. There was a rack filled with brochures advertising everything from skyline tours to sunset cruises to bike rides down the volcano.

The grocery store was a bit far, Mary told me, but there was a convenience store just down the street. As for an Internet café, I'd have to go into Lahaina, which meant waiting until Jimmy returned.

The road to the convenience store was leafy, narrow, and overrun by rental cars. I jumped into the bushes twice to avoid getting run down. By the time I arrived, I was breathing heavily and sweating profusely. Also, I was starving. It was still morning in Maui, but my stomach hadn't gotten the memo. Praying I wouldn't get food poisoning, I bought a chicken teriyaki bowl from a roadside vendor and wolfed it down on the spot.

This was not the kind of morning I had envisioned when I'd drawn up my itinerary.

Fortunately, the convenience store had everything I needed, at only two or three times the price I would have paid on the main-land. I bought cereal, milk, orange juice, yogurt, minibananas, a bunch of tropical flowers, a bottle of sunscreen, and a cheap snor-keling set with flippers (just so we're clear, by "cheap" I am refer-ring to quality, not price). Packages of homemade baked goods sat on the counter. I chose pineapple-mango scones.

I barely noticed the condo's ugliness as I unpacked my grocer-ies and arranged the flowers in a chunky glass vase. Nesting al-ways makes me feel better.

When I was done, I balanced a scone on a square of paper towel and headed to the office. Mary laughed in delight and said *"mahalo,"* which means "thank you" in Hawaiian (eighteen hours here, and I was practically fluent). She took a bite and nodded. "Mm—'s good."

The door opened, and a couple walked in. They were about my age, maybe a little older, and dressed almost exactly the same, in denim shorts and white logo T-shirts. The woman snagged a whale watch brochure. She had blond hair, stringy at the ends, with about an inch of dark roots.

Her husband leaned on the counter, his underarm hair tufting out of his sleeveless shirt. He smelled like banana mixed with co-conut mixed with car grease. Really, he should have spent the ex-tra two bucks on better suntan lotion. "We got a problem with our air-conditioning," he said to Mary.

"What air-conditioning?" she asked.

"Exactly," he said.

She blinked at him. "Excuse me?"

"The AC," he said. "Pfft." He sliced the air with his hand. "Not working."

Mary bit her lip. "The units aren't air-conditioned. Did you try opening the window?"

He stared at her. "Of course not! I didn't want to let out the air-conditioning! So you're telling me—oh, man!" He threw back his head in disgust.

"I told ya we shoulda stayed at a hotel," his wife muttered, slipping the whale pamphlet back into the display.

"We have electric fans," Mary said. "You want one in your room?"

"What for?" the guy grumbled. "So we can move the hot air around?"

Mary kept a pleasant smile on her face.

"Hair dryer," the woman prompted under her breath.

"Oh, yeah," the guy said. "You got a hair dryer my wife can use? She didn't pack hers 'cause she figured you'd have them."

Mary shook her head. "Sorry."

The guy grunted in disgust. "This place blows."

"Well, that was rude," I said once they left (even if I did agree with the assessment).

Mary waved the air with her hand. "That was nothing. Some guests, they come here expecting room service, a heated pool . . ." She chuckled. "In-room massages."

I laughed along with her. (In-room massages? I could totally go for that.)

She continued, "So I say, sorry, we don't have that, and they get mad." She shrugged. "Ah—well. It's a job."

"Could you get another job?"

"On Maui? Probably not. Nothing better, anyway. I'd have to leave the island. Lot of my family's moved to Las Vegas."

I thought of Vegas: the neon, the cigarette smoke, the sprawl. "Isn't that a bit like trading heaven for hell?"

She laughed; a full, hearty sound. "Me, I think there's things more important than a fancy job and a big house. I don't mind working here. Most guests are nice." She picked a crumb off her paper towel. "Some even bring me food."

She looked at me, considering. "You still need to use the Internet?" she asked. "'Cause you can use my computer. Long as you don't tell nobody."

*   *   *

After I read Bob Wills's e-mail and sent back my comments, I asked Mary for directions to the nearest beach. She told me that if I walked along the rock wall, I'd eventually reach a small stretch of sand.

Back at the condo, I stuffed my tote with a rough, white bath towel (Maui Hi did not supply beach towels); my new snorkeling set and flippers; a bottle of No-Ad suntan lotion; and a paperback; some frothy story about a city girl looking for love. My swimming attire—board shorts over a navy-blue racer-back tank—was uninspired. I'd save my other suit—floral print, bikini top, little, flirty skirt—for Jimmy.

The beach was a bit farther down than Mary had said. It was nothing special, at least by Maui standards, but it was fairly empty, and the sun felt warm on my exposed skin. I sat on the towel and read for a while. When I got hot, I pulled out my snorkeling gear and adjusted the strap on my new mask. I spit on the glass to keep it from fogging up, a tip I'd learned while vacationing in Mexico a few years back.

The water was colder than I expected, but it didn't take long to get used to it. I swam over to the darker water, searching for fish. A wave splashed over my head and into my snorkel; I sputtered and blew the water out. A yellow fish darted between the rocks; another chased it. A school of silvery-white fish sped by, looking like swimming coins. Water seeped in along the sides of my mask.

Back at a sandy spot, I stood up, awkward in my flippers. I pulled off the mask, tightened the strap, and put it back on. I swam back to the rocks, where I saw a black fish with little white dots, a white angelfish, the yellow guys again. My mask fogged.

Emerging from the water at the shoreline, I shivered. I pulled off my mask and smoothed back my hair. Far out in the water, there was a splash; another whale. My face felt funny: I was smiling. Here I was, alone on a little beach, abandoned by my boyfriend, with nothing but a flimsy towel to dry me. My condo sucked; my mask leaked. I should be cranky, whiny, and disillusioned. But it was impossible—because I was finally here, in Maui.

Chapter 5

When Jimmy announced that he was taking me out to dinner, I tried to keep my expectations in check. In our five months together, he'd taken me out only a handful of times, always to places he described as "fun." He claimed that no restaurant could match my awesome cooking (he was especially fond of my chicken parmigian) and that he liked nothing more than sharing a cozy evening at home with me. Between his business lunches and his side job waiting tables, fancy restaurants had lost their allure.

"Something nice," Jimmy said when I asked him what I should wear. He had a fresh sunburn on his nose because his lunch meeting had been by a hotel pool.

"What does that mean? Nice shorts or a nice dress?" According to my guidebook, there was a restaurant in downtown Lahaina called Hamburger in Paradise. That sounded like Jimmy's kind of place.

"Just—nice." He was wearing white linen shorts and a pale yellow silk shirt. It didn't look like hamburger attire.

Philippe's was a first-date kind of place, in the same league as the oceanfront spot in Laguna Beach where I had met Jimmy. Our table, covered with a white tablecloth and decorated with a candle and an orchid, was on a patio right next to a beach. The golden sun, low on the horizon, made me squint.

"I should have brought sunglasses," I said as the maître d' helped me into my chair.

"I've got mine," Jimmy said. "Here—sit on this side. It's not as bright."

There were a few groups on the beach, enjoying the end of the day. A tiny girl with flyaway brown hair ran around wearing nothing but a swim diaper, holding an orange sand shovel over her head like a torch. An enormous white cruise ship sat anchored offshore.

"Nice spot for a cruise," I said.

Jimmy stared out at the ocean, his chin resting on his hand. "I don't know. I'd hate to be cooped up like that."

"Yeah, our place is much nicer," I said.

Jimmy shot me a sideways glance. We both laughed.

He reached for my hand. "You've been really great about that. I know it's not what you expected."

I smiled. "I don't need a fancy resort. All that matters is that I'm with you."

A waitress came to take our drink orders. She was a pretty girl, with exotic Hawaiian looks: shiny black hair, full lips, almond eyes. Her flowered halter dress showed off a tiny hibiscus tattoo on her shoulder. I checked Jimmy's face, steeling myself for any expression of lust, but he was merely polite, ordering a bottle of champagne before returning his gaze to me.

"Champagne," I said. "What's the occasion?"

"Any day with you is an occasion." I beamed at him, forgetting for an instant that our usual occasions involved beer and pasta.

On the beach, the little girl's mother rubbed the sand off her back with a frayed towel and pulled a pink T-shirt over her head. The little girl danced in place, the orange shovel still clutched in her hand. It made it harder to get the T-shirt over her arms, but the mother managed, somehow. The mother's hair was brown and flyaway like her daughter's. She wore a tank top over her bikini, an intricate tattoo blooming between her shoulder blades. The little girl's father was there, too, folding up the beach chairs and throwing empty potato-chip bags in the beach tote. He had a tattoo, also. I was starting to feel like the only person in Maui without one.

"Could you see yourself staying here?" Jimmy asked.

"At this restaurant?"

He reached out as if to chuck me under the chin but didn't actually touch me. "No, I mean here. In *Maui*."

"You mean—to live?" What was he asking me, exactly?

"Yeah. Could you see that?"

"Well . . . I have my job." I considered that for a moment. "Not that it would break my heart to leave it, but I don't know what kind of work I could find here." I looked at him and then dropped my gaze flirtatiously. "Plus, I have this boyfriend in California. I wouldn't want to leave him behind."

"What if he came with you?"

"Then I'd . . . I'd think about it."

The waitress came and opened the champagne. Jimmy kept his eyes on me. My whole body felt hot. My heart raced.

When the waitress left, Jimmy held up his glass. "To the future. Whatever it holds."

I gulped some champagne to give me courage. "Could you move your business to Maui?" I asked as casually as I could manage.

He shrugged. "Probably. Or maybe I'd just—I don't know. The business takes so much out of me, I'm starting to wonder if it's worth it."

"But it's your dream," I said, feeling oddly alarmed.

He shrugged. "It was. But . . . what's wrong with just being a waiter? With just enjoying every day as it comes?"

"Nothing," I said, my voice cracking slightly.

"And you could get a job in a kitchen," he said, leaning forward. "I mean, you're a really good cook."

"I—couldn't see that." I drained my champagne.

"Why not?"

I poured myself another glass of champagne and topped off Jimmy's. "The hours would get to me. The pace. I like quiet evenings." Wow: could I sound any more boring? The real reason I liked quiet evenings was that I had such busy days. In my job. My real job. That I had worked ten years to achieve.

"You could open a bakery, then," he said. "Hasn't that always been your dream?"

"No," I said. "But it's something to think about." I thought about it: it sounded awful.

We ordered our food: scallop ceviche, pork with pineapple, mahimahi. The sun turned red and slipped below the horizon. The cruise ship lit up like a Christmas tree. Jimmy and I stopped talking about moving to Maui—but I didn't stop thinking about it. Maybe Jimmy was right. Maybe we should forget ambition, seize the day, catch the wave. We could live in a little house and have children who ran naked on the beach. The more champagne

I drank, the better I liked the idea. I could work in a restaurant kitchen, chopping lettuce, breading fish. Sure, why not?

By the end of the meal, Jimmy and I had scooted our chairs next to each other so that we were both staring out at the ocean. I leaned my head against his shoulder. I felt pleasantly fuzzy all over. We drank coffee, trying to sober up for the drive back to the condo.

When the waitress brought the bill, I reached for it out of habit, but Jimmy stopped my hand. "This one's on me."

"You sure?"

"Business has been good lately. Really good. Plus, I think I just got a new account today." He reached into his back pocket and pulled out his worn blue canvas wallet. He slipped out a credit card and dropped it on the bill without even checking the total. "From now on, I pay the bills."

I blinked at him and smiled, not knowing what to say. An hour earlier, he was ready to ditch his career and become a waiter on Maui. Now he was embracing the idea of himself as a thriving businessman. I wanted to love him either way, to say that I'd follow him to the ends of the earth no matter what path he chose, but I had to admit: I liked the ambitious Jimmy better than the slacker Jimmy.

The waitress whisked away the bill. Jimmy put his arm around me. He smelled like coconut mixed with lemon.

"I could get used to this," I said.

"I'm already used to it," he said.

The waitress reappeared. She cleared her throat. "Uh, sir?"

"Mm?" Jimmy turned around. The waitress looked apprehensive.

"Your Visa? It, uh, wasn't accepted. Do you have another card I could put this on?"

Suddenly we were both sober. Jimmy reached for his wallet and then stopped. "I don't—I mean, not with me. It's back at the hotel. I've got some cash but probably not enough." His voice cracked. He blinked furiously.

"It's okay," I said, reaching behind my chair for my purse. "I've got it."

"I didn't want you to," Jimmy said.

"It's no big deal," I said. "You get the next one."

"Thanks," he mumbled.

We were quiet on the ride back to the condo—not a comfortable silence, but an awkward "are we still friends?" stillness.

"I've been putting a lot of business expenses on my card," Jimmy said, his eyes on the road. "Must have exceeded my limit."

"It happens," I said casually. "No biggie. You've got another card, you said."

"Right," he said. "Except the thing is, that one . . . I know I've already hit my limit. I just got some new office furniture—Ana's desk was a piece of crap, and Scott's got a bad back, he needed one of those ergonomic chairs. I probably should have waited, but I like to treat my employees right."

"You're better to your employees than you are to yourself," I murmured.

"Is that bad?"

"No, it's good. It's why I—it's what makes you the person you are." Suddenly I wanted to make him feel better. "Tell you what. Tomorrow I'll cook dinner. Fish, maybe. We don't need any fancy restaurants. I mean, we're in Maui. What else could we possibly need?"

Chapter 6

As I once told anyone who would listen, I met Jimmy on a blind date . . . with someone else. That is the punch line. Let us now pause to chuckle.

Technically, it wasn't really a blind date, at least not in the traditional sense. I met Geoffrey on MySpace. And yes, that's Geoffrey with a *G*. His MySpace tagline was "Geoffrey with a *G*!" The first time he called me, he said, "Hi, this is Geoffrey with a *G*." Actually, that's what he said every time we talked.

I posted a MySpace profile because it seemed less desperate than joining any of the traditional Internet dating services. Designing my profile was kind of fun. I chose a background picture of a tropical island (ironic, in retrospect) and uploaded a fuzzy photo of myself laughing at the company picnic.

The lead-up to my date with Geoffrey started as these things do: with a friend request (from him) and a few perky messages.

Hey, neighbor! I saw you live in Brea. I'm down here in Orange.
I love the beach, too. Don't get down there enough, though.
Maybe we can go together some time. LOL. Drop me a line.

-- Geoffrey w/a G.

Hi, Geoffrey with a G!
Thanks for the friend request.

-- Jane with a J

Jane with a J—LOL, that's really funny. Do you like living in
Brea? I go to the Improv there sometimes.

-- G. w/a G

GG,
Love the Improv. The Square in Orange is nice, too.

-- JJ

Inspired? Hardly. But you have to appreciate the context. The
only other guys who contacted me wrote stuff like, *Hey their
pretty lady, I'm Dan 36 Riverside, new in town and looking to make
friends, Id like meet you sometime, lets talk.*

Geoffrey's profile photo looked like a passport picture (and
maybe was): button-up white shirt; short, dark hair combed a little too severely; an awkward, squinty smile. He was thirty-five
years old, a college-educated Californian, an IT manager. Status:
single. Children: someday. Here for: friends.

After a week of witty MySpace repartee (The Office *is good,
but nothing compares to early* Seinfeld), we progressed to the next
stage of modern relationships: we exchanged e-mail addresses.
Things moved quickly from there: work, cell, and home numbers;
last names.

I suggested meeting at a restaurant in Laguna Beach. The traffic was minimal for once, leaving me forty-five minutes to kill before our seven o'clock reservation. After handing my car over to the valet, I wandered down the street before pulling off my sandals and stepping onto the beach. The air was cooling down, but the sand still held some of the day's warmth. A little girl with blond pigtails chased the waves like a sandpiper. The sun was slipping in the sky, giving everything this golden glow.

When I checked my watch, I was amazed to see that it was seven o'clock: time for our dinner reservation. It was one of the few times in my life when I actually lost track of time.

I raced back toward the street, hastily rubbed the sand off my feet, and slipped on my sandals. If I'd had a few extra minutes, I would have darted into the ladies' room to comb my hair. Instead, I just ran a few fingers through it, enjoying the feeling of being sandy and windblown.

Had Geoffrey been the first man I'd come across in that sunset-addled state, I might very well have fallen in love with him. But the first man I saw was the waiter. He had shaggy, streaky blond hair, slim hips, a cat's grace. A white scar, around an inch long, ran along his jawline. Like the rest of the staff, he wore a white button-down shirt and black trousers.

The hostess was away from the stand, so I gave the waiter my name. He smiled in delight as if I had said "Cinderella" instead of "Jane" and led me to my table. Just when I should have been thinking, *I can't wait to meet Geoffrey,* my eyes wandered down the waiter's body and I thought, *Nice butt.*

Geoffrey didn't stand up when I got to the table. I'm hardly old-fashioned, but it bugged me. It was basic manners. Besides, I wanted to see how tall he was.

"Geoffrey," I said.

"With a *G*." He smiled. Sort of. I mean, his mouth turned up and his eyes scrunched, but more like he was squinting than smiling.

"Yes," I said. "Always with a *G*." Without thinking, I glanced around for our waiter. He was taking an order at the next table, his back to us. Nice butt.

I pulled out my chair. Geoffrey had taken the seat with the better view. The sun hung near the edge of the horizon like an orange balloon.

"This is gorgeous," I said.

"Long drive," Geoffrey said.

I took a deep breath and turned my full attention to him. There were no terrible surprises here, really. Unlike some other guys I'd gone out with, Geoffrey looked like his picture. Actually, he looked exactly like his picture, down to the white shirt and the squint.

"Can I get you folks something to drink?" I looked up to find the waiter smiling at me—just me, as if Geoffrey weren't even there. The sunset cast its glow on his tanned skin.

A smile spread over my face. "Yes," I said. "Please."

"I'll just have water," Geoffrey said.

"And for you?" The waiter's eyes never left my face.

"Wine," I said. "Chardonnay."

"Small, medium, or large?"

I laughed. "Extra large. Super Gulp."

At the next table, a man and woman were so intent on their conversation that their foreheads practically touched over their place settings. The man was silver-haired, fit but weathered, wearing a coat and tie. She had voluminous blond tresses and impossibly large breasts on a ridiculously skinny frame: an Orange County chiropractor's dream. I wanted to catch Geoffrey's eye, to whisper, "Isn't it nice of that man to take his niece out to dinner?" But he was busy studying his menu.

"Anything look good?" I asked.

He shrugged. "Expensive."

"Oh," I said. "Well, you pay for the view." Outside, the sun had finally slipped beyond the edge of the earth, casting a rosy glow over the clouds and the sea. (I'll say this for the California smog: it really pumps up the pinks and purples.)

"How's work?" I asked.

"Okay," he said without looking up.

At the next table, the waiter (*my* waiter) brought over a champagne bottle and silver bucket for the May-December (March-December?) couple.

"Did you finish that project you were telling me about?" I asked.

His head still bent down, he held up an index finger as if to say, *Wait a minute.* Next to us, the champagne cork came out with a satisfying pop.

"Because you said that there might be an extension," I blabbered on. "Though an extension can be good or bad. I mean, sometimes a deadline is nice, even if you're buried for a while, because it just forces you to finish what you're doing."

His head popped up from the menu. "I can't read and talk at the same time."

I smiled, thinking he meant that as an apology, expecting him to give me his full attention. Instead, he tightened his lips and resumed his menu meditation.

On the beach, there was no sign of the little girl with the blond pigtails. A couple strolled by, holding hands. How nice it must be to enjoy this setting with someone you loved. Or even liked.

"Chardonnay?" The waiter was standing over me. Looking at me. He placed a balloon glass, filled high, on the table.

"Wow, you really did bring me the Super Gulp."

"I asked for water?" Geoffrey said.

"The busboy will bring waters," the waiter said. He pulled a pen from behind his ear and did a quick flick of the head to get his streaky blond hair out of his light eyes. It was hard not to stare at him.

"I'll have the strip steak. Medium well." Geoffrey closed his menu with a snap and held it out.

"Anything to start? Salad, appetizer?"

"No."

The waiter turned to me, his eyes crinkling. "What would you like?"

I looked at him helplessly. "I haven't even looked at the menu."

"You want me to come back?"

"No!" I didn't know what seemed more unbearable: the thought of him walking away or the idea of spending that much more time alone with Geoffrey. "Do you have any suggestions?"

"You mean—for food?"

I stared at him (which was acceptable because he was talking to me). Did he mean—? His blue eyes twinkled. Yes, of course that's what he meant. "What do you think I'd like?" I asked.

He tilted his head to one side, studying me. I looked good that night, which is to say I didn't look like my usual self. I wore a blue batik-print halter dress and long dangling earrings. Bronzing powder gave the illusion that I spent my days outside rather than under fluorescent lights. My lip gloss was fresh and shiny. And my hair, of course, was windblown.

"How about if I just surprise you?" he said finally.

I nodded and made an embarrassing little mewing sound.

A short while later, as I was silently finishing up an ahi appetizer (Geoffrey and I had given up on conversation), the waiter came over, looking concerned. "Sir, what kind of automobile do you drive?"

Geoffrey paused for a moment, as if this were a trick question, before answering. "Ford Explorer."

"What color is it?"

"Dark blue."

The waiter nodded. "You left your lights on. The valet wanted us to ask around."

"The lights turn on and off automatically," Geoffrey said.

The waiter shrugged. "All I know is what they tell me."

Geoffrey stood up with an irritated grunt and dropped his napkin on the table. (He was about five foot ten, I was finally able to discern, with a small roll of fat near his belt.) "Do you mind?" he asked me.

"No, of course not!" I said, astonished that he had finally shown some manners.

"Can I take your plate?" the waiter asked me as Geoffrey walked out the door.

"Sure." I leaned back to allow him more room.

He stood there for a moment, just holding the plate. "Do you have any plans later?" he asked.

"Later—when?"

"After I get off of work. Say, ten o'clock?"

I checked the doorway: no sign of Geoffrey. "Where should I meet you?"

"How about the beach out front." He gestured outside with his chin.

We locked eyes. "There wasn't really a problem with his car, was there?"

"What car?" he asked.

*　*　*

It was almost ten-thirty by the time he showed up, sauntering down the beach with a bottle in his hand. He plopped down on the sand, handed me the open bottle, and reached forward to roll up his black trouser legs. "We're going to have to make this quick. I've got another customer meeting me here at eleven."

"It's just as well," I said. "I had another waiter here at nine-thirty, and I'm beat."

He looked up at me, surprised, and laughed. Then he leaned over and kissed me. He tasted like dinner mints.

"I don't even know your name," I said.

"Jimmy. Jimmy James."

"Your parents named you James James?"

He grinned. "My first name is really Michael. But no one calls me that except my mother."

"I'm Jane Shea," I said, holding out a hand.

"Yes, I know." The reservation had been under my name. He took my hand and pulled me close for another, longer kiss.

When he released me, I peered at the champagne bottle. "Dom Pérignon? Nice."

"Mr. Robertson's date didn't like champagne," he said. "But she didn't say so until after I'd opened the bottle. They were at the table next to you—old dude, young chick."

"Oh, yes." Now I could say the thing I'd thought while sitting across from humorless Geoffrey. "I figured she was his niece. His very favorite niece."

In the middle of a swig, Jimmy choked on the champagne and

wiped his mouth with the back of his hand. "Mr. Robertson has a *lot* of favorite nieces." He passed me the bottle.

I held it up. "Here's to Mr. Robertson's latest niece." I took a long drink. It tickled my nose. "Are all of them that well-endowed?"

"Oh, yeah. The more silicon, the better," he said.

He meant silicone. For some reason, the error seemed cute.

"You probably see a lot of interesting stuff in your job," I said.

He made a dismissive wave with his hand. "Oh, this isn't my real job."

"It isn't?" I tried not to sound hopeful. (I sounded hopeful.)

He leaned back on his elbows. "I've got my own business—designer wetsuits. It's still in the start-up phase, though, so I took this restaurant gig to make ends meet."

I checked his face in the moonlight, tried to guess his age. Twenty-seven? Thirty-seven? Either would put him within five years of me, a respectable age difference. Not that it mattered, I reminded myself: I was only having a fun conversation on the beach with a very handsome stranger.

He picked up a handful of sand and let it fall from his fist, like from an hourglass, over my foot. "Do you dive?"

I shook my head. "I tried once. Not really my thing. Do you surf?" I'd tried that, too. The experience had been less traumatic than scuba diving but no more successful.

"Nope." He pointed to the scar on his jaw. "You see this? I got it in high school. Bad wipeout. Now I stay under the water. It's safer there."

He lay back on the sand, his arms crossed under his head. "You can really see the stars tonight."

I lay down next to him and closed my eyes. "I've never seen them so clearly."

Chapter 7

When I woke up on our second morning in Maui, Jimmy was gone again. Against all odds, he had left a note.

Gone for a drive & to get a bite to eat. Back soon. J.

Had I not told him about the pineapple-mango scones? I couldn't remember. According to my itinerary, we were supposed to be watching the sunrise over Haleakala right now. And then we were going to bike down the volcano. I never should have made the itinerary: planning and Maui just don't work. Or maybe it was planning and Jimmy that didn't mix.

I took my coffee and a scone out to the lounge chairs. After two days, it felt like a treasured routine: the whale spotting, the contemplation, the soothing sounds of someone playing a guitar in a nearby condo.

When I returned to the condo and found it empty I felt a tinge of worry. The little red car was flimsy. What if there had been an accident? But a few minutes later, Jimmy strolled in, forcing a smile but looking tense around the eyes. He was taking the credit-card incident hard. He'd barely spoken when we'd returned last night, just pulled a T-shirt over his boxers, kissed me on the top of my head, and gone to sleep.

"I brought you a bagel." He held up a paper bag.

"Thanks, but I already ate."

He grimaced. "The scones. I totally forgot. Sorry . . ."

"It's okay," I said. "They were kind of dry."

He dropped the bag on the table along with my guidebook. "There's this beach up the coast I've been wanting to dive. Snorkeling's pretty good there, too. You want to do that today?"

"I'd love to!" I said, thrilled that he wasn't springing another meeting on me. The volcano could wait for another day. Or another life.

"It's this spot past Kapalua—Slaughterhouse Beach. It's supposed to be awesome, really secluded and pretty."

"Nice name. You never dove there before?"

He shook his head. "I usually dive around Kihei, further down the coast."

"We can go there if you want." I am nothing if not flexible.

"Nah." He waved his hand. "This'll be fun, and it's closer. The water's a little rougher up here, but that just means we'll have to get there earlier, before the wind picks up." He eyed the digital clock. "Shoot," he murmured.

"What?"

"Well, I have to pick up my air tank. The dive shop is in the opposite direction, toward Lahaina, so I can't just do it on the way. If we left right now, we'd be okay, but there were some calls I wanted to make for work . . ."

The credit-card incident hung between us. He wanted to be a good provider, which meant working harder. And he wanted to give me a good vacation, which meant working less.

"How about I pick up the air tanks while you stay here and make your calls?" I suggested.

His face relaxed. "You wouldn't mind?"

* * *

The guy behind the counter at the dive shop wore a faded Chicago Cubs T-shirt, soft denim shorts, brown rubber flip-flops, and an expression of Zen-like relaxation. His sandy hair was wavy and damp. I wondered whether he had dropped out of college to come to Maui or if he had finished his education first. I wondered what his parents told the neighbors.

Farther back in the store, another guy examined a flipper display before making notes on a clipboard.

"I'm here to pick up an air tank," I said to the young, sandy-haired guy. "For Jimmy James? He called earlier."

The briefest flicker of confusion crossed his face. "We don't have anything for a Jimmy James." He blinked, the tension erased. "We had a call from a Michael James."

"Oh, right—that's his real name."

He disappeared into a back room and came back hauling a silver tank. "Just one?"

I shrugged. "I guess. If that's what he ordered."

He put the tank on the counter. "I'll just need to see his PADI card."

"His . . . what?" I remembered something about PADI from my brief foray into diving.

"His PADI card?" He held his hand up, his fingers in a *C*. "It's about yay big? It shows that he's a certified diver."

"I . . . don't have it." I glanced at my watch. If I went back to the condo to get the card, we'd be even later than we already were.

"I can't give you the tank without the card. Sorry."

The guy with the clipboard looked up. "You mean Michael James from Jimmies?"

"Yes." I blinked at him with surprise.

He stuck the clipboard under his arm and sauntered over. "Nice guy. We used to buy wetsuits from him, but . . ."

"What?"

"They were a little unreliable—at least, the people in his office were. Said things had shipped when they hadn't, sent the wrong stuff. He keeps trying to get us to give them another chance. I might take him up on it, one of these days. So you're his . . ."

"Girlfriend," I said, feeling sixteen.

He smiled and held out his hand. "Tom Paulson."

"Jane Shea," I said.

He was considerably older than the guy at the counter—about forty, I'd guess—but with the same easy, happy look. Clearly, he didn't care what his parents told the neighbors.

"Glad to see he's finding time for something besides business and diving. He's pretty driven."

I thought of Jimmy's hours, his two jobs. "He has trouble slowing down," I agreed.

Tom tapped the counter. "You can give her the tank, Connor. Her boyfriend is certainly certified. Though I'm amazed he didn't come himself. He doesn't usually miss a sales opportunity." He grinned at me.

"He'll probably call you at some point," I said. "He stayed back to make some calls so we can hit the beach before it gets too late."

"You're diving today?" Connor asked.

"I'm just snorkeling. He's the diver."

I'd taken scuba-diving lessons the year after moving to California. During my first open-water dive, in the cold waters off Dana Point, I got water up my nose while kneeling on the ocean floor, adjusting my mask. I freaked out and sucked even more water into my sinuses, at which point I shot to the surface. When my instructor caught up with me, he said I should never, ever pop up like that. When I calmed down enough to speak, I told him it wouldn't be an issue since I would never, ever dive again.

Connor said, "You won't see much today. I was out this morning—the vizz was real bad."

"Vizz?" I asked.

"Visibility," Tom said. "The surge is pretty strong today, too. You might want to wait until tomorrow."

* * *

Back at the condo, I told Jimmy what Tom and Connor had said about diving conditions, but he didn't want to wait. "I've been dreaming about this dive for a month."

I didn't want to wait, either. If he didn't dive, Jimmy might leave me for another sales call.

He pulled his license out of his blue canvas wallet and stuck it in a pocket of his swim trunks. He threw the wallet into his duffel bag, which he had yet to unpack or even move from the middle of the room. "You don't want to take anything valuable," he told me. "Stuff gets stolen out of cars and sometimes even off the beach."

"Gotcha," I said, thinking, *I bet stuff doesn't get stolen off Kaanapali Beach.*

* * *

We parked the red rental car next to two others in a tiny lot. The road was high, narrow, and twisty. A stand of rugged trees blocked the beach below. The instant I opened the door, a gust of wind hit me in the face.

"Maybe we can find someplace more sheltered," I suggested.

"Nah," Jimmy said, lifting his tank and dive bag from the trunk. "It won't be bad on the beach. The cliffs will break the wind."

I made my way to the top of the steps and peered through the trees, catching a glimpse of steel-blue water and whitecaps. "It looks kind of rough."

Jimmy opened the back door and sat down, leaving his feet on the pavement. He reached in and pulled out a worn wetsuit. Once black, it was now more of a smoky gray.

I raised my eyebrows. "Don't you, uh, sell wetsuits?"

"I know." He smiled. "I have a couple of nicer ones at home. But this was my first, and I'm sentimental."

He stuck his feet into the legs and pulled up the black rubber like panty hose, leaving the suit open and hanging at the waist. He peeled off his T-shirt and tossed it onto the backseat. He yanked on his booties. Next came the diver ritual: he propped his BCD (that's the "buoyancy control device," otherwise known as the inflatable-vest thingy) on the pavement and attached the tank to the back, pulling on a strap to make sure it wouldn't slip out. He attached the regulator (that's the air hose) to the tank, checked the tank, checked the mouthpiece, and clipped his hoses into place. The mask was easy: he pulled it over his head and let it hang around his neck before slipping his arms into the BCD and hauling it onto his back. He'd adjust it on the beach, after he zipped up the wetsuit. Finally, he snagged his flippers, which he'd put on in the water.

Now you know why I preferred snorkeling. Well, that and fear of drowning.

"You look like the Creature from the Black Lagoon," I said. "In a good way."

He tossed me the keys. "Hang on to these. We'll leave the car unlocked—someone might break the windshield otherwise."

We worked our way down the concrete steps, holding on to a green railing for support. Above us, heavy tree branches blocked the sky. The steps eventually gave way to a narrow, sloping, dirt-and-rock path. I was glad I wasn't hauling any heavy gear on my back; my tote was bad enough.

"This looks like heaven," Jimmy said when we finally reached the beach, practically shouting to be heard over the wind and waves.

I made a noncommittal "mm" sound. The pictures of the Hyatt looked like heaven. Kaanapali Beach looked like heaven. This looked . . . scary. It was beautiful, certainly, a crescent-shaped, white-sand beach surrounded by lava-rock cliffs and low-hanging trees. At the edges, sea spray exploded against soaring boulders; closer in, angry breakers rammed the beach. On a sunny day, the water would be a brilliant blue, but the gray clouds cast a foreboding glow, and whitecaps dotted the steel-colored water like peaks of meringue. If there were any whales jumping today, I wouldn't be able to see them.

There were two other groups of people on the beach, their belongings clustered by some loose lava rocks. Jimmy led me down the sand, and I placed my tote bag next to a large boulder. Tough, scruffy pine trees grew straight out of the cliff and would have provided shade had there been any sun. There were no palm trees, no hibiscus—nothing to remind you that you were in the tropics. It looked more like Big Sur than Hawaii—and as beautiful as Big Sur is, I wouldn't want to swim there.

Jimmy shrugged out of his BCD and placed it on the sand. He

slipped his arms into the wetsuit and pulled on the long cord to zip it up the back.

"You going to snorkel?" he asked.

"Well, yeah," I said, thinking: *What else am I supposed to do?*

"Watch out for the coral," he said. "It can really cut you up."

"I will," I said, thinking: *No shit.*

A gust of wind, stronger than the others, knocked over my tote bag. Sand stung my legs. "Are you sure this is a good idea?" I asked. "Aren't you supposed to dive with a buddy?"

I trailed him to the water. Down the beach, one of the other groups began to pack up. Jimmy took a couple of steps into the surf, peering at the water in an attempt to find a sandy entry.

"I dive alone all the time," he said. "I'd never dive a cave or a wreck by myself, but a little beach dive? It's no big deal." He took a few steps to the left. "I'm not going very deep, which means I can stay out for a while. Honolua Bay is right around the corner—it's got tons of awesome fish and coral. Might even see some sharks."

A wave broke near the shore and pummeled our ankles. Jimmy took another step to the left and leaned over to check the entry. "It's sandy right here. You'll be okay as long as you get your feet up fast. Use the waves."

"It looks rough out there . . ." I said for the second time.

"On top of the water, sure. But twenty feet down? Not a problem. You remember that big tsunami in Asia? There were people diving when it happened, and they didn't even know about the big wave till it was over."

"You're right," I said. "I'm just a worrier."

"I know," he said. "And I love that about you."

A wave swelled and broke, and he plunged in before another could knock him over. His back to the breakers, he pulled on his flippers in one smooth motion and then, still facing the beach, kicked back toward the open ocean, his inflated BCD keeping his head bobbing above the waves. He grew smaller and smaller until he made it past the rock outcropping.

He waved. I waved back.

And then he disappeared below the surface.

*　*　*

Jimmy's "just rough on the surface" line was a load of crap. The sea bottom churned below me, fogging the water with sand and driving the fish who knows where. Maybe they were out in the deep water with Jimmy, I told myself. Where the ocean was calm and safe.

I don't know how long I was out there. It probably felt longer than it was, what with clearing my leaky mask and gagging on the water when the waves broke over my snorkel.

Finally, I gave up and swam back to the shore, trying (and failing) to get in without being smacked by a wave. Back on land, I coughed out some of the salt water and dried myself as best as possible with my rough bathroom towel. Maybe on the way home we'd stop off at the ABC store and buy a couple of beach towels. Ten dollars each: only the best for my Hawaiian vacation.

I hadn't brought an extra towel to sit on since the plan was to spend the entire time in the water. Jimmy's dry white towel was tempting, but I left it in the tote. Even with the wetsuit, he'd be cold when he got out.

Bag in hand, I scooted under a tree with low branches and settled myself on an exposed root. My cell phone was at the bottom of my bag. According to the screen, it was 1:43 P.M. in California, which meant it was 10:43 here in Maui.

The tree provided some small protection from the wind. Shade wasn't a factor since the murky clouds had obliterated the sun. Would that affect Jimmy's visibility? And if so, would he cut his dive short? I doubted it, somehow. Jimmy had a tendency to get caught up in the moment. I pictured him in the depths, gliding past coral, staring at a puffer fish, hovering over a moray eel.

When my bathing suit went from soaking wet to merely clammy, I pulled on my terry cover-up, wishing I'd brought something warmer. Jimmy's T-shirt was in the car, but I didn't want to risk being away from the beach when he came out of the water. With surf this rough, he might need help getting out.

Above me, the dense clouds darkened. The remaining blue sky, to the left of the beach, seemed far away. Farther down the sand, the last of the beachgoers packed up their gear and disappeared up the path.

I thought about dinner, about what I might make in that dinky little kitchen. Fish, certainly—Mary told me the best stuff came from Safeway. Lemon. Bagged salad. A loaf of nice bread. A crisp Chardonnay. Sometimes simple meals are the best. We could eat out on the lounge chairs again, assuming it didn't rain. Or I could do something cold, crab salad maybe, which we could take someplace idyllic and quintessentially Hawaiian, one of those spots that I'd dreamed about from California.

Like: the Hyatt lobby.

It began to rain. I said a bad word. When that didn't make me feel any better, I said a worse one. That helped, but only a little.

According to my cell phone, it was 1:56 in California, which made it 10:56 in Maui. What time had Jimmy gone under? I wished I'd checked before snorkeling. He'd have a timer and an air gauge with him, but knowing Jimmy, he'd stay under as long as he could, till he was almost, but not quite, out of air. You never want your air to run out completely. You need to keep some in reserve to get you back to the surface. But even if Jimmy's air did run out, he'd be okay. His dive was so shallow, he could shoot up without risking decompression sickness, otherwise known as "the bends."

I tried to remember how long a tank would last. A lot depended on the depth of the dive; the deeper you went, the faster the air ran out. But Jimmy was an experienced diver, and slow, measured breaths could make his air last longer.

I needed to distract myself. Had it been a weekday, I would have called Lena because she always made me laugh. Instead, I called my sister, Beth, in New Jersey.

After three rings, a girl's voice said, "Hullo?"

"Hi . . . Samantha? This is Aunt Jane."

"This is Savannah."

"Savannah! Wow. You're starting to sound so grown-up." Savannah, Beth's second girl, was twelve. Or maybe thirteen? I'd lost track.

When Savannah didn't reply, I said, "It was nice seeing you at Christmas."

After a pause, she said, "Yeah."

"Did you use the Gap certificate I gave you?"

There was a bit of static, and then, "No." I tried to think of something else to ask her, but she saved me. "You want to talk to my mom?"

"Hello?" Beth sounded harried. Beth always sounded harried.

"I'm on the beach in Hawaii," I said.

"Isn't that a Ziggy Marley song?"

"It's raining," I said.

"You're looking for pity?"

"And the hotel lost our reservation, so we're in a crappy condo." I heard the sound of running water, dishes clinking. "Did I interrupt your dinner? What time is it there?"

"It's almost dinnertime, but no one's eating. Sierra and Sindy have the stomach flu. Eleven times they've thrown up today. Samantha was home all week with a sinus infection, and now she's locked herself in her room so she doesn't start puking. Savannah says she feels nauseous, but I think it's just because she wants attention."

"Okay, you win," I said. "Your day sucks more than mine. Where's Stacey?"

"Slumber party."

"Sal?"

"Nauseous. But I think that's just his personality. And, oh—Mom was supposed to come to dinner tonight, and when I called to cancel, she said she could tell all along that I didn't really want her to come, so I'm probably glad to have an excuse."

My phone beeped. "Oh, crap—battery's low. Anyway. Just wanted to say hi. Jimmy's diving, and I'm stuck on the beach waiting."

"My heart bleeds for you," Beth said, sounding a touch more chipper than she had at the beginning of the conversation.

I threw the phone back in my tote and stared out at the water. The sun peeked through in patches, the rays reaching through the raindrops like a child's drawing. When I thought I saw Jimmy's head pop out of the water, I hurried to the water's edge and peered out, but it was just a whitecap.

The rain slowed to a mist. It was 11:09. Figuring that Jimmy went under at around ten-thirty, and his air would last around forty-five minutes, I decided he would resurface no later than eleven-fifteen.

The rain stopped. At eleven-fifteen, I reconsidered the shallowness of the dive plus Jimmy's diving expertise. He could probably stay under for an hour, which meant he'd be up by eleven-thirty. I wouldn't tell him I'd been worried. I wouldn't even let him know I'd been cold.

At eleven-thirty I decided that Jimmy had begun his dive later than I'd assumed. He'd had to swim pretty far out. And maybe I wasn't in the water for as long as I'd thought. I'd been nervous, after all, and time slows down when you're afraid. Surely Jimmy would return to the surface no later than 11:40. I'd act a little annoyed, but not enough to ruin the rest of the afternoon.

On the way back to the condo, I'd ask him to stop off at Safeway. I'd buy fish.

I wouldn't tell him I'd been worried. Because it was just so crazy to think that something bad might have happened.

At eleven forty-five, there was still no sign of Jimmy.

That's when I knew: he was gone.

Chapter 8

I shouldn't have called my sister. Without those minutes, there would have been enough charge left in my battery to call 911. If Jimmy was trapped underwater, every second counted.

I should have checked the time when he went in.

I should have left my cell phone charged.

I should have gone for help sooner.

It didn't even occur to me to blame Jimmy for breaking a basic safety rule by diving alone. I didn't want to be angry at him.

I ran up the concrete steps, tiny red ants swarming at my feet. Even without any sun, the air in the car was humid. I ran my hand under the seat and yanked open the glove compartment. Surely Jimmy had brought his phone along. But then I remembered him tossing it on the table at the condo: he didn't want it to get stolen.

Adrenaline made my body shake and my heart race. My breathing came in strangled gasps. I stepped into the road and looked both ways, but Jimmy had chosen a deserted stretch, and there was no traffic. Driving away was out of the question: I couldn't leave Jimmy.

I ran back down the stairs, just far enough so I could see Jimmy if he had reappeared. In my mind I pictured him staggering breathless onto the beach and falling into my arms. I'd hold him tight, not caring that he soaked my already-damp terry cover-up.

Already, though, I knew that wouldn't happen. He had been down too long. Everyone needs to come up for air.

I was about to get back in the car when a tan sedan appeared around the bend. I dashed into the street and held my arms up. The car jerked to a halt.

The man who got out was silver-haired, older but not old. I think his wife had silver hair, too, but I can't be sure. So many details escape me. All I could think about was Jimmy. All I could see was Jimmy in the ocean, kicking away from me.

The older couple stood there quietly, their rental car's engine humming, as I dialed 911 on their cell phone. "My boyfriend is gone!" I sobbed, tears appearing as if from nowhere.

When the operator asked where I was, my mind went blindingly white. I couldn't remember the name of the beach. "Do you know where we are?" I pleaded with the silver-haired couple. The husband took the phone and gave directions to Slaughterhouse Beach. His wife offered to stay there to flag down the police so I could go back to the water. Just in case.

Stupidly, I still felt hopeful as I ran back down the path. Jimmy could be there. It wasn't impossible.

He wasn't there, of course. And he wasn't there fifteen minutes later when the rescue workers arrived: police, fire, coast guard, lifeguards. All those people could have made me feel optimistic.

Instead, the swarms made me realize just how bad things were. I felt numb and cold—so cold.

The beach was no longer deserted. Divers barreled out beyond the waves, dragging a flag-marked float along to mark their descent. If only Jimmy had brought a float. If only he had picked up the air tank himself, he would have thought of it.

"Did your friend have any health issues?" a firefighter asked me. "Any problems with his heart?"

"Nothing," I said. "No problems at all." Why were there firefighters here? Where was the fire?

The buzz of Jet Skis filled the air. They'd launched from Flemings Beach, just down the coast. (Lifeguard? Coast guard? I couldn't keep them straight.)

I kept my eyes on the water, but it was so hectic out there, Jimmy could swim to shore and I wouldn't even notice.

And then: hope. The currents were strong today, a lifeguard said. He was a young guy, on the short side, with a wide, smooth chest, dark hair, and kind eyes. It's easy to get lost underwater, he told me. My friend could have popped up down the shore. He could be a mile away, sitting on the beach and trying to figure out how to explain this without sounding stupid.

I took this as good news. Great news. I began to laugh with hysterical relief. "You think he's okay?"

"We're checking the beaches along the coast," he said. "See if he's turned up."

He hadn't turned up.

But he could be floating around somewhere, another lifeguard told me later, when I had retreated to my spot under the low-hanging trees. Someone had brought me a blanket, but nothing could warm me.

"So you think you'll find him?" I pleaded.

The lifeguard paused a long time before replying, very carefully, "Yes, I think we'll find him." He didn't say any more. He didn't have to.

Someone offered to get me a sandwich, but I wasn't hungry. I wasn't thirsty, either, but a paramedic—a woman, I think—made me drink a can of overly sweetened pink lemonade.

"Is there anyone we should call?" a policewoman asked me. I shook my head. I had no one local, of course, and calling my friends or family from home made it too official. As long as no one knew that Jimmy was missing, he still might come back.

"Do you want a ride somewhere?" the policewoman asked me.

I shook my head: I wasn't leaving. As long as Jimmy was in the water, as long as there were rescue crews about, I would sit under my tree.

I sat there. And I sat there. My bladder began to hurt from the lemonade, but I ignored it.

The sun, which had finally come out, slipped below the horizon: a beautiful Hawaiian sunset made especially magnificent by the elaborate clouds. Rescue workers on Jet Skis buzzed over pink-tinted water and disappeared around the corner. Divers emerged from the depths and pulled off their masks. A crazy yellow bird danced in the branches above me.

"It's getting dark," a firefighter told me. "There's nothing more we can do tonight."

Chapter 9

On Sunday, I awoke just before daylight and had an instant of peace. *Jimmy's slipped out for another one of his meetings,* I thought. *Maybe he'll bring me breakfast—the scones are getting stale.*

And then, cruelly, the memories washed over me like an icy wave. Had they found him? *Please, please let him be alive,* a voice inside my head begged. He could have washed up somewhere in the night, unconscious, injured, but still alive. I pictured him lying on the beach, moaning, whispering my name.

Blood rushing in my ears, I reached for the phone, the number for the Maui Police Department filed in my memory, perhaps forever. The woman at the switchboard put me through to a detective.

Search crews had resumed their search this morning, but they'd found no traces of Jimmy, Detective McGuinn said gently. But in the next several days I could probably expect some things to—(he paused to find the least hurtful phrase)—appear.

"Appear?" I croaked (I hadn't even had my coffee yet).

"Wash up."

I didn't say anything in response. My voice had stopped working.

"You might want to make some calls," he said. "We can do it for you if that would make things easier. Family members, close friends . . . we should give them a heads-up before this hits the wires."

"Can't we wait before we make some kind of announcement?" I pleaded. "I'd hate to upset people if it's for nothing. Maybe he's lying on a beach, unconscious. Or he could have amnesia. I mean, it happens, right? And not just in movies?"

The detective paused, trying to find the right words. "We've already alerted the press. Last night. It's best in these kinds of situations—so people keep their eyes open. Miss Shea, you've got to understand . . . I know this is hard to accept, but the chances of Mr. James turning up alive—they're not good."

"But not impossible."

"Miss Shea." The detective's voice hinted at exhaustion. "Had you noticed any . . . changes in Mr. James recently?"

"What kind of changes?" I asked, confused.

"Had he seemed troubled at all? Depressed? Was he dealing with any personal problems or financial difficulties?"

Jimmy had been acting strangely in the last few weeks: distant, preoccupied. I'd feared he was pulling away from me, but maybe there was something else going on. And then there was that incident with the credit card . . .

"Jimmy owns his own business," I said. "Finances had been tight lately, but I think that goes with the territory." I didn't tell him how preoccupied Jimmy had been. He didn't need to know.

Suddenly I realized what he meant. My hands began to shake. "You don't think that Jimmy killed himself?"

"We don't know what to think. But we can't rule out the possibility. For an experienced diver to go off alone in such rough conditions—it doesn't quite make sense. Especially since he didn't even take a marker out with him. Also, Slaughterhouse Bay isn't a great dive spot. It's right next to Honolua Bay, true, but he'd have to swim against the current to get there. Why not just go in at Honolua instead?"

"It was because of me," I said, eager to talk him—and myself—out of the suicide scenario. "He knew I wanted a nice beach to sit on. And as for the float—I picked up the air tank for him, and I didn't think to get him one." *But,* a little voice nagged, *he never told you to.*

"It was probably just an accident," the detective said gently. "I'll call you if we hear anything."

How could Jimmy be gone when his duffel bag was sitting in the middle of the room, just where he'd left it? When his toothbrush was still in the bathroom? After I got off the phone, I started to go through the bag, to look for an address book with his family's phone numbers, but as soon as I pulled something out—the pale blue polo shirt he'd worn on the plane—I smelled him, and the sadness hit me so hard that I couldn't do any more.

A few minutes before eight o'clock, Mary, in her oversize muumuu, knocked softly at the door, the local newspaper in her hands. On the front page was a photo of Slaughterhouse Beach. The headline: MAN DISAPPEARS WHILE DIVING OFF WEST MAUI COAST.

I grabbed the door frame to steady myself. Somehow, the newspaper report made it all real.

"Oh no, it *is* your man," Mary said. "I recognized the name from when he checked in. But I'm thinking, Michael James is a common name. Maybe it's a different one."

"It's him," I said. "It happened yesterday. He went under and just—never came back." My voice cracked.

Without a thought, Mary took me in her arms. I wheezed in despair but felt too numb to cry.

"Can I do anything for you?" she asked. "Anything at all?"

I started to say no but then remembered the duffel bag. "I'm supposed to get phone numbers," I said. "For the police. I never even met Jimmy's parents. They live in Arizona. He's said in the spring—maybe in the spring we'd go visit."

"Does he have a computer?" she asked. "Cell phone?"

"He didn't bring a computer. His cell-phone battery is dead, but maybe he has an address book or papers or, I don't know— something in his bag. It's just—earlier I tried to look . . ." My voice trailed off.

"You want me to see if I can find anything?" she asked.

I nodded.

Mary knelt down on the brown carpet, next to the duffel bag. Just a few days ago, I'd been stationed at the baggage carousel, waiting for this bag to appear, convinced that losing our luggage was the worst thing that could happen.

Perched on the edge of a chair, I watched Mary go through Jimmy's things. It seemed wrong somehow, as though Jimmy were going to come back and complain about the invasion of privacy.

On the floor, Mary neatly stacked Jimmy's possessions: a base-ball cap, a pair of sunglasses, some tired-looking sneakers. Swim trunks, T-shirts, shorts, a belt. A cell-phone charger for the car. A box of condoms. (I was so numb that I didn't even feel embar-rassed.) And then . . .

"What's this?" It was tiny. Square. She handed it to me.

I stared at the black velvet box in the palm of my hand. Surely it was just a pair of cuff links or a tie clip. Had I ever even seen Jimmy wear a tie?

But, no. It was a ring, an emerald-cut diamond flanked by sapphires, set in platinum. Jimmy had taken me to Hawaii to propose. The man I thought would never commit wanted to marry me. He didn't just love things *about* me—he loved me. And now he was gone.

Now I knew why Jimmy's card had been turned down at the restaurant. He hadn't exceeded his limit on new office chairs. He had exceeded it on my engagement ring.

My tears broke loose, sliding down my cheeks like a hot waterfall.

"Are you going to put it on?" Mary asked.

"I don't think I should," I whispered. "He never actually proposed."

"He'd want you to wear it," she said.

It was a little tight, but I managed to shove it on my left ring finger. It made me feel better, somehow, connected to Jimmy for one last time. Plus, there was relief: if Jimmy had been prepared to embark on a new life with me, there was no way he would have killed himself.

Mary let me use the computer at the registration desk to look up Jimmy's office number. Scott and Ana would need to be told. Maybe Ana would have contact numbers for Jimmy's parents. I would never again be jealous of Ana, I thought, fingering my ring.

Ana answered on the fourth ring: "Hey, this is Ana—hold a sec." And then she cut me off. Next time she picked up after only three rings, having shortened her spiel to a simple, "Hold on." This time she put me on hold.

"Are you okay?" Mary whispered. I nodded, clutching my cell

phone. Today's hold music was rap. I was treated to two "mother-fuckers," a "bitch," and several "hos" before Ana picked up.

"Hey, this is Ana—what's up?" she said.

"I—this is Jane," I croaked.

"Sorry—what? I think we have a bad connection."

"This is, this is—" I paused to collect myself.

She hung up. I burst into tears.

"You want me to do it?" Mary asked. All I could do was nod. "Speakerphone?" she asked. I nodded again.

Ana picked up without putting Mary on hold: "'Sup?"

"Aloha?" Mary said.

"Yeah, this is Ana. Whassup?"

"Aloha," Mary said. "I am calling about Mr. Michael James."

"Not here," Ana said. "He's in Maui this week."

"Yes, I know," Mary said. "I'm in Maui, too."

"Oh, you want his cell? Or the number where he's staying?"

She meant the Hyatt. Would things have been different with-out the reservation mix-up? We could have spent yesterday on the beach or around the pool. Jimmy could have walked down to the Sheraton and gone diving at Black Rock.

"That won't be necessary," Mary said. "You see, the reason I'm calling is—I'm calling for Miss Jane Shea."

"Who?"

"Mr. James's fiancée."

"He has a fiancée?" Her voice sounded hollow over the speaker-phone.

"It wasn't official yet," Mary conceded. "Miss Ana, the reason I'm calling is to give you some very sad news. Mr. Michael James went scuba diving yesterday morning, and he never came back."

There was a pause. "He never came back to his room?"

"No," Mary said. "He never came back to the beach. He went under and . . . now he's gone."

"But who was he with?" Ana demanded.

"He was with Miss Shea. But she stayed near the beach, snorkeling."

"*He went diving alone?* Why the hell didn't she dive with him?" Her voice cracked.

"I don't dive," I whimpered. "I tried a few years ago and it . . . it scared me."

There was a pause as Ana digested the fact that she was on speakerphone. Or that Jimmy had gone diving alone. Or that I'd let him. Or that Jimmy was missing. Jimmy was dead.

"It might be in the newspaper," Mary said quietly. "We didn't want you to find out that way. Also, we hoped you might have a phone number for his parents." Ana didn't say anything. "Do you think you might have that? A phone number?"

"I don't—I don't know," Ana said, sounding dazed. "I can look in his office. But he doesn't like people going through his things." She gasped. "Though I guess he's not going to care if . . . if . . . Is he dead?"

"They haven't found his . . . They haven't found him," Mary said.

Chapter 10

This was the second time I'd worn an engagement ring without a proposal. The first time, I was twenty-eight, and I'd been "in a relationship" for two and a half years. That's what I used to say: "I'm in a relationship," as if the relationship mattered more than the man—which, I suppose, it did.

Steve was an ophthalmologist. ("I'm in a relationship with a doctor.") We'd met in the frozen-food section at the Brea Trader Joe's. Steve was buying a handcrafted Thai chicken pizza. I was on the other side of the aisle, buying orange chicken. We backed into each other. We apologized. We talked about frozen halibut and chickenless chicken nuggets. About hormone-free milk and health supplements. About restaurants in Brea. About what we were doing on Saturday night.

Two and a half years later, on a Saturday just after Thanksgiving, we were talking about cell-phone chargers. Steve needed one for his car. I suggested we go to the RadioShack at the mall. Afterward, we could have dinner at California Pizza Kitchen—you know, really make a night of it.

Parking was awful; even the lot by the Red Lobster was full. Steve circled several times while I said, "We could go somewhere else. You want to go somewhere else?" Finally, we snagged a spot, and I said, "Whew! I'm glad we didn't go somewhere else."

The mall was done up for Christmas: carols blasting from the speakers, big metallic balls, elaborate wreaths. Santa sat in his big chair while young women dressed as elves kept children of every conceivable ethnicity in line. Outside, it was seventy degrees; earlier in the day, it had reached ninety.

We had to wait an hour for a table at CPK. When we finally sat down, it was too loud to hold a conversation. We finished our meal forty-five minutes before the mall was due to close—plenty of time to pick up a cell-phone charger. Plenty of time to window-shop.

The jewelry-store window was packed with diamond rings: simple stones set in platinum, elaborate designs surrounded by gold. Diamond solitaires, diamond bands, diamonds flanked by other jewels. A hand-lettered sign read THE GIFT OF A LIFETIME. I slowed and then stopped. Steve walked a few paces before realizing I wasn't with him. He retraced his steps and stood next to me, silent.

We had never discussed marriage. It was the elephant in the room, in the car, and now, in the mall. Plenty of people had urged me to give him an ultimatum, but I wanted him to propose because he wanted to, not because he felt he had to.

"RadioShack is going to close," he said finally.

"Not for forty-five minutes." I was sick of that elephant. "The rings are making you nervous, aren't they?" I tried to keep my tone playful.

"Only an idiot would buy a ring at a mall. They double the price." He was trying to keep his voice casual. Or maybe he didn't have to try.

"Would someone who's *not* an idiot buy a ring somewhere else?" I asked awkwardly.

"I don't know—I guess." He looked at his watch.

"That would be a no."

"I don't even know what you're talking about." A ridiculous statement: he knew exactly what I was talking about.

"Am I wasting my time here?" I asked. (Did I mention? I'd had two glasses of wine at California Pizza Kitchen.)

"I just want to go to RadioShack and then go home," he said coolly.

"I'm not talking about RadioShack. I'm talking about the rest of our lives."

"Do we need to decide this right now?" His voice was getting tight.

"You've had two and a half years to decide this." (Inside my head, a little, sober voice was saying, *Shut up! You'll ruin everything!*)

I was about to drop the subject, to huff off to RadioShack, when a man came out of the jewelry store. He had smooth olive skin, carefully cut black hair, a double-breasted suit. His cologne was too strong, but it smelled nice, like a forest. "Can I help you? You like to try on some rings, maybe?" He had a Middle Eastern accent and bright white teeth.

"Yeah, sure—let's look at rings," Steve said, crossing his arms.

I should have walked away right then, but my left ring finger itched with desire.

"Okay," I said. "If you think we have time."

He shrugged.

The store was quiet, carpeted, and cool. It smelled of the salesman's forest-y cologne. The cases were blond wood and glass. The salesman—he called himself Frank—offered us cushioned beige chairs.

"That one," I said, pointing to a simple solitaire in a platinum setting.

He unlocked the case and plucked out the ring. "Fits you perfectly—doesn't even need to be sized," he said after I had slipped it on my finger. "We could send you home in that ring tonight," he continued, as if he were selling me a sporty roadster.

I shifted my hand this way and that. The diamond caught the light and twinkled.

"Is just under a carat," Frank said. "So is good deal for the money. Price goes way up once you hit a carat."

I bit my lip. When it came to diamonds, did size really matter?

"You want, we could put you on a payment plan," Frank purred. "You give me down payment tonight, you pay a little bit every month after. Is beautiful ring, huh?"

"It is," I murmured, though I was thinking: *I'd really like a full carat.*

"You want to try on another one?" Frank asked.

"No, we're done," Steve said.

Frank and I both looked up at him in surprise, like we'd forgotten he was even there. Was this the big moment? Would he drop down on one knee?

"I'm not buying the ring," Steve said in a flat voice.

Frank smiled and shrugged. "Well, if you change your mind . . ."

Steve looked at me. Through me. "I'm not going to change my mind."

"Do you just mean . . . this ring?" I asked. "Or . . ."

"I'm not going to buy you a ring. Any ring." He ran a hand over his face and then said, "I'm sorry." He didn't sound sorry. He cleared his throat. "We can still make it to RadioShack. I mean, if you still want to go."

I nodded. Who would miss an opportunity to visit RadioShack?

The ring slid off easily. How could Steve be calling off our engagement when he'd never proposed in the first place?

We walked out of the hushed, heavily scented jewelry store and back into the chaos of the mall without speaking and made our way to the electronics store. Steve managed to buy the charger with fifteen minutes left before the mall closed. "You want to go into the bookstore?" he asked, considerate to the end.

"Sure," I said, wondering if we were going to pretend the ring incident had never happened, wondering if we could just continue as before, a flicker of hope still burning in my heart.

I bought a detective novel. He flipped through magazines but left the store empty-handed. He drove me home without speaking. His car smelled like leather. He slid a jazz CD into the stereo. *At least if he dumps me I can stop pretending to like jazz,* I thought.

At my door, he kissed me on the cheek and said, for the second time that night, "I'm sorry." He put his hands in his pockets. "I should have said something sooner, but I figured we'd get through Christmas . . ."

I nodded. The jewelry store hadn't changed anything. It had just sped things up.

He touched my cheek one last time. He looked sad. He didn't love me, but he didn't want to hurt me. "You'll find someone," he said.

Steve was right: I had found someone.

And now he was gone.

Chapter 11

Ana called back within the hour. I was still in the condo and didn't plan to leave all day. What if Jimmy came back and I wasn't there? Mary had offered to bring me something to eat, but the thought of food made me nauseous. Light made me slightly nauseous, too, which was why I'd left the blinds closed.

"Is this . . . Jane?" Ana said.

"Yes," I said, still feeling hurt that Jimmy had never mentioned me. I rubbed my engagement ring with my thumb. He cared. Even if he didn't know how to express himself, his feelings ran deep.

"This is Ana. From Jimmies." She paused. "I'm so sorry." Her voice sounded hoarse, as if she'd been crying. "It just blows my mind that . . ."

"I know," I said.

"I feel so bad that I never even met you," she said. "That's just like him, though, not to tell anyone what was going on in his life outside of work. I didn't even think he *had* a life outside of work.

Though I guess I'll probably meet you at . . ." Her voice trailed off, but the unspoken word, *funeral,* hung between us.

I started to correct her, to say, *He may still be alive,* but I couldn't get the words out. I closed my eyes and tried to steady my breathing.

"Anyway," she said. "I got the number you wanted. For his parents." She paused. "That's going to be a rough phone call."

"Yes," I said. "It is."

*   *   *

"Hello, Mrs. James? This is Jane. Jane Shea."

"Yes . . . ?" Clearly, she didn't know who I was; no big surprise.

"I'm calling about your son."

"Douglas or Michael?"

"Um—Michael." I'd forgotten that she called him that.

"Are you his secretary? He couldn't call me himself?" Her words were brisk, clipped. Somehow, I had expected a western drawl.

"No—he couldn't." I was trying to break the news gently, slowly, but she wasn't reacting quite the way I'd expected.

"Do you know if he's coming to his father's birthday party?" she demanded. "Because he was supposed to let me know by last week. The caterers need a head count."

"A party?" I croaked. He'd never even mentioned it. "No—he won't be able to make it."

She made a sound somewhere between a sigh and a snarl. "It's his father's *seventieth birthday,*" she hissed. "Surely he can get away for a couple of days."

"Mrs. James, your son is missing," I blurted.

There was a long pause, after which she said, "Did you try his cell phone?"

"No." I tried to keep my voice steady. "I'm not his secretary—I'm his . . . girlfriend." She didn't need to know about the ring, at least not yet. "We're in Maui. Your son went diving yesterday, and he just . . . he never came up."

"Try his cell phone," she said again, sounding more insistent this time. "He doesn't always answer it, but I know he checks his messages."

"Mrs. James, you don't understand. I was on the beach. Waiting for him. I watched him go in the water. And he never came back."

The line was dead for a moment. *"But where is he?"* she finally demanded.

"I don't know. In the water—under the water." I started to cry. "I stayed there all day."

"Why isn't anyone looking for him?" she shrieked. "Why didn't anyone call us sooner—we know people, we could have *done* something. *Why isn't anyone doing anything?"*

"They are, Mrs. James." I was sobbing now. "They've got the police out, the fire department, coast guard, lifeguards. Everyone's looking. They searched all day yesterday and since sunrise this morning. But he's just . . . *gone.*"

"No. Oh, no," she moaned, suddenly understanding. "I told him that scuba diving was dangerous. I told him to be careful." Her voice caught. "Not my baby. Not my boy."

"We were going to get married." It seemed right that she should know.

"You were?" Her voice went up, as if that gave her a ray of hope: surely her son wouldn't miss his own wedding. But then the reality hit her and she began to cry like a little girl.

Chapter 12

When the police called a few hours later, I knew it had to be bad news.

"I think you should come down to the station," the detective said.

"Did he . . . did you find him?" I croaked.

The detective paused for an excruciating moment. "It's really best if you just come down here."

Mary offered to drive, and I probably should have let her. The way I was crying, I could barely see the road. Jimmy's cell phone sat on the seat next to me, charger attached. When it was juiced, I could play back his message, hear his voice a final time. It was a poor substitute for the man I loved.

The police station was up on a hill, past some tennis courts and just beyond the community center. The building was clean and pale, blocky and low. It looked like a town swim complex.

In the parking lot, I took a few minutes to compose myself. I looked awful: puffy eyes, sallow complexion. I'd managed to spend three days in Maui without getting anything resembling a tan. My hair was lank and dirty. My clothes—a yellow Lands' End T-shirt and navy shorts—were rumpled.

Everyone looked up when I walked in the door, and then a couple of officers immediately looked at the ground. Two phone lines rang at once, a police radio blared, desk drawers jangled, a computer printer whirred. I heard the terms *domestic incident, stolen bicycle, smashed windshield, assault and battery.*

Detective McGuinn came to me. "Good morning, Miss Shea." He was about my age, a little chubby, with curly brown hair, dark eyes, and a kind face. I nodded to him, unable to speak. *He didn't say aloha,* I thought absurdly.

"You probably saw the newspaper this morning. I hope it didn't take you off guard. But when someone goes missing, we like to get the word out. The more eyes the better." He motioned to the back of the room. "Please—come with me."

I stood still for a moment, the now-familiar sensation of cold-ness washing over me. As long as the detective didn't tell me that Jimmy's body had been found, he might still be alive. I couldn't let him tell me.

Fighting the urge to flee, I finally began my slow walk across the room. I didn't notice her until I sat down: a young woman, in her twenties, with long dark hair cut in elaborate layers and streaked with gold. Her generous lips were pillowy, as if she'd been crying. Carefully arched eyebrows framed light brown eyes accented by (apparently) waterproof mascara. Unnaturally large breasts spilled out of a black halter top, the top of a tattoo peeking over the fabric. Her tiny shorts and high heels were both white.

"Miss Shea, I'd like you to meet Tiara Cardenas. Miss Carde-nas, this is Jane Shea."

I tried to force a smile but couldn't. Her eyes flickered over me and then returned to the floor.

"We received a call from Miss Cardenas early this morning. Her boyfriend is also missing."

I felt a sudden bond with this sniffling, big-breasted woman. "Oh God—I'm so sorry. Did he—was he in the water?"

"I don't know," she whimpered. "Last I saw him, he was in our"—here she paused to sob—"hotel room. We'd just"—*sob*—"made"—*sob*—"love." She began to wail.

The detective cleared his throat. "When Miss Cardenas's boyfriend left their hotel room yesterday morning, he told her he was planning to scuba dive."

"The currents were so strong!" I said. "There should have been signs up. Warnings."

Tiara nodded, too wrecked to speak.

Suddenly I realized why Tiara and I had been brought together—and it wasn't to form a support group. I gawked at the detective. "You found a body, didn't you?" I gasped, comprehension dawning. "But you don't know which one of them it is."

Tiara looked up, horrified. We locked eyes and then glanced hurriedly away, both struck by the same thought: *Let it be her boyfriend, not mine.*

"Does either of you have a picture of your companion?" the officer asked.

"I don't," I said. For a while I'd kept some shots on my cell phone. I'd flashed them proudly while visiting my sister at Christmas (she'd long since deleted the one I'd e-mailed). I'd never printed the pictures, though—it seemed too possessive, too serious—and I'd deleted them in anger one evening after Jimmy canceled our plans so he could take a customer out to dinner.

"How about you, Miss Cardenas?" the detective asked. "Any photos?"

Tiara bit her hand and sniffled. "I can't show them to you."

"It would be very helpful," the officer said, not explaining the obvious: a picture might save one of us from having to view . . . whatever was left. At least the damage couldn't be too gruesome if a snapshot was enough to identify the body.

"In the pictures I have of him—I'm in them, too," Tiara said, nibbling on a bright pink fingernail.

"That's really not a problem," the officer said. "Unless you're— oh!" His eyes popped.

"It was just a—it was a private thing," Tiara said. "Between consenting adults."

I can't wait to tell Jimmy about this girl's naked pictures, I thought for an instant before realizing he wasn't here to tell. Jimmy would have thought this was hysterical. If only it were all a joke, if only there weren't two men missing, at least one of them almost certainly dead. The diamond felt heavy on my left hand. I rubbed it with my other hand as if doing so would yield three wishes. Right now I'd settle for one.

"Perhaps you can describe your boyfriend, Miss Cardenas," the officer said.

"He was beautiful, like . . . like an angel," she said. "Or a surfer. Except I don't even know if he surfs. God, I can't believe I don't even know that!" Her crying resumed full force.

"How about his height?" the officer asked.

"I don't know," she said. "Tall."

"Tall as in six feet? Six foot three? Six foot six?"

"I don't know. Maybe."

The officer blinked twice, the slightest flicker of irritation showing through. "Miss Shea gave us a description of her boyfriend yesterday. Let me read it to you." He pulled a sheet of paper off his desk. "Thirty-four years old. Five eleven and one-half inch. One hundred seventy pounds. Dark blond hair. Blue eyes. Athletic build. Scar on chin." Here he paused and frowned at the paper. "Detached earlobes." (They'd asked for distinguishing features; I was just being thorough.)

"I don't understand what all of this has to do with Jimmy!" Tiara blurted.

"Jimmy?" I said.

"Having two men go missing in twenty-four hours—that's pretty unusual," the detective said, crossing his arms. "Even more unusual is when both missing men are named Jimmy James."

"Jimmy's real name is Michael," I said, as if that cleared things up. "My Jimmy, I mean."

Tiara stared at me. "Same thing with my Jimmy."

I grabbed the side of my chair. The room spun. There must be some misunderstanding. Some terrible mistake. "Do you live here?" I asked when I could speak. "Does your—your Jimmy live here?"

She shook her head. "California. I live in Irvine. Jimmy lives in Laguna Beach."

"Oh my God," I whispered, covering my mouth with my left hand.

She yelped. "You have a ring!"

I held out my hand and blinked at the diamond as if I'd never seen it before.

"You and Jimmy were *engaged*?" she wailed.

"He wanted to marry me," I whispered, hiding the ring with my right hand.

She stuck a knuckle in her full mouth and made sounds like a wounded animal.

"Miss Cardenas arrived in Maui three days ago," the officer

told me. "Same day as you. Her boyfriend flew in separately, said he was on business and staying in a client's condo but he'd visit her at the hotel."

Jimmy's disappearances returned in a flash: the early morning meetings, the sales calls. And then it hit me. It couldn't be. Oh, no.

"Where are you staying?" I asked slowly.

"Huh?" She fluttered her damp eyelashes, too dazed for a moment to speak. And finally, the answer: "On Kaanapali Beach. At the Hyatt."

That did it: total emotional overload. My head buzzed. My breathing came in gasps and spurts. Everything grew fuzzy and pale.

"Can we get some water over here?" the detective called out. Someone brought it and made me drink. I gagged but got it down. The detective asked us more questions, and I'm sure I answered them, but I'm not sure what was said. Mostly I remember waves of nausea, catapults of emotion: pain, anger, confusion, more pain.

"This doesn't really change anything," the officer said in closing. *Doesn't change anything?* That may have been the stupidest thing anyone had ever said. "We still have a man missing. And probably—" He looked from me to Tiara and back to me. "Probably dead."

I tightened my mouth and nodded shakily as Tiara burst into a fresh round of sobs.

The officer stood up. "The search crews are out today—we'll send them out again tomorrow if necessary. You're free to go. We'll be in touch." In touch. As if we were completing a job interview. I stood up. Tiara remained hunched in her chair, her wails growing louder and, quite frankly, annoying.

"Oh, Miss Shea," the detective said. "Did you get any more

contact numbers for his friends and family? Maybe someone can send me a recent picture."

"I talked to his mother already," I said. "And his office manager. I told them what was going on."

"You know his mother?" Tiara asked weakly.

"We've spoken," I answered after a pause. "I charged his cell phone on the way over," I told the detective, wanting to change the subject. "I've got it right here." I dug the phone out of my purse and hit the power button. Somehow, I didn't expect it to work, as if it needed Jimmy's life force to function.

But the screen came to life with its made-for-teenagers greeting, WHERE YOU AT? *I'm in the innermost circle of hell,* I thought miserably.

The phone's battery was low—the drive to the station had been short—but there was enough of a charge to check the contact list. I zipped right down the list to the *T*s. And there she was: TIARA. Home number, cell number. No photos, thank God. Then I backed up to the *J*s, just to make sure I was there, that Jimmy hadn't erased me from his phone in preparation for erasing me from his life. But there I was: JANE SHEA. My name is short: easy to enter in its entirety. And yet, it bothered me. Tiara was just Tiara. I was "Jane Shea." I could be anyone—business acquaintance, hairdresser, one-night stand.

The detective crossed the room; I handed over the phone.

"You know a Scott?" he asked, flicking through the numbers.

"Work."

"Bryan?"

"Roommate."

He ran down the list (omitting my name and Tiara's). I knew some names, coworkers from the restaurant, mostly (Bunny, Chaz, Luis). There were girls' names (Holly, Simone, Tammi). What was their story? I wondered. Were they one-night stands from Laguna Beach? Or were they holed up at yet another hotel? (And if so, was it nicer than the Maui Hi?)

"Nothing for his parents," the officer said finally, shutting the phone and handing it back to me. "They'd probably be the best bet. Can you get me that number?"

I nodded. "I've got it back at my room."

Tiara staggered across the floor, dabbing her eyes with a wad of toilet paper (the station had run out of tissues). "So you never met his parents?" she asked in a little voice.

I shook my head. "Did you?" It was ridiculous how badly I wanted her to say no. And she did. But it didn't make me feel much better.

The detective put his hands in his pockets. "That will be all for now. Thanks for coming down."

We both looked at him, bewildered.

"If I hear anything else, I'll call of course. And, Miss Shea, I'd appreciate you calling me with that phone number."

I nodded. Tiara and I continued to look at him. How could he just send us off like this? What were we supposed to do?

"You two might want to sit down together," the detective suggested. "Someplace else, someplace neutral. And compare notes." He saw my expression. "Or—not."

Not, I thought.

But Tiara said, "That would help me. Really. I'm staying at the Hyatt." (As if I'd forgotten.) "Maybe you can come over, and we can talk. I have so many questions."

I did, too, of course, though I wasn't sure I was ready to hear answers.

Tiara blew her nose into the wad of toilet paper. "Please come with me. I don't want to be alone."

Chapter 13

So I finally got to see the Hyatt, though the experience wasn't quite what I had envisioned.

"It never even occurred to me to rent a car," Tiara sniffled from the little red car's passenger seat as we glided up a long, palm-lined driveway to the hotel. It was the first thing she had said since leaving the police station.

"I mean, why would I need a car?" she continued. "All's I was gonna do was lounge by the pool and make love to Jimmy. Maybe stroll down to some restaurants if we got hungry. But mostly, I figured, we'd just get room service."

"Welcome to the Hyatt," the valet said, opening my car door. "Will you be staying with us?"

"She is," I said, nodding toward Tiara.

After one look at Tiara, the valet practically yanked me out of my seat, leaving me stranded in the driveway as he raced around to assist her. He opened her door and leaned forward eagerly. She held out her limp, manicured hand. "Let me help you," the valet murmured.

Standing in the lobby was a major déjà vu moment—not because I'd been there in this (or any) life, but because in the past month I'd spent so many hours poring over photos in guidebooks and on the Web.

Alo-fucking-ha.

The photos hadn't done the Hyatt justice: pictures couldn't capture the soaring open-air atrium, the ocean breezes, the smell of hothouse flowers, the chirping and cawing of brightly colored birds. Reddish flagstones lay underfoot, interrupted here and there by towering palm trees and antique canoes.

"You wanna see the penguins?" Tiara asked. "Because I think that's just really cool. You know—penguins in Hawaii."

What was she—my tour guide? My enthusiasm for penguins had diminished over the last couple of days, but I followed Tiara, her heels clicking on the stones, until we reached a gold railing surrounding a leafy enclosure.

"See?" Tiara put her hands on the rail and leaned forward. "Penguins." She sounded proud, as if she owned them. As if we had nothing more important to think about than exotic birds.

The penguins were smaller than the usual tuxedo kind, their markings more muted. Plus, they didn't stink the way penguins usually do.

"Nice," I said.

"There's flamingos, too," she said. "And swans. You want to see them?"

"Not really."

"Oh." She looked stumped, confused—like she couldn't remember why we were here.

"When did you meet Jimmy?" I asked. Wasn't that what we were supposed to discuss?

"Not that long ago. Sometime after Christmas," she said, still gazing at the penguins. "I can't remember, exactly."

"Was it still December?" I asked. "Or January?" For some reason, the timing felt important, something I had to know. Did Jimmy pull away from me because he'd met someone else? Or did he look elsewhere because I'd begun to bore him? Maybe he just got lonely when I left him to go to New Jersey for Christmas.

She looked at me, baffled. "Maybe."

"Maybe what?"

"I'm not sure. January?"

I remembered Jimmy once saying that I was smarter than the girls he usually dated. No shit.

"Was it before or after New Year's?" I said, speaking slowly.

"Oh! It was after." (Comprehension: yay!) "Because for New Year's? I was dating this other guy."

"Mm." I nodded. "And how long before you and Jimmy . . . were intimate?" I couldn't bring myself to say *made love*.

"Oh, we fucked the first night," Tiara said. "Four times."

I felt like I'd been punched in the stomach. No wonder Jimmy had lost sexual interest in me. He'd been exhausted. In the penguin enclosure, one of the birds waddled into his plastic igloo. I longed to follow him.

The questions continued to jump around in my brain. Did Jimmy take me to Maui because he felt guilty about Tiara? Or had he met her after booking the tickets?

"It would help me," I said, "if you could tell me the exact day you met Jimmy. I could—better understand things, maybe."

She shook her head, confused. "I really haven't a clue. I mean— do you know when you met him?"

"September eighteenth," I said. "Seven p.m."

She squinted. "Huh."

"Don't you have a planner?" I asked. "A calendar? Something?"

Her eyes widened. "Kind of. It's in my room."

*   *   *

Tiara's room (*my* room) was in the main tower, high above the atrium. Once off the elevator, I peered down to the stone floors far below. A person could fall from here, but what a way to go. Besides, if a person splattered in the Hyatt lobby, at least there would be no missing-body issues.

The room had a kick-ass water view, a lanai, and pretty, Asian-inspired furniture that didn't smell. There was a comfy-looking sofa covered with soft green velour and a dark wood coffee table that, I was pleased to see, was a bit worn around the edges. The walls were covered in a paper that looked like ivory linen. A Hawaiian quilt decorated the wall behind the bed, which had a white coverlet and enough pillows for three people.

Ew.

I don't know what pissed me off more: Jimmy's infidelity or this room. In a flash of self-protective and entirely deluded thinking, I considered for a moment that he'd put me in the condo because it had a kitchenette and he really liked my cooking.

And then Tiara peeled off her top and every device of psychological self-defense failed. "I'm going to change into something more comfortable," she said, like a coy character from an old sitcom. "This shirt is so tight it's, like, cutting off my circulation."

Tiara got the nicer hotel because Tiara had bigger boobs than

I did. Actually, Tiara had bigger boobs than pretty much anyone I'd ever seen—and I belong to an Orange County health club. It was unclear whether she was just uninhibited or whether she was showing off.

I could see her full tattoo now, a five-point star on her left breast that said TIARA. Was that to make sure that no man, on the morning after, ever asked, "What was your name, again?" She could have been more straightforward and tattooed "Hello, my name is:" above it.

Tiara kicked off her white heels. One of them almost hit me in the shin. When she started unbuttoning her shorts, I headed for the lanai, but she stopped me. "So you and Jimmy had been going out for a while?" she asked, sounding like a sad little girl.

"Yes." I looked at her out of reflexive politeness and then looked away because—you know. When she didn't react, I peeked over again.

She dropped her shorts on the floor. I looked away, but only after I'd seen that she wasn't wearing any underwear.

"I haven't known him long," she said. "But right away I was certain—I just *knew* he was the one. He was my Prince Charming, the man I've been dreaming about since I was a little girl."

"But your prince already had a queen," I said, feeling like the witch who gave Snow White the poisoned apple.

"I didn't know about you, I swear," she whimpered. After a pause, she said, in a tiny voice, "When did he ask you to marry him?"

I looked at her in surprise, training my eyes on her face—though some dark recess of my brain registered *Brazilian bikini wax,* to which another, more primitive, recess responded, *Ouch!*

"It was . . . a while ago." As I said it, the realization hit me— rather late, I'll admit, but remember, I'd been under a lot of stress:

Jimmy might have bought the ring for Tiara. In fact, Jimmy proba- bly bought the ring for Tiara. Then again, if Tiara got a room at the Hyatt, it only seemed fair that I got a diamond.

I scurried toward the sliding-glass door, suddenly desperate for fresh air. There was a big mirror over the dresser; passing it, I shud- dered. My hair looked even flatter and greasier than it had this morning, and dark circles had formed under my eyes. I looked like I had been through hell. But then, I had.

Beyond the sliding door, the lanai had a triangular glass table and two chairs. The view was spectacular, of course. The resort had winding stone paths, a rope bridge, and a humongous pool—a *Flintstones*–meets–*Fantasy Island* creation of caves and boulders surrounded by lounge chairs and lush landscaping: bougainvillea, magnolia trees, palm trees, all kinds of pink and purple flowers. It was like a rain forest, only without the poisonous snakes and exotic parasites. Hammocks and cabanas overlooked the beach, which wasn't nearly as wide as I expected but that, all things con- sidered, didn't suck.

Beyond the beach lay the Pacific, the island of Lanai rising in the distance. The blue water was gentle today, the waves not crashing so much as stroking the shore, as if they were too polite to make a lot of noise. A powerboat buzzed by pulling a parasailer, the giant parachute a lemon-yellow decorated with two eyes and a smile. Have a nice day, my ass.

"Which do you think?" Tiara asked from behind me. I turned. She stood in the doorway to the lanai, stark naked, holding a teeny bikini top, one white, one pink, in each hand.

"Ahh!" I yelped.

"What?" She looked genuinely hurt.

"People can *see* you."

She shrugged. Perhaps that was the point. She turned and

strolled back into the bedroom. Her ass, I noticed uncharitably, was puckered with cellulite.

"I think I'll wear the white one," she said, slipping it on. I didn't bother to tell her that her nipples were slightly visible behind the light fabric. That would make her happy. I didn't tell her that her butt looked cottage cheesy in the back. That made me happy—and happiness was in short supply right now.

"You're going *swimming*?" I asked. "I thought we came up here so you could check your calendar."

"Oh—that. It's not a calendar, exactly." She shrugged. "I'll get it in a minute. But anyway, I'm not going in the water. I'm not in the mood with all that's happened, plus it took me like an hour to do my hair this morning. I'm just really *hot,* and I can't bear to wear clothes right now. You want to borrow a suit?"

"Thanks, but I don't think your bathing suits would fit me." I crossed my arms over my A-cup breasts.

"Oh, no—here's the thing." She crossed to the dresser, yanked open a drawer, and rummaged around until she pulled out another white bikini, identical to the one she was wearing. She brought it out to the lanai. "When I buy bikinis? I have to buy two sets because my top and bottom are such totally different sizes. What I'm wearing is a sixteen on top and a six on the bottom. So—you could just wear the pieces that I'm not using."

I opened my mouth, but no sound came out.

She bit her cushiony lip. "Was that rude? I didn't mean to say—what I mean is, there's nothing wrong with being more, um, natural." She made fluttering gestures around her chest. "Actually, you're lucky—I mean, you're starting from scratch, so if you ever do decide to get some enhancements, you can get some that are more proportionate. Makes it easier to buy dresses. Anyway, I bet this would fit you."

She held up the size-six bikini top. I have coasters that are bigger.

I shook my head. "I think the bottom would be too loose." I waited for her to agree. She didn't.

"Besides," I continued. "It seems wrong—to act like we're still on vacation, while Jimmy . . ." My voice trailed off as my gaze fell on the big, comfortable bed. I thought of Tiara and Jimmy on the bed. I thought of their pictures. "Do you want to get a drink?"

"There's all kinds of stuff in the minibar," she said. "Beer and wine and those cute little bottles. Jimmy said to take whatever I wanted. Help yourself." She sat down at the triangular table.

I stayed standing. "Thanks, but I'd rather go somewhere else." A few days ago I couldn't wait to get into this room; now I couldn't wait to get out of it. "After you've checked your calendar, I mean."

"Oh—that." She popped up from her chair. I followed her into the room but waited while she went into the bathroom, returning with a round plastic case.

"Birth-control pills?" *That* was her calendar?

"Mm." She squinted and then looked up for a moment, calculating. "We met twenty-four days ago," she finally announced.

Three and a half weeks. That would have been days after Jimmy had booked the Maui tickets. So, he hadn't planned to bring both of us over; he made the decision after meeting Tiara. Did that make things better or worse? Did it matter?

*   *   *

Downstairs, next to the penguin enclosure, there was an open-air lounge—the Weeping Banyan, it was called, after a giant, twisting tree that grew in the middle, providing shade for fashionable guests and a perch for birds looking to poop on them. Unfortunately, the Weeping Banyan served as an espresso bar until five o'clock (when it turned into a bar-bar) and it was just shy of four. I definitely needed something stronger than an espresso.

"Guess we'll have to hit the pool bar," Tiara said with fake disappointment, tossing her dark hair off her face. She was dressed for the pool area, of course. She'd topped off her white bikini with a cover-up—one of those fishnet things that doesn't actually cover anything, just softens the edges. As for footwear, she'd gone with bright pink high-heeled flip-flops.

"Maybe I should just leave," I said, suddenly craving darkness and solitude.

"Oh, no!" She turned on her rubber heels and grabbed me by the wrist. "We still have so much more to talk about!"

It was true: we did. I'm not one to leave questions unanswered, so it was best just to get it over with. Perhaps we could find a quiet seat at the pool bar—under an umbrella, maybe, away from the crowds.

Or—not.

"YOU DIDN'T TELL ME THE BAR WAS IN A CAVE." I had to shout to be heard over a waterfall. There was another one at the end of the man-made cavern, where swimmers could splash through to the biggest section of the pool. In the shadowy water next to the bar, a pale, hefty couple snuggled on a ledge, sipping frothy drinks from plastic cups.

"I KNOW—ISN'T IT COOL?" Tiara said. "IT'S CALLED THE GROTTO BAR."

When Tiara sat down, the men a few chairs down swung their heads to look at her, even though her tummy got all poochy when she sat.

The bartender gave her a big, friendly smile. He gave me a big, friendly smile, too, which just demonstrates the Power of the Tip.

When two women joined the men at the end of the bar, the

men wisely turned their attention away from Tiara. I had to admit: she wasn't merely beautiful, she was interesting-looking. Her mouth was full and wide, her nose child-small. Her light brown eyes, almost gold and flecked with green, were practically iridescent against her naturally tan skin.

Tiara ordered a banana daiquiri. A daiquiri seemed too festive under the circumstances, so I ordered a mai tai instead.

"Jimmy and I came here on our first morning," Tiara said wistfully (and right into my ear so I could hear her over the waterfall). "After we made love. I had a piña colada, but he had a Coke because he didn't want to get too sleepy."

That would be the morning when I went to the convenience store. I remembered Jimmy coming back to the room with damp hair. He said he'd been calling customers from the beach. He said he'd jumped in the ocean.

"Did Jimmy swim in the pool that morning?" I said into her ear. Weirdly, it would feel like less of a betrayal if he'd told the truth about an ocean swim.

She looked up, considering. "Nope. He went in the ocean instead, which I thought was kind of weird."

A family—mother, father, two squealing boys—came from under the waterfall and walked through the pool next to the bar. "Cool!" one of the little boys yelled. "There's a TV in here!" It flickered on the wall behind the bartender, captions running along the bottom. There was an aquarium, too, filled with tropical fish. It seemed sad, somehow, for the fish to be cooped up here, so close to the ocean.

"How did you meet Jimmy?" Tiara asked me.

"I'm not ready to talk about it."

"Do you need a few days?"

"No, I need a few mai tais."

She laughed. It was the first time I had heard her laugh. Actually, it was the first time I had seen her smile. She had a beautiful smile: bright white, with teeth just imperfect enough to give her some character, and a little dimple on her left cheek.

Bitch.

"I met him at the restaurant," I said. "He was my waiter." What had once sounded free-spirited, fated, and funny now seemed cheap.

"Me, too," she said, sounding wounded.

We didn't say anything for a moment. It was too painful. Plus, there were several blenders going at once, and it sounded like we were in a subterranean machine shop.

Tiara signed the drinks to the room. "Jimmy said I could sign anything to the room from anywhere in the hotel, even the shops. You like my shoes?" She stuck out a leg to show off a pink high-heeled flip-flop.

"Mm," I said.

"Sixty dollars. But he said I was worth it."

Did she not remember who I was and why we were here?

The bartender turned on another blender.

"Do you want to take the drinks outside?" I asked.

"What?"

"LET'S GO OUTSIDE."

"What?"

The bartender turned off the blender. "OUTSIDE!" I screamed, my voice echoing off the walls of the grotto.

"Sure," Tiara said. "You just had to say so."

The pool lounges had cushy green pads and white frames. We claimed two under a thatched tiki umbrella and put our drinks on a white plastic table. From there, we could see the children's pool (complete with gravel beach and pop-up fountains) and the outside of the waterfall, bougainvillea spilling around the edges. Beyond a suspended rope bridge, a waterslide expelled shrieking riders. Around us, half-naked, dangerously pale adults glistened with suntan oil while their children scurried around, damp and squealing.

Day one of my itinerary: hang around the Hyatt pool. So the vacation wasn't a dead loss, I thought grimly.

At her request, I gave Tiara a brief synopsis of Jimmy's and my relationship, and then I asked, "How did you and Jimmy get together?" I didn't really want to know, but it would have been rude not to ask.

She slipped on oversize sunglasses and leaned back on her lounge. "Kinda like you, I was going out with this guy, supernice, totally into me, bought me lots of shit, but the sex just wasn't that hot, you know?"

She turned to me and slipped her sunglasses down to make eye contact. Then she pushed them back up. "Plus, he was married, and even though he said he was thinking about leaving his wife, I had this feeling like he was leading me on. He was really rich, though. That was cool. But he was, like, a lot older than me, so I kept feeling like I was screwing my grandpa."

I sucked on my mai tai straw, only to realize that the plastic cup was empty. "Yeah. That sounds exactly like my situation. Except for the grandpa bit." I held up my hand to get the waitress's attention. She wore blue board shorts and bright white sneakers. She raised her eyebrows as if to ask, *Another one?*

"Just a Diet Coke," I said (I had to drive). "And charge it to her room."

"So, anyways," Tiara continued, fluttering her pink nails. "We're at the restaurant, Jimmy's restaurant, and I'm just taking my first sip of champagne—the good shit, really expensive—and

I hear this voice say, 'Excuse me, is this your purse?' 'Cuz it'd dropped off my chair. Jimmy wasn't even my waiter, but he just, like, came to my rescue, like a knight in shining armor." She took a deep breath, which made her chest even huger, and let out a long sigh. Then she slipped a finger behind her big sunglasses to wipe away a tear.

Old guy. Champagne.

"Wait a minute. The guy you were with—silver hair, distinguished-looking? Ate there a lot?" I remembered the sugar daddy. "Mr. Richardson?"

"Mr. Robertson."

"Right. Jimmy said he was a regular. Brought in a new young woman every month." Tiara looked stunned. "But maybe he cared about you," I said quickly, not wanting to hurt her, in spite of everything. "Maybe he really would have left his wife for you." (And, gee, isn't that a romantic thought.)

"It's not that," she said. "It's just—if Mr. Robertson brought in all these other girls . . . how many of his dates do you think Jimmy picked up? Just the ones who dropped their purses on the floor?"

I remembered how Jimmy tricked Geoffrey into leaving me alone. It seemed cute at the time. "Maybe you didn't drop your purse, after all. Maybe he knocked it over when you weren't looking."

There were two of us here; how many more were in California? And that waitering job: was it really for the extra cash? Or did he just do it to meet women?

"That first night—did Jimmy make love to you on the beach?" I asked.

Her face crumpled. "I had sand in my crack for days."

I crossed my arms over my chest. "What an asshole."

"No!" She really looked upset by that assessment. "What Jimmy and I had was real."

"Sure it was," I muttered. "He just forgot to mention that he had another girlfriend."

"I thought there might be someone else," she said quietly.

"Why?"

"He was always changing plans at the last minute or hurrying off with some lame excuse. But I didn't want to screw things up. I figured, if I just gave him time, he'd realize I was his perfect match. But . . ." She looked up from under her long lashes before dropping her gaze to her long legs. "I never wanted to hurt anyone. If I'd known you then . . ." She let the sentiment go unfinished. "Do you really think there were others?"

I thought back to my nights alone and my anonymous phone call to his office. "I always wondered about Ana."

"Who?"

"You know, the office manager. He made a big deal about me not calling his office."

"Me, too," she said, nibbling on a long fingernail.

"I worried it was because he had something going on with Ana," I said. "Or maybe he was juggling so many women that he didn't want to get caught."

"Do you really think there are more women?" Tiara squeaked, sounding hurt again.

My diamond—if it was mine—caught the light. How many rings could he possibly afford? "It was probably just you and me."

On top of the tiki umbrellas, birds hopped around, chirping and pecking, hoping to score a stray potato chip, content with a lifetime of crumbs. The ocean breezes tickled us from behind. My eyes stung with tears; not just for the loss of Jimmy, but for the loss of hope: for a better man, a better me.

Tiara suddenly sat up and gasped. "What time is it?"

I checked my watch. "Almost six."

She popped off the lounge. "I've got to get to check-in at the cabanas—I'm scheduled for an oceanfront massage."

"A *massage*?"

She adjusted her mesh cover-up. "I scheduled it my first day here. I forgot to cancel it, which means they'll charge me, anyway." The cabanas were right behind us, at the edge of the beach, little teak rooms draped with canvas for privacy.

"I know Jimmy would want me to go," Tiara said. "Especially since I've been under all this stress." She paused to blink back tears. "It was supposed to be a couples' massage. We were each going to have our own masseuse."

"Nice," I said sarcastically.

She touched my arm. "Why don't you come? You can take Jimmy's place."

I tried to say no, but I was thinking, *Ew.*

"New," I said.

"It would be fun," she chirped, squeezing my arm (and pinching me just the tiniest bit with her talons). "We'd be like sorority sisters. Or sister-sisters." On any other day, the thought of Beth and me getting a couples' massage in Hawaii would have cracked me up.

"Jimmy would have liked that," I said, making no effort to keep the bitterness from my voice.

"So you'll come?"

"New," I said.

Chapter 14

That night, I dreamed about Joey Ardolino.

Joey and I went to the same high school, but we traveled in different circles. He was a second-string football player, a C student, a heavy-metal fan. I was a viola-playing honor-roll student, a baton twirler, and president of the French club. I'd known Joey since freshman year—our school wasn't that big—and he seemed nice enough. We'd smile when we passed in the hall or say hi if we bumped into each other around town. He was undeniably cute, with lush lips, giant brown eyes, soft olive skin, and a wiry build, but I was hung up on a trombone player and didn't give Joey a lot of thought.

Until junior year, that is. The second week of September we had an all-school assembly—a chance for club presidents to push their extracurricular offerings on the apathetic student body. (With yearbook photos scheduled for October, the pressure was on.) As president of the French club, I had three stomach-clenching minutes to say, "*Bonjour, mes amis,*" and describe the club's up-coming activities—in French, no less. (Geeky, yes, but my adviser made me do it.)

It went pretty well—which is to say that nobody in the audience laughed or threw spitballs—and attendance at the next French-club meeting was respectable enough for me to consider the speech a success.

Joey didn't come to the French Club meeting—I think he took Spanish—but he showed up at my locker the next morning, hands in the pockets of his faded blue jeans, work boots stubbing the ground. He wore a dark blue hooded sweatshirt even though the days were still summer warm, and he smiled shyly.

"You did really good yesterday," he said. "You know—at the assembly."

"Thanks," I said, surprised. "I was nervous."

"You didn't look it." He blushed and dropped his eyes to the ground.

"It helped that I had to speak French," I said. "If I messed up, no one would know."

He beamed at me as if that was the cleverest thing he'd ever heard (which, maybe, it was).

I pulled out a textbook covered with brown kraft paper and shut my locker. "I'd better get to class." I wasn't trying to ditch him; even then I hated to be late.

"I can walk you," he said, apparently lacking my fixation on punctuality. "What class is it?"

"Trig."

"Cool."

Things went on like this for a couple of weeks. He'd show up at my locker, bat his thick eyelashes, make small talk (I mean, really small), and walk me to class. He thought it was cool that I played the viola, cool that I was in honors English, cool that I watched *Quantum Leap*.

We were a mismatched couple—him in his hoodie and work boots, me in my Docksider shoes, Gap jeans, and oxford cloth shirts. "I never would have put you two together," my best friend, Regina, said—but the way she looked at him, long and hard, left no doubt that she would have been glad to have Joey lingering at her locker instead of mine. The trombone player did a double take when he saw us whispering outside the music room, and I didn't bother trying to hide my smile.

After two weeks, Joey finally asked me out on a date. We went to his friend's house and watched TV, and then we drove around town with his friend and his friend's girlfriend until we found a shadowy spot to park behind the public library. There we spent a good half hour necking while Nirvana played on the radio.

The following Monday, I bounded into school with a big smile: I had my first official boyfriend. I'd been to formal dances and group movie dates, but this was the real thing. I expected some hand-holding to go along with our new status, perhaps a chaste peck when he dropped me off at trig class, but things continued as before: the random locker visits, the strolls down the hallway.

He was busy the next weekend—family stuff, he said—but he called me twice, and the next week he continued to spend quality time with me in the four-minute breaks between classes.

"I need to talk to you," Regina told me at the beginning of orchestra one day. A harpist, ballerina, and aspiring anorexic, Regina was the only person I've ever known who could make me look laid-back. "It's about Joey."

"Mm." I rested my viola on my shoulder and made a show of tuning the strings, which were pretty much in tune to begin with. In the past few weeks, my honors and music friends had warned me that Joey had been known to cut class and skip school on occasion. There was even a rumor that he'd been caught smoking pot after a football game sophomore year, but I didn't believe it.

"Joey's dating Katie Rothman," Regina said. Her face was tight, anxious—I mean, even more than usual.

"No, he's not," I said calmly. "He's dating me." *Why can't she just be happy for me?* I thought.

"But he's dating Katie, too." She detailed the chain of information, which began with Katie telling someone about her Saturday-night date with Joey and ended with us there in seventh-period orchestra.

"It's not true," I said, believing my words. "Joey likes *me*." You'd think I'd be less trusting, considering that I'd so recently had a front-row seat to my parents' divorce, but this was different. My mother was middle-aged, messy, sagging at the edges, while I was young, accomplished, and well groomed. Besides, I spoke French. On top of that, Katie was a little, well, quirky—an artist with a tiny lisp who favored tinted glasses and thrift-shop clothes. There was no way Joey could like her.

But Regina was right, of course. Joey was dating me *and* he was dating Katie.

"I'm so confused," he moaned when I confronted him after school that day, his big brown eyes looking genuinely pained. "I didn't plan it this way, you know? It just, like, happened. I like both of you. I mean, you're cuter and sweeter, but Katie is exciting because she's *different.*"

I held back a mouthful of biting comments because I was supposed to be the sweet one. If I called him a cocksucker, I'd be left with nothing but my cuteness to recommend me. And I wasn't even all that cute.

The next day, Katie smiled when I passed her in the hall. She had a wide mouth and funky-crooked teeth. I thought, *What does she have to be happy about?*

A couple of days later, while I was still (stupidly) waiting for Joey to make his choice, I ran into Katie in the lunch line (it was pizza day) and she said, "I guess we've got something in common." She laughed sweetly. (And *I* was supposed to be the sweet one.)

I said, "Yeah, I guess," and grabbed a salad because it got me out of line faster. If she was happy, it could only mean one thing: Joey had chosen her.

But he hadn't. In the end, he drifted away from both of us. For the rest of high school, Katie continued to smile at me, while I did my best to avoid her.

The summer after my freshman year of college, I took a job at a local clothing store only to discover that Katie worked there, too. She had just finished her first year of art school; her short hair was now streaked with pink, and she had three holes in each ear.

"I hated you in high school," I confessed one day while we were dressing a mannequin. (Katie wanted to glue a metallic stud to the mannequin's nose, but I talked her out of it.)

"Why?" She looked genuinely confused.

"Because of Joey," I said. "Because he liked you."

"But that wasn't my fault," she said. "I didn't even know about you till after he asked me out. Besides, he was a jerk to both of uth." (Her lisp only came out now and then.)

"I know," I said. "But it just bugged me. He was the first guy— well, the first cute guy—who saw something in me, but I wasn't enough for him."

"Or maybe he was just an ath-hole," Katie said, her piercings glinting under the fluorescent lights.

She was right, of course, but I was left with the nagging feeling that I was not special enough to be loved—that I, alone, would never be enough for anyone.

Through college, Katie and I kept in touch—writing letters and getting together on Christmas and summer vacations. She'd call me when she needed advice; I'd call her when I needed to laugh. Regina's parents had moved away the summer after graduation, so I didn't really see her anymore. By the time I finished college, Katie was my closest friend from high school. She urged me to move to New York with her after graduation, but she was already involved with Ron, the man she would eventually marry (an investment banker, of all the unlikely choices) and I didn't want to get in the way.

A year after moving to California, I flew back to be a bridesmaid in Katie's wedding. It was the first time I'd met Ron, who sported a goatee and a gold hoop earring.

I didn't know many people at the rehearsal dinner, so Katie was pleased to see Ron and me laughing together. He either found my stories about high school in New Jersey extremely funny or he was just really drunk.

When it was time to leave, he said, "I'll help you get your coat." I thought he was just being nice. Katie was across the room, laughing with her sisters. I waved to her and went down the hall with Ron. Once I'd retrieved my coat, he followed me around the corner, grabbed my shoulders, and laid his mouth on mine.

I pushed my hands against his chest and pulled my head away.

"Where are you staying?" he asked urgently.

"You're getting married!" I said, suddenly sober.

"Yeah," he said. "So we'd better hurry. Tomorrow it's all over."

I didn't sleep with him, of course. I gave him a brief, inarticulate speech about how lucky he was to be marrying someone as wonderful as Katie and how stupid he'd be to throw everything away. The next day, I took my place in the bridal lineup, taking care to avoid Ron's eyes (not hard, since he was avoiding mine as well). It was a modern ceremony: no "do you have any objections" moment. But I wouldn't have said anything even if I'd been asked.

The truth was, I had never hated Katie for dating Joey; I had hated her for telling people about it. I wanted to believe Joey was all mine. Whether it was true or not didn't really matter.

After the wedding, I let my friendship with Katie lapse, afraid that my memory could somehow poison her happiness. Ron was not the man she thought he was, but she'd be okay as long as she never discovered the truth about him.

And now, in Maui, that's how I felt about Jimmy—and Tiara. For all my insistence on research, on clarity, on lists, there were times when I craved complete ignorance.

Chapter 15

I awoke early, Joey Ardolino's long lashes still fresh in my mind. After a couple of hours spent trying to get comfortable in the hard bed with its rough, overbleached sheets, I finally got up and turned on the lights. It was too early to call the police station, not that there was much left to ask or say.

I took a long hot shower, and then swore when I remembered there was no hair dryer. But then, did it really matter what I looked like?

Once dressed, I brewed a pot of coffee and called the airline. If the police needed someone to identify a body, they could call on Tiara, who was obviously content to remain in Maui for the rest of the week, getting volcanic mud treatments at the spa and buying expensive shoes. As for me, I had a good job to go back to, a nice condo, and a pleasant set of work friends.

Unfortunately, they'd have to wait. The flights between now

and my scheduled departure on Thursday were booked solid. I was stuck in Maui.

Shortly after I got off the phone, there was a soft knock on my door. Mary stood there, holding a small loaf of bread.

"I saw your lights on," she said. "Figured you were up." She held out the loaf. "Banana bread. Thought you could use some home-made comfort food."

"You made this?"

She smiled, her square teeth very white. "Well, not me person-ally."

I took the loaf. "Would you like some coffee?"

"I should get back to the office, but, well . . . a few minutes wouldn't hurt." She followed me over to the kitchenette. "Any news about Mr. James?"

I shook my head. "Still missing."

There was some news, of course, and I might as well get used to saying it. Keeping my eyes on the fake-wood-grain cabinet, I said, "Though I did find something out. He was seeing another woman. And she's here on Maui."

A lump clogged my throat. I pulled a couple of mugs out of the cabinet and poured the coffee, trying hard to steady my hands.

"I know," Mary said quietly.

"You know?"

Eyes on the ground, she nodded. "It was in the paper this morning."

"Oh God." I took a deep breath. "Can you show it to me?"

MISSING MAN AT CENTER
OF LOVE TRIANGLE

LAHAINA—The case of Michael "Jimmy" James, the La-guna Beach, CA, man who allegedly disappeared while scuba diving on Saturday, took a bizarre twist yesterday. Initial police reports indicated that Mr. James had been traveling with "a friend." New information reveals that Mr. James was splitting his vacation time between two women, Jane Shea, 32, of Brea, California, and Tiara Cardenas, 24, of Irvine, CA. Both Ms. Shea and Ms. Cardenas maintain that they knew nothing about each other before yesterday *(story continued on page 6)*.

I looked up at Mary. "Allegedly?"

"Huh?" She was getting a carton of milk out of the refrigerator.

"It says Jimmy 'allegedly' disappeared while scuba diving. Are they saying that he may not have disappeared? Or that he maybe wasn't scuba diving?"

"I think you should read the whole thing," she murmured.

I turned the pages. "Oh my God!" There were separate photos of Tiara and me outside the police station. She looked ready to go clubbing. I looked like I lived in a house without a mirror. "Who took these? Was there someone waiting outside the police station?"

Mary shrugged helplessly.

"I look like shit," I said.

"It's not a good angle," Mary conceded.

LOVE TRIANGLE *(continued from p. 1)*

According to Lahaina Detective Fernando McGuinn, "We are surprised that the body has not turned up yet. We are asking all Maui residents to alert us immediately if they have any information."

Police surmise that Mr. James met both women in California, where he owns and runs Jimmies, Incorporated, a wetsuit design company.

Ms. Shea is a registered guest at the Maui Hi condomini-
ums on Lower Honoapilliani Road. Ms. Cardenas is staying
at the Hyatt Regency on Kaanapali Beach. Neither woman
was available for comment.

Hands shaking, I gave the paper back to Mary. "Now everyone knows where to find me."

"You're not exactly Britney Spears, honey. I think you'll be
fine."

"You're right," I said, trying to smile.

"Let's get you out of here," she said. "It's nice outside. And
Martin should start playing right around now. How 'bout we take
our coffee out back and look at the water?"

Martin, it turned out, played the guitar music I'd heard drift-
ing out of a ground floor unit.

"He came here on vacation," Mary explained, putting her
coffee and the banana bread on a plastic side table. "It was 1995,
1996—something like that. And he just never left." She settled
herself on a slightly damp lounge chair, tucking her oversize polyester muumuu around her legs.

"Wow," I said, settling onto the lounge next to her. "People always talk about doing something like that—getting out of the rat
race and moving to the tropics, embracing the simple life. But I
didn't think anyone actually did it."

My coffee was warm and sweet. Mary had added sugar without asking me. It tasted surprisingly good.

"Ha!" She laughed. "You hang around Maui for any length of
time, you find lots of people did just that very thing. Works for
some of them."

"And the others?"

She shrugged. "They go home. When they find they can't make a living here, when they get sick of the sunshine. Some people think they can run away from themselves—that if they come here, they're going to be a whole new person."

"Wherever you go, there—you are," I said, thinking of my cross-country move. I'd never really felt at home in California until I moved into my pristine little condo, the exact replica of which I probably could have bought in New Jersey or Boston.

I'd gone to Jimmy's house only once. We'd just finished an early dinner at a Mexican restaurant in Laguna, and he wanted to pick up a change of clothes before heading up to Brea. I was excited about seeing the house, having wondered why we didn't spend any time there. It was within walking distance of the beach, after all. He'd told me it was a fixer-upper, but how bad could it be?

Pretty bad, as it turned out. While the house must have cost a lot of money—he never told me what he'd paid, but everything in Laguna was expensive—it looked like a shack. Several blocks up from the Pacific Coast Highway, it was a sad, squatty bungalow crammed between two renovated beauties. The paint was a dingy yellow, the walkway cracked concrete.

"Bryan's home," he muttered as we walked hand in hand to the front door. Jimmy had a roommate to help with the mortgage.

"How do you know he's here?" I asked.

"His car." He motioned to a black Mercedes SUV parked across the street. "Trust-fund kid," he explained.

The smell of marijuana smoke hit me the instant Jimmy un-locked the front door. Bryan sat slumped at the kitchen table, mouth hanging open, glazed eyes glued to a laptop. On top of the marijuana, the room smelled like old pizza, stale beer, and miscellaneous decay. Empty pizza boxes and crumb-covered plates covered the yellow Formica counter.

Bryan glanced up when we walked in the room. "Hey."

Bryan would have made a great bouncer. He was a big guy, both in height and width. Thick, dark, wiry hair peeked out above his sleeveless T-shirt and below his nylon basketball shorts. He was playing a game on the computer, something involving simulated shots, explosions, and screams.

"This is Jane," Jimmy said.

Bryan nodded without looking up again. "Hey."

"You want anything?" Jimmy asked me. "A glass of water or something? I think we've got orange juice."

The tiny sink was crowded with plastic plates and beer mugs. Once white, the refrigerator was a streaky gray. "No, thanks," I said.

Jimmy's dark bedroom, awkwardly situated off the kitchen, wasn't much better. He'd left his double bed unmade. Dirty laundry littered the orange shag carpet. The entire room smelled like socks. I reached out to open the window blinds and then thought better of letting in the early evening light: there are some things you're better off not seeing.

Jimmy shoved some clothes into a shopping bag and then asked, "You want to hang around here some more or . . ."

"Let's go to my place," I said. (Screw the easy beach access.)

"I would have cleaned if I'd known you were going to see it," he said.

"I'm not sure it would have made much of a difference," I answered honestly.

"It's a dump, I know. But you can't beat the location. And someday, when my business takes off . . ." He gazed around, and we both thought about how the room—and the whole house—

would look fixed up. All it would take was time and money. And maybe a woman's touch.

(But which woman? I wondered now.)

"You could get another roommate," I suggested later.

"Yeah, I know. But Bryan's quiet, at least. And to be honest, he's paying way more rent than he should—it comes close to covering my mortgage. Besides, it's not forever." He smiled, and I wondered if the word *forever* could ever apply to us, never dreaming how little time Jimmy had left.

* * *

Mary and I sipped our coffee and looked at the water, which changed colors and textures as the sun rose higher in the sky, the blue broken every now and then by the distant splash of a whale. Martin started playing, finally—a Jack Johnson tune. Mary handed me a slice of banana bread. Within seconds, little chirping birds swarmed around us.

"This is delicious," I said. The banana bread wasn't quite as good as mine (just being honest here), but I was touched by the gesture and almost ridiculously grateful to have someone doing something nice for me, for a change.

Martin finished his song and moved on to an old Simon and Garfunkel tune. The tension between my shoulders let up, just a little.

A sturdy Hawaiian man wearing a polyester shirt—the print matched Mary's muumuu—came around the corner. I recognized him as the kind-faced man I'd seen working around the grounds.

"There you are," he called to Mary with a smile. "Lying in the sun while I'm working my tail off."

"Mm-hmm," she said, smiling a little as she sipped her coffee. "Do me a favor, Albert, and go check the front office—make sure no one needs anything from me." She peered inside her coffee cup. "And if you could make us another pot of coffee, maybe? I'm getting low."

"How's the banana bread?" he asked, coming toward us with a big grin.

Mary handed him a piece. "Better with macadamia nuts."

"We were out." He took a bite and shrugged. "Tastes good to me. I'll get that coffee." He shot Mary a sly look. "Your Highness."

"He made the banana bread?" I asked when Albert left.

"Mm-hmm." Mary put the last bite in her mouth and slapped the crumbs off her hands. The little birds went wild.

"Is he your boyfriend?"

She swallowed her banana bread and licked a crumb off her lips. "Husband. Four years in April."

I snuck a peek at her but still couldn't guess her age. Her brown skin was smooth, and her black hair showed no signs of gray. Still, she seemed too calm and wise to be really young. "You're lucky to have someone like Albert."

"I know," she said matter-of-factly. "But it works both ways. I treat him good, too."

It never seemed to work both ways for me.

"Was Albert your first boyfriend?" I asked.

She laughed. "Hardly."

"Did any of the others ever cheat on you?"

"Nope," she said confidently.

"How can you be sure?" I could only think of one of my boyfriends—Steve the ophthalmologist—who didn't fool around, but maybe he did and I just never found out.

"I've got a good feeling for people, I guess," she said. "I can tell the difference between what's flashy and what's real. Some guys who asked me out, they were good-looking, nice dressers, they could dance—but I could tell that they'd never like me half as much as they liked themselves. So I just said no."

"You met Jimmy, right?" I asked.

"Sure," she said. "I was here when he checked in. Worked a double shift that day."

I paused before asking, "What did you think of him?"

Mary frowned in concentration, remembering Jimmy. Were his flaws obvious at first glance? Did she see something I had missed?

"I thought he had a nice ass," she said finally.

When Albert came around the corner again, he didn't have a pot of coffee. And he wasn't smiling.

"There's a message on the answering machine," he said. "From the police."

Mary and I both sat up abruptly.

"They want Miss Shea to call them," he said. "They said it's important."

Chapter 16

"We found Michael James," Detective McGuinn said.

"Is he . . ." I couldn't finish the sentence. The image that flashed in my mind was so grisly, it made me dizzy. I sat down on a stinky green chair, afraid I would fall over.

"We'd like you to come down to the station," he said.

* * *

Tiara, dressed in a buttercup-yellow halter dress, climbed out of a taxi just as I pulled up. Out of respect for her missing boyfriend, she wore flats instead of heels, and her glossy black hair was held back chastely in a clip—a rhinestone clip, but still. She pulled a tissue out of a big yellow bag dotted with metal studs and dabbed her eyes.

"They said that they found him," she whispered. "They didn't say he was dead, but . . ."

"I know." I took a deep breath. "And it's going to be hard to hold it together, but just so you know—people will be asking us questions. Not just the police." I did a quick scan of the parking lot but didn't see anyone hiding out with a camera. "Our pictures were in the paper today."

"Really?" She spun her head to look at me, sounding more pleased than was appropriate under the circumstances. "How did I look?"

"You looked—fine." Actually, she looked gorgeous, but that didn't matter right now. "Did the police say anything else about Jimmy?"

"No. Just that I needed to come down here." Her gaze grew distant for a moment. "Jane?"

"Yes?" I said, feeling a momentary bond: after all, we were going through the exact same thing.

"Did you save a copy of that newspaper? I'd really like to see it."

*　*　*

The entire station went quiet when we walked in the door. Detective McGuinn came over to greet us. "Ladies."

"You said you found Jimmy." I couldn't bear the suspense any longer. My eyes swept the room, searching for Jimmy, but of course he wasn't there. A fresh wave of pain washed over me. In a dark, stupid corner of my brain, I'd been harboring a fantasy: Jimmy would be here, looking cold and confused but alive. And Tiara would see him and say, *No, no, there's been a terrible mistake. That's not my boyfriend. I've never seen this man before.*

The detective scratched his cheek, considering. "Did I say we found him? What I should have said, I guess, was that Michael James found us."

I stared at him. "Do you mean . . ."

"He's alive?" Tiara gasped.

The officer looked across the room. "I have Michael James

waiting in the interrogation room. Not that we're interrogating him," he explained. "Just—that's our only other room."

"Alive," I said for confirmation.

"Very much alive," he said.

I put my hand on my chest. "Thank God."

Something inside me lifted, lightened. There'd be no happy reunion, I realized, immediately abandoning my two-different-Jimmys fantasy. And I wasn't going to sit around hoping that Jimmy would choose me over Tiara. But at least now I could go home and hate him with a clear conscience.

Tiara covered her mouth with her hands and began to sob.

"There, there," the officer said, folding her in a loose hug.

"I thought," she sobbed, "I'd never"—*sob*—"see him"—*sob*—"again." She gasped and blubbered some more.

Around the room, the other officers, along with a guy being booked for drunk driving, watched with expressions of misty sympathy, like they were witnessing the last ten minutes of a *Hallmark Hall of Fame* special.

"Can we just get this over with?" I asked. The mistiness evaporated.

"Of course," the officer said, releasing Tiara.

*   *   *

When you learn to scuba dive, the first thing they teach you is, never hold your breath. I didn't even realize I'd stopped breathing until we entered the room and my chest began to hurt. I gulped air. And then I looked around. The interrogation room was small and rectangular, dominated by a long table. I scanned every inch of the room, even glancing under the table, but Jimmy wasn't there—just another police officer sitting in a plastic chair and a tall guy with dark hair who was talking to himself. He looked upset by whatever he was saying. Then I realized: oh, a cell phone. He had one of those little earpieces that always throw me. Was he talking to Jimmy? Was Jimmy in the hospital—in the ICU, perhaps? The thought of Jimmy injured, Jimmy in pain, made me tremble despite all that had happened.

I'd wait till Jimmy made a full recovery, and *then* I'd start to hate him.

The guy with the earpiece frowned at us. "Don't know," he said into the air. "Complete mess . . . Unbelievable." He spoke quickly, in clipped tones. No sooner had he turned off his phone than it rang again. "Yeah?"

Tiara entered the room behind me, mewing like an injured kitten.

The officer cleared his throat. The guy on the phone scowled and held up a finger as if to say, *One minute.* He was in his thirties, I'd guess, long and lean with square shoulders, dressed in khaki shorts and a black polo shirt. His dark hair was cut conservatively. His eyes were sharp and brown. Most of all, he looked really, really annoyed.

Finally, he pulled the receiver out of his ear, stuck it in his pocket, and folded his arms across his chest.

The detective motioned to the seated policeman. "This is Sergeant Hosozawa," the detective said. "He works out of the Wailuki station."

Sergeant Hosozawa rose out of his chair, his bearing erect and vaguely military. His black hair was so short his scalp showed through, and his mocha-colored skin was acne-scarred. His eyes were so dark it was almost impossible to tell the pupil from the iris. Just being in the same room made me suck in my stomach and stand straighter.

The sergeant held an arm out toward the tall man in the black polo shirt. "Ladies, I'd like you to meet Michael James."

Chapter 17

"That's not Jimmy," I said as steadily as I could. Tiara began to wail. The detective helped her into a chair.

"Have you ever seen this man before?" the sergeant asked us.

"No," I said. Tiara made a gulping, gagging sound and shook her head.

The tall guy tapped his foot. "Can I go now?"

The sergeant ignored his question. "I take it you don't know these women, Mr. James."

"No."

"It's a different Michael James," I told the detective evenly, doing my best to keep the "duh" out of my voice.

The officer cleared his throat. "Mr. James, can you tell us where you work?"

Before he could answer, his cell phone rang, the tone like a cat's purr. Michael James pulled the phone out of his pocket and checked the screen.

"I gotta get this." He stuck the bud back in his ear and pushed a button on the phone. "Hey . . . Yeah, I know—I just talked to him." He grimaced. "My mother just about had a heart attack." His eyes popped wider. "You're kidding me. When? How much? . . . Oh, my God." He ran a hand through his short hair.

"Mr. James owns his own business," the sergeant said. "Scuba gear."

"Just like Jimmy," I said.

The sergeant cleared his throat. "Mr. James is thirty-four years old. His scuba company is located in Laguna Beach," the sergeant said. "I think you know what it's called."

No. It couldn't be. "Oh my God." I put a hand on the table to steady myself.

"What?" Tiara squeaked.

"Jimmies," I said, not making any attempt to keep the "duh" out of my voice.

She looked at Michael James, still talking on his phone, and said, "His company has the same name as Jimmy's?" (I think I actually heard someone in the room say, "Duh," but maybe it was just my imagination.)

The sergeant crossed his arms and pulled his shoulders up even higher. "Mr. James watched the news last night. He was kind of surprised to find out he was dead. Even more surprised to find that his American Express miles had been cashed in to pay for a room at the Hyatt."

Michael James pulled the piece out of his ear. "Actually, I was more surprised to find out I was dead." He shoved the phone back in his pocket and looked from Tiara to me. "Does either one of you know anything about a really expensive ring bought in a jewelry shop at the Hyatt a few nights ago?"

I instinctively covered the diamond with my right hand. I had tried to yank the ring off this morning—it seemed absurd to wear it at this point—but it was so tight I couldn't get it off.

"No," Tiara said. I didn't say anything.

"I just talked to my assistant," Michael James said.

"Ana?" I asked, hoping he'd say no, hoping that Ana really worked for Jimmy, that something he'd told me was true.

"Yeah." He blinked. "How did you know that?"

We locked eyes. Something like dread spread over his face.

"This isn't just about credit cards, is it?" he asked. I shook my head.

"What's this about a ring?" the sergeant asked him.

"Someone used my American Express to buy a diamond ring at the Hyatt a few days ago," Michael said. "The same card was used at the ABC Store in Whaler's Village." (My muffin, I thought. My anklet.)

"And my frequent-flier miles are gone," he continued. "Used for two first-class tickets." He closed his eyes and sighed. "I was going to use those for a dive trip to Australia."

I held out my left hand. "This is the ring," I mumbled, my head down.

Tiara swung around to look at me. "But you said you and Jimmy had been engaged a long time!"

I shook my head and blushed with shame.

"So when did he propose?" she demanded.

"I—he—" I looked at the faces around me and then back at the floor. "He never actually proposed. I found the ring later. In his luggage. After he disappeared."

The room was silent for a moment. "So he may have bought the ring for me!" Tiara burst out happily.

"*He* didn't buy the ring for anybody!" Michael James said. "*I* bought the ring."

I pulled on the ring. It hurt. "You can have it back."

"Thanks so much," Michael muttered.

The sergeant spoke. "Before Mr. James—the other Mr. James, Jimmy—disappeared, did anything strange happen? Anything to indicate maybe he knew he was in trouble?"

I stopped pulling on my finger. The restaurant: of course. "We were out to dinner. They turned down Jimmy's credit card."

"How did he seem after that?"

I considered. "Upset. Distracted."

"So he might have guessed he was in trouble," Detective McGuinn said.

"Do you still have his personal effects?" Sergeant Hosozawa asked me. "His wallet, his license?"

"Yeah, they're in my condo."

"Would you mind if we took a look around?" He said this casually, but I felt like I'd been punched in my gut. If I said no, he'd look around anyway, but he'd need a few hours to get a search warrant. *Allegedly disappeared.*

"Of course not," I said cooperatively. *I had nothing to do with this.*

"Oh, and Ms. Shea?"

"Yes?"

"We're still going to need that ring back."

*   *   *

"I feel bad," Tiara said when she walked into my condo. I'd driven back with two police cruisers in tow: Michael rode with Sergeant Hosozawa, while Tiara hitched a ride with Detective McGuinn. ("Can I try on your handcuffs?" I heard her say before she shut the car door.)

I was feeling bad, too. Well—obviously. But just when I thought

I couldn't sink any lower, I was hit with a new wave of humiliation. Having finally seen the Hyatt, the Maui Hi seemed even sadder than before. It made me feel shabby by association. Any fool could see which woman Jimmy preferred. Tiara was the five-star lover. I was the budget girl. I put the *ho* in HoJo.

Tiara sat down on one of the rattan chairs with the orange cushions, perching on the edge to minimize skin-to-fabric contact.

"The green ones are cleaner," I said. "And they don't, you know. Smell."

"Oh!" She popped up and moved over to a green chair. I remained standing, as if I were hosting an impromptu neighborhood get-together. Sergeant Hosozawa dug through Jimmy's duffel bag, emptying the contents onto the nasty brown carpet and running his fingers over every edge to check for hidden pockets. His latex gloves made me think of the kind of yearly doctor appointments that I dread for weeks beforehand.

Detective McGuinn, meanwhile, opened drawer after drawer even though I'd told him that Jimmy had never unpacked. He ignored me, digging uninterrupted through my bathing suits, T-shirts, and sensible cotton underwear.

"Can I get anyone coffee?" I chirped, disappointed when the police said no.

Michael stood outside the door, talking to himself again, like a well-groomed schizophrenic. With nothing left to do, I settled onto a green chair, noting almost subconsciously that it actually smelled just as bad as the orange ones.

"Jimmy didn't invite me to Maui," Tiara muttered, picking at her fingernails.

"What?" I wasn't sure I'd heard her right.

"He didn't invite me. I kept expecting him to. I mean, your boyfriend tells you he's coming to Maui and doesn't even ask you to come with? I kept saying stuff like 'We could make love in the ocean,' and 'I could lick piña coladas off your—' Well, you know. But he didn't pick up on it."

"Perhaps you were too subtle," I said, thinking, *Pina coladas?* Wouldn't that be awfully cold and, you know, sticky?

"So, anyways," she continued, "I'd just been reading this article in *Cosmo* about how guys really like it when a girl takes the initiation." (I didn't correct her. I think I get points for that.) "So I bought my own plane ticket and checked into the Hyatt. I wasn't even going to tell him. I was just going to wait for him in the room—naked, you know."

"With a piña colada," I said.

"Or Jet Puff. You know the marshmallow spread? One time we—you probably don't want to hear about it."

"Not so much," I said. "So . . . when did Jimmy find out you were here?"

"He called me from the airport. Said he'd just landed and was missing me and wishing I was in Maui with him. I was so excited, I just couldn't keep the secret, so I said, 'Baby, I have a big surprise for you.'" She sniffled. "We called each other baby."

"What did he say when you told him you were here?" I couldn't believe I cared. I didn't want to care.

"He was, like, totally bummed—saying, 'You're putting me on, right? Tell me you're putting me on.'"

"Really?" I sounded too pleased, I realized, making an effort to lower the timbre of my voice. "I mean—you must have been hurt."

"Well—yeah! I mean, especially considering that the last time we'd been together we didn't leave my room for, like, eighteen hours. My mother was all, 'Are you guys going to stay in there all day or are you going to come out for something to eat?'"

"Your *mother* was there?"

She shrugged. "A lot of people my age live at home. It's not like she was in the bedroom with us. She totally respects my boundaries."

"Did someone say something about coffee?" Michael James, off the phone at last, entered the room.

"Yes!" I hopped out of my chair. "It's Kona coffee—pretty good, actually."

He followed me over to the coffeemaker. "And, if you have any painkillers—aspirin, Aleve. Morphine."

"Headache?"

"Mm."

I started the coffeemaker and then went into the bathroom, but the detective had taken my cosmetics bag into the main room.

"Um, Detective—have you seen a bottle of Aleve?"

He tilted his head to a spot next to the bed. "On the floor over there. Between the diaphragm and the condoms."

"Thanks ever so much." I snatched up the bottle and crossed the room to Michael.

"You're pretty prepared." We both knew he wasn't talking about the Aleve.

"Yeah, well, I don't like surprises. By planning ahead, I can make sure nothing goes wrong."

He snorted with laughter and then rubbed his head, as if the strain had worsened his agony. He popped open the bottle and swallowed a couple of tablets dry.

"I guess this is stressful for you, too," I said, just as his cell phone rang. He checked the number and stuck the phone into his pocket.

"Probably not as bad as it's been for you, but, well—yeah. I've spent half the morning answering calls from people who want to know if I'm really dead and the other half calling people to let them know ahead of time that I'm not dead."

I poured his coffee into a blue mug with white hibiscus flowers. "What do you say, exactly? 'Just calling to tell you I'm not dead?'"

"Pretty much, yeah."

"I'm sorry about upsetting your mother." I handed him the mug. "Milk or sugar?"

"Thanks—black is good." He took a careful sip of the coffee, which was lukewarm at best. "My mother said you were nice about it." A smile tugged at the corner of his lips. "And she's really looking forward to our wedding."

Could I sink any lower? And then I remembered: "Oh. By the way, she needs to know if you're going to your father's birthday party."

"Oh, crud." His eyes widened. "I completely forgot about it. When is it?"

"She didn't say," I answered stiffly. What was I—his secretary? But then I thought about his mother and how upset she'd been. "It's got to be pretty soon, though. You were supposed to let her know by last week—the caterer needs a head count."

He bit his lip, thinking.

"You should really try to make it," I said, pouring myself some coffee. "It's his seventieth."

Sergeant Hosozawa strode over, Jimmy's wallet in his latex-gloved hands. The wallet was two-toned blue canvas, frayed at the edges, with a Velcro clasp. Clearly, this was a wallet no business-man would carry—it would be far too embarrassing to pull out. I'd seen the wallet countless times before. Why didn't I realize something was off?

"I've got Jimmy James's credit cards here," the sergeant told Michael. "You got yours?"

Michael put down his mug, reached into the back pocket of his crisp khaki shorts, and pulled out a silver money clip. He fished out a few cards and handed them to the sergeant. "I've already canceled two of these."

"You're sure I can't get you some coffee, Officer?" I chirped. If Hosozawa said yes, it would mean he didn't suspect me of anything: murder, identity theft, or a cover-up.

He looked up from the cards briefly and shook his head. Oh, crap.

"The American Express is a match," he told Michael. "But we figured that since it's the card he used to buy the ring."

Without thinking, I rubbed my left thumb against my naked ring finger.

"What's this other American Express?" the sergeant asked, holding up one of Michael's cards.

"That one's for personal expenses. It's the only one I haven't canceled."

"I don't see a match in Jimmy James's wallet. But that doesn't mean he didn't have one. Miss Shea, do you remember what card he tried to use at the restaurant?"

"It was a Visa," I said. "I remember he said he had another card back at the room. I assumed he only had the one Amex, but I don't really know."

"Oh, great," Michael moaned. "That means I have to cancel this card, too, and it's the only one I've got right now."

"Don't," the sergeant said. "Not just yet."

"I don't follow."

"I doubt Jimmy James would try to use the other Amex. It's already been turned down once. But if he gets desperate enough, he might try to use the Visa number, even without the card—or, who knows? Maybe he has your other Amex account. Or your ATM card, even."

"Wait a minute," Michael said.

I stared at the policeman. "Are you saying . . ."

Sergeant Hosozawa shrugged. "Maybe he really did drown. The currents were strong that day, and nobody saw him come ashore. Still, given this new twist, we have to consider the very real possibility that he faked his own death, snuck off somewhere. If he's hiding, he'll need money eventually."

"Jimmy might be alive?" Tiara yowled.

The sergeant narrowed his eyes. "Yes. I just said that."

She shook her head violently. "No. He wouldn't fake his own death. I know Jimmy better than that. He'd never do anything to hurt me."

We all paused and then silently agreed to ignore her.

"I think we're done here," Sergeant Hosozawa said. "Detective?"

"I'm through." He crossed the room and peeled off his gloves. "And I'd love a cup of coffee, if there's any left."

Michael's phone purred. He checked the display. "It's the second time he's called. I'm going to have to . . ." He opened the phone without finishing the sentence.

"Hey, Rick, how's it going?"

The guy on the other end was so loud, we could hear him yelling, though we couldn't make out the words.

I poured coffee for the detective. I apologized for the absence of Sweet'n Low; he apologized for using up my milk.

Michael closed his eyes and rubbed the back of his neck. "It wasn't me," he told the person on the other end of the phone. "Some guy stole my credit-card numbers and, well, kind of my identity and—*what?*" His eyes popped open. "What channel?"

Seeing him scanning the room for a television, I pushed the power button on the little set and handed him the remote.

There he was on the set, poorly lit and unsmiling: Michael

James—the real Michael James, that is—under the caption MAN LOST OFF MAUI COAST.

"We'll keep you updated with any new developments," the newscaster said.

Michael flipped to another station. There was his unflattering photo again—he looked seriously cranky—next to a shot of Slaughterhouse Beach. The caption this time: SPECIAL REPORT: SCUBA TRAGEDY. A newscaster was in the midst of his narration: "According to the coast guard, the beach is known for riptides and dangerous currents. Search crews continue to comb the area, though officials admit that it is unlikely that they will find Mr. James alive . . ."

The next station Michael checked had a soap opera that couldn't even begin to compete with real life. Within a minute, all of the stations had resumed their regular programming. Michael ended his phone call and turned off the TV, but we all stood there silent for a moment, just staring at the blank set.

"Do you think they mentioned my name?" Tiara asked.

"You looked pretty unhappy in that photo," I said to Michael, trying to lighten the mood.

"I was unhappy. I'd just spent three hours at the DMV. It's my driver's-license photo." He was still staring in disbelief at the blank television.

"Since neither of you ladies could provide a photo, we contacted the California DMV," Detective McGuinn said casually. "Good coffee, by the way."

"It's Kona," I said.

"We will continue to present this to the press as a presumed drowning," Sergeant Hosozawa said. "If Jimmy James is still alive, we want him to relax a little, let his guard down. If he's alive, he may try to contact one of you." He looked at Tiara, then at me.

Then he looked back at Tiara, as if betting on which of us Jimmy would call. "If he does, I want you to pretend to be happy."

"But I would be happy," Tiara said.

"Miss Cardenas, identity theft is a felony. Aiding Jimmy James would make you an accessory to a crime."

"That's not all it would make you," I muttered.

"If he offers to meet either of you somewhere, say yes and call us immediately. Also, we need a photo of Jimmy James," Sergeant Hosozawa said. "To release to the press. If Jimmy James is out there, we'll need extra eyes."

"I don't have a photo," I said. "I'm sorry."

"Miss Cardenas?"

She nodded and reached into her oversize purse, pulling out a tiny silver camera. "They're on here."

Maybe it was just my imagination, but I think I saw the detective smile.

Before the police drove her back to her hotel, Tiara took my arm and said, "Call me."

I paused for a moment before saying (somewhat rudely, I admit), "Why?"

"We could, like, get together," she said. "Talk about old times."

"We don't have any old times."

"I mean, with Jimmy. There's no one else I can really talk to about him. Plus, you and me, we're both alone here, you know? It might be nice to have someone to hang out with. For, like, dinner. And manicures, and stuff."

"Thanks," I said. "But—I don't think so."

Chapter 18

After everyone left, I did what I do best: I restored order. I washed and dried the mugs and put them back in the brown plastic cabinets. I cleaned the coffeemaker and took out the garbage. I folded my clothes precisely (a skill acquired that summer when I worked in a clothing store with Katie Rothman) and stacked them in the appropriate drawers, and then I gathered my toiletries and jewelry from their piles on the carpet and put them back into their quilted cases. When I got to the anklet Jimmy had given me, I stopped cold. He'd bought it after spending the morning with Tiara, I now realized. It wasn't a token of love, as I'd assumed. It was a token of guilt.

I picked up Jimmy's clothes one by one—his board shorts, his T-shirts, his boxers and flip-flops—and threw them against the wall, grunting as I did so. I kicked his duffel bag as hard as I could. It barely budged.

I collapsed on the floor and cried for a really, really long time.

And then I got up, washed my face, gathered Jimmy's clothes, and tucked them neatly into the bag, which I shoved into the back of the closet, where I wouldn't have to see it. Having handled the clothes, my hands smelled faintly of Jimmy, so I scrubbed them with a bar of the Maui Hi's cheap white soap.

Next I made a grocery list: milk, coffee, crackers. The list was so short there wasn't really any need to write it down, but putting everything down on a piece of paper felt so routine and normal that it gave me the faintest sense of control.

The Safeway was a couple of miles down the road, just where Mary had said it would be. It was just like grocery stores on the mainland, only it carried a lot more suntan lotion and beach mats, plus all the customers were so happy. Well, everyone except me, of course. Sunburned families strolled the aisles, negotiating over breakfast items. "But we always get Pop-Tarts on vacation," I heard one kid say.

Inspired, I took a box of frosted strawberry Pop-Tarts off the shelf and dropped it into my cart. They were my favorite when I was a kid. It had been years since I'd bought them, but what the hell: you only live once.

I was about to go to the checkout stand when I saw the rack of sundresses in the front of the store. I don't normally buy clothes in the same place I buy my milk (well, except for Target, of course), but these were so perfectly Hawaiian—filmy rayon things in all different colors. I scooped up a long blue one patterned with green turtles. It had spaghetti straps and fringe at the hem.

That was two things I bought that weren't on my list. Oh, yeah, I was living on the edge, all right. But it was Monday, and I was stuck in Maui until Thursday night: I might as well pretend to be on vacation. As for a revised itinerary, tonight I would stroll through downtown Lahaina and grab a casual bite to eat. Tomorrow I would drive to the volcano in the morning and sit on Napili Beach in the afternoon. On Wednesday, I'd explore Wailea. Thursday, my last day, I would walk down the coast from the condo and find the beach where I'd spent my first morning, spotting whales and struggling to remember what it felt like to be happy.

All this assumed that Jimmy was in hiding and wouldn't be found. I replaced the mental picture I'd been carrying around— Jimmy drowning, terrified, encircled by sharks—with an image of Jimmy in a lava rock cave, scratched and muddy, out of his mind and perhaps even talking to a volleyball named Wilson. For some reason, I thought of Katie Rothman and what she would call him: "Ath-hole." It almost made me smile.

The news crews in front of the condo complex ruined my itinerary—not to mention my emotional equilibrium. A newswoman, looking incongruous in a pale blue suit, stood by the Maui Hi sign, fiddling with her microphone. Assorted guests loitered about, thrilled by the distraction. No pool, no beach, no hair dryers or air-conditioning, but the Maui Hi had reporters! What a deal!

I turned the red rental car around and headed for the main road, not knowing where I was headed. Lahaina wasn't far. I'd planned to change into my new dress before heading downtown, but there was no reason I couldn't just go as I was (rumpled and grubby). But there was the problem of the milk. If I left it in the car, it would spoil. For some reason, I couldn't stand the thought of letting new milk go sour, of allowing one more thing in this world to go bad.

At the turn for the Kaanapali Beach resorts, I hit my blinker. Tiara's room had a minifridge. Besides, I suddenly craved human companionship, and right now Tiara was my only option.

"I was thinking we could have decaf in that lounge downstairs,"

I said once she let me into her room. I didn't really feel like coffee, but it was too early for cocktails, and I wasn't ready to commit to dinner.

"I'd love to!" she said. She wore a low-cut white tank top that almost entirely exposed her "Tiara" star tattoo and pink velour shorts that said JUICY on the butt. I said a silent prayer of thanks that I hadn't been here to watch her change her clothes.

"But why decaf?" she asked. "What's wrong with real coffee?"

I motioned to the clock. "It's after four. Too close to bedtime."

She didn't say anything—just gave me a look that let me know I was the least-fun person in the whole entire world.

The milk fit easily in the small refrigerator since there was nothing else in there. I left the rest of the stuff in a grocery bag on the floor. Then I casually mentioned the reason I couldn't use my own refrigerator.

She got so bouncy with excitement I feared she'd hit the ceiling. "So, are you sure it was two news vans? Or could there have been more?"

"I'm pretty sure it was two," I said, wishing I hadn't mentioned it. "But I hurried out of there pretty fast."

"Do you think they're still there? If we leave right now, maybe we can catch them." She reached for her big yellow handbag.

"Tiara." She stopped. I made her look at me. Her greenish-gold eyes sparkled with excitement. "We are not going to the condo." I paused to make sure she understood. "We are not talking to any reporters." I paused again, still holding her gaze, using the same look I give people when they "borrow" office supplies or take too long a lunch break.

Once she looked vaguely cowed, I said, "Jimmy broke the law. If he is alive, he is in big trouble. If the police think you and I helped him, we could get in trouble, too. Don't you understand?"

She tilted her chin up and swallowed, as if she was trying not to cry.

"This is hard on everyone," I said gently. "But we have to keep our heads. Tomorrow will be a better day." I find platitudes highly effective during emotionally charged situations.

She dropped her chin and nodded. Then she looked at me from under her dark lashes. "Did you bring that newspaper, by any chance? With our pictures?"

I shook my head. Coming had been a mistake: that much was obvious. But I'd already asked her to have coffee with me. Besides, the reporters and photographers were probably still at the condo, and I had no place else to go.

Coming off the elevator, we walked almost immediately into Michael James. He looked from me to Tiara and back to me. If he had any raunchy thoughts about seeing us together, he was classy enough not to let it show in his expression.

"We're just going for coffee," I explained.

"There were news crews in her parking lot!" Tiara gushed.

I rolled my eyes as an antidote to Tiara's enthusiasm. "Are you staying here?" I asked Michael.

He shook his head. "I've got an old friend from prep school with a place on the island. He lets me use it when he's not here." He stopped and wrinkled his nose. "Did that sound really obnoxious?"

"Which part?" I asked. "The reference to prep school or the bit about 'a place on the island'?"

He grinned. A faint sunburn warmed his cheeks and nose. It softened him, somehow, made him seem more approachable. He wore a short-sleeved black silk shirt, oatmeal-colored linen trousers, and manly brown sandals.

"I'm meeting a customer here," he said. "His shop was my first account on Maui. His parents are in town, and they wanted to go to a luau." He looked mostly at me, I noticed, and when he looked at Tiara he kind of kept his eyes over her head, as if he was trying really, really hard not to stare at her breasts.

"A luau? Fun!" Tiara chirped.

A luau. That was scheduled for day four of my itinerary, after parasailing.

"I had to call in about five favors to get tickets," Michael said. "They were completely sold out." He looked at his big black diver's watch and pulled out his cell phone, like he'd self-destruct if he went five minutes without dialing.

"Yeah, it's me," he said into the phone. "Yes, for real. Didn't you get my message? . . . Well, rumors of my death are premature." He forced a laugh. "I know—crazy. And it'll be funny in about . . . twenty years. At any rate, I'm not only alive, I'm at the Hyatt. Check-in for the luau begins in"—he checked his big watch—"ten minutes. But the show doesn't start till five o'clock, so it's no big deal if you're a little late."

He paused. And then he scowled.

"Wanna leave?" Tiara mouthed. I shook my head, wanting to hear the rest of the conversation.

"But—I'm not dead," Michael said. He frowned and crossed his arms, the phone sandwiched between his shoulder and his ear. "Yeah, the cloud cover at Haleakala can be a bitch." His jaw looked tense. "Well, Mama's Fish House is a terrific restaurant, but it's not a luau."

Finally, he gave up ("We'll do it some other time. Yeah, you have a good evening, too") and shut the phone.

"Problem?" I asked.

When he spoke, his voice was quiet and even. "So this morning my customer—but really, I think of him as a friend—turns on the news and finds out that I'm dead." He slipped the phone into his pocket. "He was so overcome with grief that he drove his parents up to the volcano. Which sucks for them because the peak was covered in clouds, and they couldn't see anything. So they had lunch at Mama's Fish House instead."

"But you're not really dead," I said.

"But he thought I was. So he went sightseeing. And out to lunch. So now they're tired and too full for dinner. On the bright side, he says he's really happy to hear that I'm alive, and he hopes we can get together before I head back to the mainland."

"People deal with grief in different ways," I said lamely.

Tiara leaned forward. "You can take us to the luau!"

Michael looked horrified. "That sounds—fun. But I think I'll try to get a refund, or maybe just exchange the tickets for another night."

* * *

At the Weeping Banyan, I ordered an iced nonfat decaf latte, while Tiara got something that looked like a milk shake.

"Just charge it to the room," she said when I pulled out my wallet.

"Uh, Tiara—the room is on Michael's credit card. You're going to have to pay for it." I made a mental note to call the airline and car-rental companies to switch the charges to my Visa. Also, I'd have to explain the situation to Mary. The worst week of my life was going to cost a fortune. On the bright side—if you can call it that—a week at the Maui Hi was a lot cheaper than a week at the Hyatt.

"Don't be silly," Tiara said. "Detective McGuinn told me that the credit cards have, like, protection." (Forgive me, but I immediately pictured a credit card encased in a condom.) "So, Michael won't have to pay. Nobody will have to pay." She lifted up her shoulders in a perky, no-worries gesture, bringing her star tattoo that much closer to my face.

"Nice tattoo," I said, partly because it felt like it deserved some kind of comment and partly because I didn't feel like lecturing her about her financial responsibilities. I'd leave that pleasure to the Hyatt's front-desk staff.

"You like it?" She stroked the star lovingly.

"It's, um . . ." I tried to think of an appropriate adjective and finally just said, "It's—yeah."

"I got it two years ago to remind me of what I'm going to be."

I waited for her to explain. When she didn't, I asked, "What?"

"A star!" She said. "See?" She stroked the tattoo again. "The shape, the letters—it's like on the Hollywood Walk of Fame."

"You want people to walk on your breasts?" (Okay, that was mean of me and not even very clever. But, remember, I'd had a really bad week.)

She pursed her lips and sipped her coffee without looking at me.

"Kidding," I said. Her eyes flicked to me and away. I was going to have to try harder if I wanted her to like me. Did I want her to like me? "Tell me more about it," I said reluctantly.

Good enough. She put her cup down, beamed and smiled: all was forgiven. "I know this sounds crazy," she said, "but ever since I was a little girl, I've known I was going to be famous someday."

"Really," I said, followed by an interested "mm" sound.

"It was just this feeling I had." She wiggled in her seat and fluffed her hair (it was down now) with long, shiny fingernails. "That I was special, somehow. And my mother? She told me later— this was, like, a couple of years ago—that she went to a psychic when she was pregnant. And you know what the psychic said?"

"That you were going to be a star?" I ventured.

"Yes!" She leaned over the table, her purple-rimmed eyes popping. "Isn't that wild?"

"Wild." My iced latte was giving me a brain freeze, but the sooner I finished it, the sooner I could get out of here.

"That article in the paper—did they say I was a model-actress?" Tiara said.

"I didn't read it that carefully, but . . . I don't think so. Is that what you are?"

"Well, yeah," she said. "I mean, I spend half my life at open-call auditions. And at the Anaheim auto show last year? I helped represent Toyota. I've got pictures in my room if you want to see them."

I smiled noncommittally. (Tiara. Pictures. Shudder.)

"A modeling agency signed me," Tiara said. "In L.A."

"Uh-huh."

"Some people say you shouldn't pay for an agent," Tiara continued, shaking a stray clump of hair off her face. "But at this point in my career, I'm really looking for a foot in the door." She giggled. "I almost said 'foot in the mouth.'"

I peered at my cup: almost gone, thank God. "You shouldn't pay for an agent." That was as far as I was going to get dragged into this conversation.

"The problem?" she said. "Is these." She grabbed a breast in each hand. Nearby, a waiter almost dropped his tray. "Runway and catalog work are out—clothes don't fit me. Everyone says I have a unique look, though, so I'm hoping that sets me apart."

"Did you grow up in California?" I asked, studying her ethnically unidentifiable face.

She nodded. "Yup, I'm a Cali girl—second generation on my father's side. My mother was an immigrant."

"From where?"

"Wisconsin."

The latte went straight to my sinuses.

"Oh—you mean before that?" she asked. "My mom's parents were German-Norwegian. And my dad's came from Cuba and the Philippines. So I'm pretty much a mutt." Only someone who looked like Tiara could make the word *mutt* sound so sexy.

She took a gulp of frothy coffee. "Anyway, working the auto show felt like a big career step, a chance to move on to bigger things, but that was a few months ago, and I haven't gotten any more work." She sighed. "I just really hoped I'd be able to quit my day job by now."

"Your day job?" That caught my attention. What could it be: Hooters waitress? Erotic massage therapist? Strip-o-gram performer?

"I'm a dental hygienist," she said.

Shit. Could life throw me any more disappointments?

I saw someone out of the corner of my eye and was prepared to tell the waiter that we didn't need anything else when I realized it was Michael.

"It was too late to get a refund," he said. "You want the tickets?"

*   *   *

We had ten minutes to change our clothes and get back downstairs. Tiara offered to lend me a dress that she described as "adjustable." I was about to take her up on it when I remembered the blue Hawaiian dress I had bought at Safeway. It was like this night was meant to be.

Not that I was so excited about going to a luau, mind you. It would only remind me of the-week-that-would-never-be, my romantic interlude with Jimmy. Besides, a luau seemed a tad inappropriate under the circumstances—but no more inappropriate than, say, taking two women to Hawaii and then faking your own death.

Still, it was better than sitting in my smelly unit at the Maui Hi, plus it would give me a chance to talk to Michael, to figure out how much of what Jimmy told me was real and how much he made up.

That was the argument that convinced Michael to join us. He'd said no at first. "Take the tickets. I can't use them. And I can't stand poi." But he, too, wanted to know how many of his personal details Jimmy had stolen.

I changed my clothes in Tiara's bathroom, staying in there for a little longer than was necessary to ensure that she'd be clothed when I came out. There was no mirror in the bathroom, but I glimpsed myself as I came through the separate vanity area. My dryer-deprived hair was still flat, of course, but my cheeks had a little color and my dress was downright adorable. Not bad, I thought. Not bad at all.

And then I rounded the corner and saw Tiara. I stopped feeling cute immediately. Her hair was slicked back in a bun, an enormous, fragrant flower behind her right ear. ("They had a big bowl of them at the spa," she told me.)

Her eyeliner was a deep green, which brought out green undertones in her eyes. Her eyelashes didn't look fake but had to be; I would have remembered if they'd been that lush before. Diamond studs glittered in her ears.

Her sundress, not surprisingly, was low-cut, her star tattoo fully exposed. The dress, green with a pink hibiscus pattern, was made of silk, cotton, or some other natural fiber not stocked at Safeway.

"Wow," I said. "You got ready fast."

She shrugged. "Being a model, I've had practice."

Maybe a quiet evening at the Maui Hi wouldn't have been so bad, after all.

*   *   *

There were hundreds of people waiting to go into the luau. I kept checking faces, half expecting Jimmy to appear—though surely he had enough sense to avoid large crowds. Men, meanwhile, kept glancing our way—well, Tiara's way. She noticed: you could tell by the way she flashed her smile and fluttered her fingernails. A path ran next to us, the white-sand beach and the Pacific beyond. The sun, falling low in the sky, made Tiara's eyes and earrings sparkle.

"Nice earrings," Michael said when he saw the diamonds.

"Thanks." She touched them lightly.

"Did I buy them?" he asked casually.

She tilted her chin up. "No. They were a gift."

"From Jimmy?" I asked.

She narrowed her eyes. "I think I already answered that."

Oops. "Right," I said, shaking my head as if I hadn't been following the conversation: better to look clueless than to seem bitchy, at least some of the time.

The line began to move forward. "The earrings were from my old boyfriend Mr. Robertson," she said. "For Christmas."

"You called your boyfriend Mr. Robertson?" Michael asked Tiara.

She touched an earlobe again. If she kept it up, she was going to knock one of the diamonds out. "He was real formal—a gentleman type. Kind of old-school. He told me to call him by his first name, but I just couldn't."

I snorted. "He wasn't old-school. He was just old. Like, eighty."

"He was fifty-nine," Tiara said evenly.

And I'm twelve, I thought.

"Did you talk to your credit-card companies this afternoon?" I asked Michael.

He nodded. "Yeah, they were cool about it—everything will end up covered. I was a little worried because some of the charges went back all the way to September—nothing big, just some dinners out—but they said it was okay."

"You had fraudulent charges that far back and you never noticed them?"

He shrugged. "I don't have time to look over every little detail on my credit-card bills."

"Wow," I said, because, really, that was all I could say.

Early on, Jimmy had taken me out a few times. There was a Mexican spot overlooking the Pacific, a pizza place overlooking a Wal-Mart. How odd to realize that he could have taken me anywhere—he wasn't paying, after all—and that's what he chose. I almost asked Michael James if he remembered any of the restaurants listed on his credit-card bill, but I decided against it. If Jimmy had gone to other, nicer places, I would just wonder whom he had taken.

We reached the front of the line, and a young, lean, Hawaiian man in a flowered shirt gave us a bright white smile, an "aloha," a string of shell beads, and a mai tai in a plastic cup. Another young man led us past rows of long white tables that were filling fast. The tables were in a vast, flat pit surrounded by lava rock and vaguely reminiscent of a volcano (not that I'd ever seen one). Around the perimeter, torches burned brightly even though it was still daylight. A big stage rose on one side, empty for now.

"Jimmy would have loved this," Tiara sighed as we sat down in plastic patio chairs, Michael on one side of the table, Tiara and me on the other.

"No doubt," Michael said. "Especially if I were paying." He slipped on a pair of aviator sunglasses. With his short hair, sharp cheekbones, and erect posture, he looked like an FBI agent in a TV show.

"There's a luau in Lahaina where you get real flower leis," Michael said. "But that one's even tougher to reserve."

"You've been to a lot of luaus?" I asked.

"More than I'd like. I've hit every one around here at least twice. Never been to a real pig roast, though—you know, like the locals do. They dig a big pit in the ground, roast a pig all day, then have a giant feast at night. That I'd like to see."

"All the time you spend on the island, you're bound to get invited to one sooner or later," I said.

He shook his head. "Nah, I'm *haole*—white. I don't live here, not that it would matter if I did. This is their island—they just let us use it. But some things they get to keep for themselves—the pig roasts, some hidden beaches. You can't really blame them."

A young woman took our drinks order; we went for another round of mai tais. A large group filled up the rest of our table. Fortunately, they showed no interest in saying more than a casual hello to us. On the stage, the chief luau guy briefly welcomed everyone—and then asked that all guests turn off their cell phones. Something like panic crossed Michael's face. He pulled out his phone, stared at it as if it were a beloved old relative he was about to send out on an ice floe, and pushed the power button.

"So, you've got all your accounts straightened out, then?" I asked him.

He shrugged. "Well, my credit cards. And I called my bank—they're changing my account number and my PIN. The airline's moving a little slower, but I think they'll eventually reinstate my miles. My real concern is that this Jimmy guy could be opening up new accounts under my name, taking out loans—who knows? It could really do a number on my credit rating." He shook his head in disgust.

"Unless he's dead," I said.

"It would make things easier," he said, a little too matter-of-factly.

"Have you figured out where he got your information?" I asked.

He shook his head. "I've never been to the restaurant where he works. And the mailboxes in my condo complex are locked at all times. I haven't got a clue."

"Do you have a roommate?" I asked. Maybe someone had gone through his things while he was away from home.

"I'm a little old for roommates," he said. I thought of Jimmy's dark and dirty little room. He was a little old for roommates, too.

"Oh, by the way," Michael said. "The police called me—they got hold of your boyfriend's roommate."

"Bryan?" I pictured Bryan in the filthy kitchen, hunched over the laptop and barely visible through the cloud of marijuana smoke.

"They didn't tell me his name. And they said it was hard to get much information out of him because he was stoned out of his mind."

"Yeah, that's him."

"The police said Jimmy's just been living with him since July—it's Bryan's house, not Jimmy's. They met partying at a bar. Jimmy needed a place to stay. Bryan had a spare room and he needed the money. Jimmy always paid his rent in cash—Bryan didn't even know his last name."

"Okay," I said.

"Okay?" he asked, confused.

"It makes sense." In my mind, I ran through more incidents

when Jimmy's behavior didn't make sense. "When's your birth-day?" I asked abruptly.

"October."

"The twenty-first?"

"Oh God." He sounded worn out. "So he knows that, too."

I nodded. "When we were first dating, I asked Jimmy when his birthday was. He looked confused for a minute, like he couldn't remember."

It was late on a Saturday morning. Jimmy and I were in bed, eating pancakes. There were crumbs and syrup on my sheets, and I didn't even care.

"And then he finally blurted out October twenty-first," I continued. (After he said that, he jumped out of bed and headed for the shower.) "I should have known something was up."

"Just from that?" Michael shook his head. "You couldn't possibly know."

But it wasn't just that. What I didn't tell Michael was that when October 21 came around, I got up early to make Jimmy a three-layer chocolate cake with whipped-cream frosting. We hadn't discussed his birthday; in fact, I had pretended to forget it (which would have been completely out of character). When he walked into my condo that evening, he saw streamers and balloons hanging from the light fixtures and candles flickering on the tables.

He froze in the doorway, completely baffled. He was wearing soft blue jeans, a white T-shirt, and flip-flops. It was drizzling outside, so he was a little damp, his hair curling at odd angles. He was the most beautiful man I'd ever seen.

"You thought I forgot," I said.

He shook his head in confusion. *I overdid it*, I thought. *He thinks I'm getting too serious.*

"At work, I'm known as the birthday queen," I babbled. "I always make the cake and buy the card and get everyone to sing. I just think it's nice to feel special for a day."

He peered around the room, and his face finally softened. "You did this for my birthday." It wasn't a question, but a statement—an oddly obvious thing to say, in retrospect. It never occurred to me that he'd lie about his birthday. But then, it never occurred to me that he'd lie about a lot of things.

He stood there for what felt like a really long time, his mouth slightly open, just looking at the room. Finally, he took me in his arms. "This is the nicest thing anyone's ever done for me," he whispered.

* * *

Now, at the luau, Michael asked, "Did Jimmy say or do anything else that seemed weird?"

I thought back over the past few months. "I kept trying to talk to him about his business and offer suggestions, but he didn't want to hear it. I thought it was because he didn't value my opinion."

"Like—what kind of suggestions?" Michael asked.

"Well, to start with, there's the name. Nothing wrong with it, really, just . . ."

I hate correcting grammar and punctuation, I really do. It makes me sound so schoolmarmish. But—he asked. So, I sat up straight and continued. "There should be an apostrophe. *J-I-M-M-Y*-apostrophe-*S*."

He shook his head. "I didn't name the company after myself. I named it after the sprinkles you put on ice cream. I thought it sounded colorful and, you know, just fun."

I hadn't heard anyone call sprinkles "jimmies" since I'd gone to college in Boston. "Let me guess," I said. "Your prep school was in Massachusetts. Or—you summered at the Cape."

"Yes," he said.

"Which one?"

He shot me a side glance, fighting a smile. "Both."

"Ha!" I said triumphantly.

"Okay." He laughed. "Now that we've got that cleared up, what were your other suggestions?"

"Your Web site has been down for at least five months," I said.

He blinked at me, and then shook his head (quickly, anxiously). "It hasn't been that long. A month and a half, maybe. Two months, tops."

"Five months," I said. "I met Jimmy in September," I said. "It is now February. Your Web site has never worked in all that time." He didn't need to know that I'd checked it at least once a week.

"Really?" He looked stricken. "Yikes."

"You should put one of your tech people on it," I said. "Or all of your tech people. Have them make it the top priority." The waitress put another mai tai in front of me.

"I don't have any tech people," he said. "I just have a general computer guy who manages the ordering system and keeps the desktops running."

"What?" Now I was confused. "How many people do you have working for you?"

"Five. Well, that's including me."

"That's all?" It was so weird, how I could continue to feel jarred. Even though I knew Jimmy didn't really own Jimmies, I still felt like the information he'd given me was true. That sounds stupid, I know, but I could only process one lie at a time.

Michael pulled himself up straight. Well, straighter. "Considering that I got my start selling wetsuits out of the back of my van, I think that's pretty good. Now we've got me and Ana—she's my administrator. There's Hank the computer guy, Lisa in purchasing—well, she's only half-time—and Pedro in the warehouse."

"But what about Scott?" I asked.

"Who's Scott?"

"In sales?" I prompted.

He shook his head. "I do all the selling."

"I wonder who Scott is, then. He was on Jimmy's cell phone. I'll have to check with the police, see if they called him yet. At any rate, you should really get your Web site fixed," I said. "I mean, honestly—if the Web site had been working, I would have realized Jimmy was a fraud months ago."

Michael stroked his chin. "So you're saying that this whole thing—the disappearance, the other girlfriend, the media storm—it's all my computer guy's fault?"

I took a long drink of my mai tai. "Yup," I said. "It's all Hank's fault."

*   *   *

Tables took turns going up to the buffet at the front of the pit. There must have been three hundred hungry people, but the flowered-shirt brigade ushered us through like seasoned marine mess officers. In turn, we loaded thick white plates with ham, chicken, fish, pork, rice, fish, vegetables, salad, bread. All things considered, it wasn't that different from the spread at the Hometown Buffet, though of course the Hometown Buffet doesn't have tiki torches. Or poi. Poi is the crushed taro-root paste that everyone says is disgusting but that actually tastes pretty good with kalua pork, which, as it turns out, is not made with Kahlúa liqueur. Who knew?

The wind picked up. Tiara had so much gel in her hair that her bun remained slick and perfect, if a little shellacked, save for one small strand that slipped out of the front and framed her face. Even her flower stayed behind her ear. What did she use—Super Glue?

Between bites, I asked Michael to fill in some more details. "So the police said you grew up in . . . Connecticut?"

He nodded. "Westport. Is that what Jimmy told you?"

I shook my head. "Lancaster."

"Pennsylvania?"

"California."

"He's probably really from there, then." He pulled out his phone. "We should tell the police." He froze and then looked at me, anxious. "Do you think anyone would notice if I kept my voice really low?"

I scowled in disapproval. He put the phone back in his pocket.

"Where are you from?" he asked.

"New Jersey."

"What exit?" he quipped.

I narrowed my eyes. "You want to know the real reason I moved to California? So I won't have to hear that stupid joke anymore."

He grinned.

"Jimmy told me he was from Texas," Tiara interjected, holding up her hand and fluttering her long nails to get the server's attention. The server, being a woman, ignored her.

"What about his parents?" I asked.

"Texas," she said. He'd told me Arizona. I was even more confused than before.

After the dessert buffet (I limited myself to three selections) and another mai tai, the show began: basically, a Vegas-meets-Maui extravaganza explaining how the Hawaiian Islands were created (from volcanic eruptions) and how they were populated (from various South Pacific islands). The sky had turned a purplish gray, showing the torches to their best advantage. Onstage, the hula dancers swayed to the raindrop-and-drum music. Next to me, Tiara downed her umpteenth mai tai and said, "That looks like fun!"

She held her arms out hula fashion—except somehow it made her look like a zombie. A really hot zombie with great hair and enormous boobs.

So I was jealous. Sue me.

After some more drums, wiggles, and don't-try-this-at-home fire tricks, the alpha-male hula dancer padded to the center of the stage, his brown legs thick and masculine beneath his grass skirt, and asked audience members to come onstage.

Tiara got up to dance. Of course she did. She jumped out of her chair so fast her napkin stuck to her dress for an instant before slipping to the ground.

"She's something," Michael said as Tiara fought her way to center stage front.

"Mm," I said.

"I'm astonished that Jimmy—or, whatever his name really is—would be attracted to both of you," Michael said.

I straightened in my chair, suddenly sober. (Well, soberer, anyway.) "That seems to be the general consensus." My voice was tight.

Michael looked at me sideways. "I meant it as a compliment."

"Oh!" I tried not to look delighted. I failed. "Thank you."

Michael returned his gaze to the stage. "She's not a bad hula dancer, though," he said, completely ruining the moment.

"If you like zombies," I grunted. "It's like Night of the Living Dancer." My sobriety had been short-lived.

Michael raised an eyebrow just long enough for me to remember that pettiness is never attractive.

I don't know what possessed me to join Tiara on the stage. Competitiveness? Jealousy? Rum? But when the alpha fire dog asked for more volunteers, I was the first one out of my seat, pausing just long enough to grab Michael's hand and say, "You're coming with me."

Give us pear-shaped girls a bit of credit: we can really shake our hips when the occasion arises. Following instructions, I held my arms out and took two steps in each direction. Then I made circles with my hips: two slow rotations followed by two fast ones. "You go, girl!" Tiara hooted. At that, I raised my arms higher and shook my, yes, boo-tay.

Up on the luau stage, front and center with Tiara and Michael, I forgot for a moment why I'd come to Hawaii. I forgot about standing on the beach, peering at the choppy water until my eyes hurt, just hoping, hoping, Jimmy would appear. I forgot about the police station. About the ring. About my lonely future.

Shaking my hips on a stage in Maui, rum coursing through my veins, I was, for a brief time, just another giddy tourist in a flowered rayon dress.

*   *   *

"Are you okay to drive?" Michael asked, grabbing my elbow as I stumbled up the red flagstone steps toward the open-air lobby. He had wisely switched from mai tais to water before dessert.

"I figured I'd just take a cab back to the condo—get my car in the morning." My balance reestablished, I continued up the wide steps, walking next to Michael.

"I'm going in the same direction," he said. "I'll drop you."

"You guys!" Tiara shoved herself between us, hooking arms.

"You're not going home! It's only eight o'clock. Let's check out some of the other hotels, maybe find a place to go dancing."

"Not tonight," I said, meaning, of course, not any night.

"I'm pretty beat," Michael said.

He likes me better, I thought.

Michael waited by a parrot while I went upstairs with Tiara to get my groceries and clothes.

"You guys are party poopers!" Tiara said, bouncing down the hall and pulling out her hair clip. She shook her head, and her dark locks cascaded around her shoulders. "I might have to go out and find something fun to do without you!" She was really pretty drunk.

At her door, she reached into her yellow handbag and pulled out a credit-card-size key. She slid it into the slot and . . . nothing.

"Huh." She looked at the key, flipped it around, and tried again. Nothing. She held it out to me. "You try."

I slipped it this way and that, but the door wouldn't open.

"These stupid keys never work right," she muttered.

Back in the lobby, I waited with Michael (and the parrot) while Tiara sashayed across the red flagstones to the front desk.

"How long are you staying in Maui?" I asked him.

"Just till Saturday. You?"

"Thursday. I'm taking a red-eye out. I mean, that's what I'm booked on, anyway. And don't worry—I'm going to call them tomorrow, have them switch it to my credit card."

He waved his hand in the air. "Don't worry about it."

"But what about Australia?"

"I'll get there somehow."

I was about to protest some more, when I heard a woman's shrill voice. Tiara, at the front desk, was making a scene.

"But the credit-card companies said they would cover it!" she shrieked. "But I have no place else to stay!"

"Uh-oh," Michael said.

Tiara was in tears, much to the fascination of the mob of Japanese tourists waiting in line behind her.

"Explain it to them, Michael!" she wailed, grabbing his arm, her fingers splayed out so her long nails wouldn't scratch him.

"I, um, uh—"

"Is this about the credit-card fraud?" I asked the young Hawaiian woman at the front desk, smiling pleasantly so she'd know I wasn't crazy like Tiara. She nodded nervously. Just like at the Maui Hi, the female staff wore muumuus, though the beige print was subtle, and the garments actually fit.

"Because Ms. Cardenas was in no way responsible for the fraud," I assured the woman. "And she is fully prepared to pay for her room here."

"What?" Tiara yelped. "I can't afford this place!"

Off to our left, a plump blond couple in competing tropical prints bent their heads together, whispering. Finally, the woman took a few steps toward me. "Aren't you the women I read about in the paper?"

I shuddered, remembering the unflattering shot and disappointed that someone could recognize me from it. "Yes," I said.

She looked at Michael. "So, is this . . . the guy?"

"No," I said. "Well, yes. It's the guy people *thought* was missing, but not the guy who was *actually* missing."

She blinked furiously, as if I'd said something confusing.

A bellman brought out a rolling brass cart stacked with Tiara's two mismatched suitcases (one red, one leopard print) and my plastic Safeway bags.

"Do you know how long the milk has been out of the refrigerator?" I asked the bellman, who was unable to provide me with a satisfactory answer.

Michael popped out front and gave his ticket to the valet while Tiara continued to cry and say, "But it's not my fault!" She hadn't been nearly this hysterical when Jimmy went missing, but she hadn't been drunk then, either.

When Michael's car arrived (a convertible!) the bellman silently (and quickly) pushed the cart out the front door and loaded everything into the trunk. I took Tiara's arm and pulled her to the curb. She was practically limp, worn out from the hysteria. "But I have no place to go," she whimpered.

"There's plenty of room where I'm staying," Michael said, handing the valet a tip. "You can come home with me."

"NO!" I said. Everyone (including the valets) looked at me in surprise. I cleared my throat. "What I mean is . . ." What did I mean, exactly?

"I understand what Tiara is going through," I said. "And I think it's important that she and I support each other. You know— talk things out. I'd like her to stay with me."

Shoot me now.

Michael shrugged and slid into the driver's seat. "Okay."

Tiara enfolded me in a hug—not easy since her enormous rack didn't exactly compress. "Thanks, Jan. That means a lot to me."

"It's Jane," I said.

Chapter 19

As it turned out, I didn't have to withstand a touchy-feely discussion with Tiara because when I came out of the bathroom after changing into my nightgown, she was passed out on my bed. In her underwear. The matching bra and panties were satin and lace, the same shade of teal as her dress.

There was no way I was getting into that bed with her. I pulled the stinky cushions off the chairs and lined them up on the floor. There were no spare sheets, of course, so I spread a couple of scratchy white towels on top of the cushions as a kind of barrier between me and the mold that inevitably lay within. I retrieved the scary bedspread from the closet and pulled one of the dust-mite-infested pillows off the bed.

Astonishingly enough, I slept. Okay, maybe it's not so astonishing when you factor in all of the mai tais.

Shortly after daybreak, the phone woke me. I lunged for the

receiver as a primitive, really stupid part of my brain thought, *Jimmy*. Maybe Jimmy had been found. Maybe Jimmy was alive. Maybe Jimmy had an explanation for the credit-card mix-up and the affair with Tiara. Maybe cats could swim and whales could fly.

It was Mary.

"I'm glad you called," I said, even though it was seven o'clock in the morning and I didn't want to hear from anyone unless it was Jimmy calling to beg my forgiveness.

"Don't leave your room," Mary commanded.

"I wasn't planning to at the moment," I said, bleary-eyed. "But I wanted to ask you—are there any more units available right now? Because there's this woman—"

"A luau," Mary was saying.

"Yes," I said. "I went to one last night."

Mary's words continued to seep through as I thought, *Jimmy's gone. Really gone.* "Pictures," I heard her say. "Video."

"What?" I needed coffee. And aspirin. And five more hours of sleep.

"Turn on the TV," she said.

I did. And there I was—again. Only this time I didn't look like the shocked and grieving fiancée. This time I was standing front and center of the hula line, leaning a little too close to Michael, and I looked like, I looked like—

"Tramp," Mary said.

"Excuse me?"

"There's this headline on the Internet," she said. "It says, 'Two Tramps. Where's the Lady?'"

"That's not even very clever," I said weakly.

"There are at least four reporters in the parking lot," Mary told me. "Plus a couple of camera crews. *Stay in your room.*"

Mary was right: there were a couple of news vans in the parking lot, along with a woman in a pink suit and a man in shades of blue and beige. Stuck in the room, I settled back on my cushions and watched my life on television. Some of the shots I'd seen before: the search crews at Slaughterhouse Beach, Michael's DMV photo. Others were new: the hula line on the luau stage. Me loading my plate at the dessert buffet. Jimmy in mid-orgasm.

I screamed. Tiara made a couple of sleepy-snorting noises and repositioned herself on the bed. She'd love these pictures. She looked great at the luau, and the porno picture of Jimmy's was hers, of course. As for the next quick video—Tiara throwing a tantrum in the Hyatt lobby (Hey! Who was hiding the camera?)— she might not be so thrilled.

When my cell phone rang, I checked the display (it was my sister, Beth) and muted the television.

"Aloha," I said weakly.

"What. The. Fuck."

"I don't think I've ever heard you use that word before," I said.

"Jane! What's going on?"

"I guess you heard about Jimmy's disappearance," I mumbled. "And about the other woman." She didn't need to know that the other woman was in the room with me.

I was embarrassed, I realized with surprise. Surely I should be feeling something darker, stronger? But my level of embarrassment was so profound it was crossing over into humiliation, which in turn crowded out a whole host of more noble emotions.

I'd last seen Beth over the holidays. After Christmas Eve dinner (a seafood-and-pasta extravaganza, all of which Beth prepared and served while her mother-in-law sat on her ass and said that an Irish girl can never cook like an Italian), Beth had advised me to give Jimmy an ultimatum: not for marriage, not yet, but for a steady, committed relationship (whatever that meant). She had asked why I didn't see him more regularly. She'd wanted to know what he was doing at Christmas, why he hadn't flown east with me.

"It's early," I'd said, scrubbing an especially noxious pot. "We haven't been going out that long."

"Early in the relationship, maybe." China clinked as she maneuvered yet another plate into the dishwasher. "But not early in your life."

She said stuff like this not as my protective big sister but as Mrs. Sal Piccolo, mother of five, devoted scrapbooker, coupon clipper, and CCD instructor at Our Lady of the Turnpike parish. (It's not really called that; I just say it to annoy her. Also, CCD isn't called CCD anymore, either—presumably because nobody ever knew what CCD stood for.)

She was just being defensive, I decided. Nobody could really believe that Sal ("We'll keep pumping 'em out till we get a boy") was better than my golden god Jimmy.

"Jimmy will come for Christmas next year," I had told Beth, putting the pot aside to soak. He'd promised no such thing, of course. He seemed incapable of planning more than a few hours ahead. But at that moment, I believed it.

"Is it on TV back there?" I asked her now, peeking through the venetian blinds. The reporters were still there.

On the muted television, a close-up of my face flashed on the screen. "Oh my God!" I shrieked. "I've got something stuck between my teeth!"

"What? So take it out," Beth said.

"Not now! Last night. We went to a luau, and someone took videos and—"

"I *know*," she said. "It was in our paper."

"You read the newspaper?" That came out wrong.

"When I get the time." That meant never. "My friend Renée called me. You remember Renée? From the PTA?"

"Yes," I said, meaning no. "I should not have bought that dress." The video had, thankfully, zoomed away from the crap in my teeth, providing a full-length shot of my Safeway couture. The dress was too straight, I saw now, too loose. It made me look like I had no shape whatsoever. Even a pear has some curvy contours.

"I can't imagine what you're going through," Beth said. "I can't believe he lied like that, and that you never even suspected—" She stopped herself before saying how lucky she was to have married Sal. "What did Mom say about it?" she asked.

"Mom? Do you think she knows?" I pictured my mother in her cramped kitchen, sitting at her oversize table. She read the paper first thing every morning, the various sections spread out in front of her, her big coffee cup filled to the brim.

"You haven't called her?"

* * *

"Hi, Mom."

"Janie? Is that you?"

"Yes. I'm in Maui."

"I know! *Everyone* knows!"

"I'm sorry I didn't call you sooner, but—"

"You were on the news this morning! They'd gotten hold of your high school picture—you know the one where your hair was all one length, the way I liked it? They said your name and where you'd gone to high school. They didn't actually mention me, but enough people know I have a daughter named Jane to make the connection."

"Oh my God, I'm so sorry."

"The phone has been ringing off the hook! All morning! I'm surprised you were even able to get through. My supervisor at Home Depot said I could take today off if I needed, but I said, no sir, I'm a team player."

"Oh, wow, Mom, I hadn't really thought about how it would affect—"

"You remember Adele Pritchard? From when we lived on East Lane?"

"Sort of," I said, meaning not really.

"I hadn't spoken to her for, what? Eighteen years? And she calls, out of the blue, says she'd seen you and didn't know you were in California and how awful this whole thing must be for our family. And she told me how brave she always thought I was, soldiering on after your father left me with two young children."

"We weren't that young."

"And so, anyway, we're going to have lunch next week, probably Tuesday, and Adele's going to call Barb Reilly, too, see if she can make it."

"Well, I'll still be here for a few more days," I said. "Just in case Jimmy shows up—or floats up, or whatever."

"No great loss," she said.

"What?" Surely she hadn't said that.

"Better you find out what he's really like now rather than after wasting twenty years of your life with him. Oops—I gotta run if I'm going to make it to work on time. I know everyone is going to have lots of questions!"

* * *

"Do you want to talk to a reporter from *People* magazine?" Mary asked me an hour later. This was after I'd talked to Lena ("The phone's been ringing off the hook. Mr. Wills hasn't left his office all day"). After I'd watched the special reports on television ("credit-card fraud . . . pornographic pictures . . . multiple lovers . . . poi . . ."). After I'd read the local paper (*Although police haven't officially named the two women as suspects in the case . . .*). After I'd talked to Sergeant Hosozawa ("We still think he's alive, but we're not ready to say that to the press").

"*People* magazine?" I said to Mary, feeling slightly hysterical. "Is this about me carrying Brad Pitt's baby? Because it's not true."

"You shouldn't joke," Mary said somberly. "It doesn't look good."

"I can't help it," I said. "It's a nervous tic. If I don't joke, I'll—" A sob escaped my lips, followed by another and another. "Lose control," I finally managed to gasp.

"I'll tell the reporter that you are too overcome by emotion to talk right now," she said.

"Good thinking," I said.

I thought Tiara would be thrilled about the news crews in the parking lot. I expected her to throw on her pretty silk dress and sprint out the door.

"I can't go out looking like this!" Tiara said, practically in tears. Her hair was all pouffy on one side, flat on the other. Her eye makeup had finally smeared. While she still looked better than I do on my best day, she wasn't up to her usual standards.

She turned on the shower (leaving the door open) and dug through her suitcases. "My product! The Hyatt people didn't pack my product!"

"Your—what?" I asked.

"My hair thickener, and the polishing milk and the spray. And the—oh my God, *they didn't pack my makeup, either!*" Once again, she was more hysterical than she'd been when Jimmy disappeared, and this time she was sober.

"You can borrow my makeup," I said. "And I've got a can of mousse."

I don't want to describe the disdainful look she gave me because it'll just piss me off all over again.

While Tiara showered (squealing when the people next door flushed their toilet, turning the spray burning hot), I called the airlines to see if I could get an earlier flight home. Tonight there was an available seat on a red-eye for a price so high I paused to consider my credit-card limit. Still, I was about to book it when the reality hit me. Going home wouldn't solve anything. Instead of news vans in the Maui Hi parking lot, there might be news vans outside my condo. And if I wouldn't talk to the reporters, they might interview my neighbors, or my coworkers, or maybe even people from my past.

Oh God.

Mary called on the room phone. "I've got Michael James on the line. I've been holding all your other calls."

"Have there been many?" I asked.

She paused for a second, counting. "Twenty-three."

"No!"

"But a lot are repeats. One guy, he called ten times, probably. I know it's him because he says his *r*'s funny. But each time he uses a different name."

"Like Wobert?" I said.

"No joking," she said, though she couldn't help chuckling.

*   *   *

"Maybe the luau wasn't a great idea," Michael said over the phone.

"You think?"

"You're a good dancer, though," he said.

"So are you."

"Not really."

I pictured him on the stage. "Yeah, but it's polite to say so."

He laughed softly. "Anyway, I know you're stuck in your room."

"How do you know that?"

"Because they keep showing your door on TV. And saying you and Tiara are in there."

That made me feel creepy. I'd seen the shots myself, of course, but it felt different to know that other people were looking at the pictures of my door, hoping to catch a glimpse of the two tramps who had been caught partying with a new man so soon after their shared boyfriend's disappearance.

"Where I'm staying, there's plenty of room," Michael said. "And it's very private. So, if you guys want to crash here, it's really fine."

I peeked between the venetian blinds. Someone had brought pink donut boxes and cardboard cups of coffee. The news crews showed no signs of leaving.

"We'll be there within the hour," I said.

Chapter 20

A door on the back wall that looked like a locked closet turned out to connect my condo to the much nicer waterfront unit on the other side.

"For fire safety," Mary explained, coming in from the other unit.

"But the door's kept locked," I said. "If there was a fire, no one could open it."

She shrugged. "So you burn. But the guy who owns this building, he doesn't get in trouble."

Mary, diplomatically carrying Jimmy's bag and one of Tiara's (leaving each of us to carry one of our own), led us through the attached unit and along Maui Hi's waterfront rock wall. We scampered over the patchy grass in front of the condos next door to the concrete walkway of the complex beyond that. We rounded a corner and came upon a parking lot slightly larger than Maui Hi's, where Albert was waiting in a blue van, the engine running.

"What about my rental car?" I asked, shoving my suitcase in the back.

"We can drive it over to you later, if you want," Mary said.

"I should get it back to the airport," I said. "It's on a stolen credit card or stolen miles—I can't even remember." Suddenly I felt very, very tired.

"Albert and I get off at four," Mary said. "We'll take care of it."

I shook my head: they had done enough. "I can't let you—"

She put up her hand: stop. "It's decided," she said kindly.

I nodded. "There's a dive bag in the trunk. You can keep it, if you like." Suddenly, impulsively, I squeezed her tight. *"Mahalo,"* I whispered.

Albert took a left out of the parking lot. I glanced to the right, afraid I'd see photographers trailing us, but we turned onto the pavement without incident. The road was bumpy, windy, and shady, lined with dingy condos that soon gave way to gates on the ocean side. Across the street, big houses with large windows loomed on the hill.

When the road curved inland, Albert turned left onto a short street and stopped in front of a black wrought-iron gate. There was a silver intercom box and a black mailbox that said Hollings-worth. Albert rolled down his window—Maui Hi's management had managed to find the last vehicle on the planet without power windows—and pushed a red button on the intercom box.

"Yes?" came a tinny male voice.

Albert cleared his throat. "I have the delivery from down the road." He turned to face us and wiggled his eyebrows.

The gates swung open like curtains on opening night. And what a show: the huge house looked vaguely Japanese, with a high-peaked roof and lots of glass. The lush yard overflowed with birds of paradise, bougainvillea, hibiscus, and a whole bunch of other plants that I didn't recognize but that probably cost a lot more than the geraniums planted on the grounds outside my Brea condo.

Albert parked the van next to Michael's rented convertible. Behind us, the gates swung shut, soundless until a final jarring clang when they snapped back into place. "WD-40," Albert muttered.

Tiara and I climbed out onto the white shell driveway and stared at the house. Through the windows, I could see all the way to the ocean.

Michael opened the front door, wearing black board shorts, a sleeveless white T-shirt, and a faded red baseball cap. Sunglasses hung from a cord around his neck. The front door opened onto the main room, an enormous space that encompassed a living room, dining area, and kitchen, the ceilings dotted here and there with lazy fans. The furniture was caramel-colored wicker with white cushions. Raffia rugs covered the pale wood floor. Directly in front of us the Pacific glinted through a wall of windows.

"This is, uh, nice," I said.

Michael grinned. "Yeah, well, every time I stay here I send my friend one of those Harry and David fruit towers, so it comes out pretty even."

"Your friend lets you stay here for *free*?" Tiara asked, pulling off her oversize eyeglasses. She had major raccoon eyes from the smeared mascara.

Michael shrugged. "I keep him pretty well stocked with dive gear, but, basically, yeah."

"You want me to get you anything from the store?" Albert asked. "Groceries or anything?"

"I'd hate to put you out," I said. "But it doesn't look like we'll be going out for many meals."

"You kidding?" he said. "This is the most exciting thing that's ever happened to me. It's like *Mission: Impossible* or something."

I checked the kitchen pantry and the Sub-Zero refrigerator and jotted down a quick list.

"Could you swing by the Hyatt?" Tiara asked Albert. "And see if they've got my makeup and my hair stuff?" She had pulled back her product-free, un-blow-dried hair. "Or maybe I should go with you," she said, biting on an arm of her sunglasses. "So if they don't have my stuff, we can swing by the mall."

"We don't have a mall," Albert said. "Not like you have on the mainland, anyway. The Cannery Mall has a Long's Drugs, though. You wanna go there?"

Tiara covered her eyes briefly, took a deep breath, and nodded.

*   *   *

"Guess that means you get first dibs on rooms," Michael said, once they had left.

There were two bedrooms to choose from. Room number one was at the end of a corridor, a bit dark, with a window overlooking some dense greenery. There was a white wood bed covered with a nubby beige coverlet, a white wicker settee, and a tiny bathroom with a shower.

Room number two's high ceiling was paneled in some kind of blond wood. A ceiling fan with fat, rounded panels lent a pleasant breeze. The bed was large and comfy-looking, covered in a quilt of the palest green. There was an overstuffed easy chair and a little writing desk. A pitcher of water sat on top of the desk, circles of lemon bobbling among the ice cubes like a crowd of happy faces. ("The housekeeper came this morning," Michael explained.)

The room had an attached bathroom, of course, with sand-colored travertine tiles, a rainfall shower, and a Jacuzzi tub.

And, oh—did I mention? Beyond a set of French doors was a kick-ass view of the Pacific, plus a lanai complete with a lounge chair and a tiny table for coffee or cocktails.

"You didn't want this room?" I asked in astonishment.

"When Trey's here—that's my friend, Trey Hollingsworth—this is where he sleeps. So, I'm just staying where I always do," Michael said. "So—which room do you want?"

I drifted closer to the French doors. "Is that a trick question?"

*   *   *

After Michael left, I spent a moment standing in the middle of my room, smiling stupidly. The room was all mine—at least for a couple of days. I poured myself a glass of lemony water and took it out to the lanai. The wind was strong today. It whipped my hair into my eyes. The air felt damp, heavy. Sweat gathered on my upper lip.

There were trees behind the house and a narrow path that led to the water. There was no sand beach, just a jumble of lava rocks.

Below me, Michael stood on some rocks near the water's edge. He tossed his faded red baseball cap behind him and then pulled off his shirt.

I stepped back into the shadows of the lanai to watch him. He was just going for a swim—nothing private—but I felt like I was spying, somehow.

Michael looked skinny when he was dressed, but now I could see that his shoulders were squared and muscular. Below his brown neck, his back was pale. I hoped he wouldn't burn.

There are two ways of entering the ocean. My preferred method starts with one toe and then moves on to a second. Michael chose the other route, standing tense and poised for just a brief moment before plunging into the water. With broad, fluid strokes, he sliced through the surface, away from the shore, his dark head getting farther and farther away until—

"*Michael!*" I was at the railing of the lanai, my heart pounding, my voice shrill. "Michael, come back!" I screamed into the wind.

He didn't hear me, of course, but continued to move through the water, farther into the bay. I clutched the railing and leaned forward, refusing to let him out of my sight. Far out, he stopped swimming and peered around: at the horizon, the shore, up at the birds.

I was being ridiculous, I realized, my heart still pounding. My hands were shaking, my palms damp. It was a nice day for a swim, if a little windy. Michael wasn't Jimmy. Michael wouldn't drown. And besides, Jimmy didn't drown anyway, right? He'd faked his death, plotted his disappearance. Isn't that what the police had said?

I'd clung to that belief for the past couple of days. It was what allowed me to feel angry, to steal moments of joy, to write Jimmy off. But now, looking at the vastness of the ocean, feeling the force of the wind, I wasn't so sure.

Michael began to swim back in. When he reached the rocks, I retreated into the room, unpacked my clothes, and put on a swimsuit: the floral-patterned one with the flirty skirt that I'd intended to wear for Jimmy.

A short while later, I found Michael sitting on a large rock, drying himself in the sun. What the beach lacked in sand, it made up for in seclusion. Only a few large houses shared the water access. On either end, jagged rock outcroppings went far enough into the surf to prevent people from strolling over.

"No sign of Albert and Tiara yet." I set my heavy floral tote on the rocks. The refrigerator had been reasonably well stocked; inside my bag were two sandwiches and a couple of bottles of iced tea—some brand I'd never heard of. Apparently, superrich people don't drink Snapple.

"I made lunch," I told Michael, reaching into the tote. "There's Brie and tomato on a baguette or turkey with cranberry chutney on whole grain."

"Thanks," he said, surprised. "Both sound good."

"There's iced tea, too." I gave him a half of each sandwich along with a napkin.

Something about Michael struck me as different—and it wasn't just that he was in wet swim trunks. "Hey—where's your phone?"

At first, I thought he hadn't heard me. I decided to drop the subject.

"The Brie should be softer," I said.

"No, it's good." He reached inside my tote for a bottle of iced tea, twisted off the cap, and took a long drink.

We were quiet for a short while, and then he spoke. "A couple of years ago, I had a girlfriend." He drank some more iced tea and squinted at the shiny ocean.

When he didn't continue, I said, "And let me guess. She wasn't who you thought she was. Plus, she was seeing someone else. And, she disappeared in a bizarre diving accident."

He smiled, just barely. "Nothing so exciting. She was always telling me to lighten up, stop being so obsessed with work. Then one day we were at the beach—not here, this was in California— and I was talking to one of my biggest customers. She was lying on a towel, looking perfectly happy, I thought, and then all of a sudden she sits up, grabs the phone out of my hand, runs to the water, and just thows it in. And then she strolls back and lies down on her towel as if nothing had happened."

I laughed. He didn't. "Did you ever find the phone?"

"Sure." He shrugged. "It didn't work, but I found it."

"And . . . did you lose the customer?"

"Nope. I told him the story—he loved it." He held my eyes for a moment and then looked away.

"And the girlfriend?"

"Her I lost for good."

"Because of that?"

"Not because of that specifically—but because of that generally. Because she wanted me to be somebody different, someone less—I don't know. Driven, I guess. But after we broke up, it occurred to me that maybe she had a point. If you can't relax on the beach, where can you?"

"Underwater?"

He smiled. "But when someone figures out how to get a signal down there, I'm all over it."

"But no more phone on the beach?" I bit into the turkey sandwich. It was better than the Brie; quite tasty, in fact.

"It's in my bag." He gestured behind him, where a black sports bag lay on the rocks. "But it's turned off." He pulled my new mask out of my bag. "This yours?"

"Pretty nifty, huh?"

"It's a piece of crap. Wait here."

A few minutes later, he was back with a mesh bag filled with several masks.

"Are these from your company?" I asked, forgetting for a moment that I knew all about his company and that they only made wetsuits.

"Nope. A lot of bartering goes on at the trade shows."

He held a black mask up to my face. "When I press it against you, suck in through your nose."

"What about the strap?"

"If it fits properly, it should hold without it, at least for a few seconds."

The mask stuck for barely an instant before falling off.

"Too big," he said. "You have a small face. Let's see . . ." He dug around in the mesh bag and yanked out another mask, pale blue this time. He pressed it against my face, and I sucked in through my nose. It stayed in place until I laughed.

"What's so funny?"

"I have no idea," I said honestly, surprised that I could laugh at all.

He got into the water before me, of course. But after putting my mask and a borrowed snorkel in place, I submerged myself relatively quickly, at least by my low standards. Treading water, I yanked on my flippers and turned onto my belly. I didn't see much at first, just brown sand and gray rocks and a few pale, darting fish.

When I looked up, Michael waved me out to him. I swam smoothly, arms at my sides, legs scissoring through the water. A rogue wave broke over my head, but the snorkel had a whizzy splash guard that kept the water out.

Far below us, a hunk of coral swarmed with fish. Because of the depth, the light was diffused, the colors dull. I pulled my head up and treaded water. Above me, the sky was a bright, clear blue. Farther inland, puffy white clouds hugged the mountains. Michael pulled his snorkel from his mouth. "You want to see something cool? Swim around the corner with me."

The "corner" was a towering mass of rocks, the surf pounding the point. Already, the rocky little beach seemed far away.

Without meaning to, I pictured Jimmy snagged on an underwater rock, his air running out. Jimmy diving into ever-deeper water, drunk with nitrogen narcosis. Jimmy in the clutches of a heart attack. Jimmy and *Jaws*.

"I think I'd feel better—" I spat out some rubber-flavored spit. "Just going in." A wave slammed against the rocks, the spray darting up like white fireworks. "After what happened the other day . . ."

He pulled his mask down to his neck so I could look into his eyes, brown ringed with copper. "Nothing happened the other day. At least not in the water." He pushed his mask back into place. "You coming?"

He was right, of course: Jimmy was alive.

"I'm coming."

The currents were stronger out beyond the rocks, and the water deeper. Michael tapped my arm and cupped a hand to his ear, making the universal sign for "listen."

I held my hands out in the universal sign for "I don't know what the hell you're talking about." He pointed to his ear again, and that's when I heard what sounded like a cross between a rusty hinge and off-key singing.

I squealed into my snorkel and popped my head out of the water for confirmation. "Whales?" I asked, the snorkel still in my mouth. ("Wawf?")

He nodded and then swam farther out, his movements so graceful that his flippers barely splashed. I hurried behind him, forgetting my energy-saving form, slapping at the water with my arms.

On the other side of the point, the water splashed over my head, and the current grew more insistent. My heart pounded. Suddenly I felt cold to my core. The ground below us was dark and rocky. Michael skin-dived way down, gliding around the rock and coral like a manta ray. I floated on the surface, wondering why I had agreed to come out here.

Michael returned to the surface in a diagonal line and flippered parallel to the rocky shoreline. I followed fearfully. The only thing worse than being stuck out here, shivering and afraid, was swimming back alone.

And then, suddenly, I forgot about everything: my fear, the cold, the slight cramp in my right foot. A sea turtle the size of a coffee table swam below me, its flippers stroking the water so gracefully it looked like it was flying: an underwater UFO. I followed without thinking about the cold or the waves or how far we were from shore. Ahead of me, it floated up until it reached the surface. I lifted my head in time to see its scaly nose peeking above the water, sucking some air. And then it was under again: down, down into the protection of the shadows.

When the turtle disappeared, Michael asked if I was getting cold, shouting over the wind and waves to be heard.

I nodded, my lips too numb to speak.

He swam over and said, "You want a tow?"

I was all set to say no when I realized just how tired I was.

"Hold on to my shoulder," he instructed. "And keep your body streamlined."

When the water was shallow enough to stand, I let go of Michael's shoulder and stood up, only to be knocked over by the first wave.

"Whoa," he said, grabbing my hand and pulling me back up. "Next time I won't keep you out so long."

I gazed back at the deep water, already missing the turtles.

Tiara was standing on the rocks. I tried to say hi, but it came out as "huh." I sat down at the water's edge and tugged off my flippers, a dinky wave knocking me back against the rocks. I slipped off my mask and handed it to Michael with wobbly arms. "Thanks," I wheezed. ("Thass.")

He made a wiping motion above his lip.

"Huh?"

He did it again. When I blinked at him, confused, he said, "You have a little . . . slime."

I reached up under my nose. Sure enough, thick, slimy mucus glazed the lower half of my face. Grunting, I wiped it with my hand and then retreated to the surf for a rinse and a moment of solitude and self-hatred.

Tiara wore her white bikini. Today the top and bottom appeared to be the same size. The bottom fit. Her hair was done up in country-and-western glamour, moving only slightly in the wind. The diamonds glinted in her ears, echoed by a rhinestone navel stud. Her star tattoo seemed sprinkled with glitter, but I couldn't confirm it without staring at her chest. Her makeup, more dramatic than usual, made her look like a doll. A Bratz doll, but still.

She did not have snot on her face.

"Guess you got your product," I said, my facial rinse completed. I pulled a green-and-white beach towel out of my tote and did my best to hide my entire body in its folds. My flirty, skirted bikini suddenly seemed far less adorable than before. "Is Albert still here?"

Tiara squirted some lotion on her hand and stroked it along one perfectly toned arm. "He said he had to get back. He put all the groceries away, though."

"That was nice of him," I said.

"Up for a swim?" Michael asked Tiara. He didn't even look tired. "There are sea turtles out there."

I felt a pang. Tiara and I had shared enough already. The sea turtles were mine.

"Oh! No." Tiara shuddered, as if Michael had suggested she bathe in goat's blood. "I don't really like the water."

Michael reached around for his bag and pulled it onto his lap, digging until he retrieved his phone.

"Just checking messages," he mumbled, like a junkie sneaking a fix. From where I stood, I could see a towel inside his bag, some flip-flops, a wallet.

I remembered Jimmy's warnings about theft. "Is that a good idea? Leaving your wallet on the shore when you're swimming?"

Michael's eyes shot to his friend's house plus the other large ones that sat on either side of it; all three had access to this spot, plus there was a tiny path that ran to the road. "I wouldn't leave it out someplace really busy, but if I'm on a little beach in Maui or a quiet cove in Laguna—sure, why not?"

Suddenly I pictured Michael's bag, left on the sand while he went diving. And then I pictured someone rifling through it. "Wait," I said. "You've left your bag unattended on a beach in Laguna? With your wallet in it?"

He began to shrug and then froze. "Do you think that—"

I stared back, speechless.

"Well, I guess that's one mystery solved," Michael said.

"What?" Tiara asked.

"Michael left his wallet on the beach in Laguna," I told her. "And then he went in the water. And Jimmy was there and he copied everything down."

Something occurred to me. "But wouldn't he need your PIN numbers to get the frequent-flier miles and the Amex points?" I asked Michael.

He pulled his aviator sunglasses from the bag and slipped them on—perhaps to avoid my gaze. "I keep a list of my PINs in my wallet. So I don't forget them."

"Mm," I said. "Good thinking."

"Guess I should call Sergeant Hosozawa." Michael sighed, pushing buttons on his phone.

"You were just looking for an excuse to use that thing," I said.

While Michael waited for the sergeant to come on the line, Tiara said, "So when Albert took me to the Hyatt? After they gave me my makeup bag? I used the showers and changing room by the pool while Albert went to the grocery store."

"Yeah—you really can't be too trusting," Michael said into his phone.

"And then after that?" Tiara said. "Albert took me back to the Maui Hi."

"I'm glad to hear that," Michael told the police. "It really has gotten out of control."

"The news crews were gone," Tiara continued. "There's some stupid surf contest on the north shore they wanted to cover." She rolled her eyes. "But a couple of photographers were still hanging out—they didn't even know we'd left the condo. And they did this whole, like *photo shoot* of me!"

She paused for a moment to let this sink in, her bright white teeth shining in the sunlight. "One of them—I think his name was Jacko—said I should be a model. And so I told him, well, I kind of already am a model! Have I told you about my modeling?"

"Mm," I said.

"Well, we're all staying away from the press," Michael told the police. "So they're bound to lose interest."

"Tiara went back to the Maui Hi," I told Michael once he'd closed his phone. "For a photo shoot." My jaw hurt from clenching my teeth.

He opened his mouth to say something, and then closed it, his nostrils flaring slightly. "I spoke to Sergeant Hosozawa," he said finally. "Assuming the body doesn't turn up tomorrow, he's going to call a press conference to say that Jimmy appears to have faked his drowning to escape legal troubles. And he's going to say that none of us is under suspicion."

He narrowed his eyes at Tiara. "And he asks that we all try to keep a low profile."

She did a little head toss so that the breeze blew her hair just so. "The photographer said we should check the television tonight."

* * *

Finding a hair dryer in the bathroom was the best thing that had happened to me all week, which says a lot about how my week was going. I spent longer than usual styling my hair. Nothing short of extensions would give it Tiara's kind of volume, but that was okay. Big hair had been out of style for twenty years.

My cheeks were so rosy from the sun I didn't need much makeup, just a little lip gloss and a coat of mascara. I hadn't looked this good in ages, I thought, slipping some dangly silver earrings into my lobes. A pale blue Lands' End tank top and a white skirt completed my casual chic look.

I checked my phone: there was a message from Lena, asking me to check my e-mail, and one from Mary, asking me to call.

"Just wanted to see how you're making out," Mary told me.

A glass of lemon water in hand, I strolled out to my lanai and settled onto the lounge. "I'm holding up. Were there any more calls?"

"About"—she paused to count—"thirty."

"Ugh."

"I told them you were in seclusion. That they should leave you alone. They were even asking me questions—where you came from, where you worked. That kind of thing. It's like they think they'll find some skeletons in your closet."

"Oh God."

"What? Is there something I don't know?"

"Of course not," I said. "I'm the dullest person in the world."

* * *

Michael's door was open. His room, large with a partial ocean view, was nicer than Tiara's but not as nice as mine.

"I don't suppose you have Internet access," I said.

He raised his eyebrows. "Wouldn't be caught dead without it." He motioned to a desk with a laptop. "I'm just going out. Help yourself." Today's black shirt was a short-sleeved cotton button-up, paired with khaki shorts.

"You look nice. Got a date?" I joked. Well, I meant it as a joke, though it came out sounding weird.

"Customer meeting."

"Tom Paulson?" I asked.

"I—no." He peered at me. "How do you know Tom?"

"He gave me the air tank. The morning Jimmy disappeared. You might want to call him. He said he liked your stuff but the shipments were unreliable."

"Really?" He looked stunned. "He always told me that my stuff was just too high-end for his store."

"You might want to call him," I said again. "Tell him you've shortened your turnaround times, contracted with some new suppliers—whatever. I mean, assuming it's true."

He bit his lip.

"Is the Web site working?" I asked.

He nodded. "I called the office this morning, really got on our computer guy's case." He paused before admitting, "He's really not very good."

"So get rid of him and hire someone else," I said.

He shook his head. "I just don't have time to interview—not to mention the retraining. I don't know—maybe in a few months."

He picked up a cardboard box from the corner of the room, put it on his bed, and started pulling out wetsuits. "What do you think?"

They were unlike any wetsuits I had seen before. There was a black one with a fireworks pattern, another with a multicolored tie-dye effect, and my favorite, a kelly-green shorty with bright pink fish swimming across the bodice. It was the kind of wetsuit Talbot's would make if they were in the business.

"Wow," I said, fingering the suits. "These are really cool."

"You should see our bridal line—they're really flying out the door. These are just prototypes of some of our new designs. Ana's really talented."

"I thought Ana was your secretary."

"*Administrator,*" he corrected. "She is. But she's also the designer."

"You've got your head designer answering your phones?" I asked. "Well, that explains a lot."

"What do you mean?"

"Ana's phone manner is awful—completely unprofessional. Plus, she cuts people off."

"I know." He sighed. "But she's been under a lot of stress. New phone system, added responsibilities . . ."

"Dead boss," I added.

He smiled. "She loses things, too," he admitted. "Phone numbers, contracts, customer orders. But until we get bigger, I've got to make it work. Anyway, I gotta run. The computer's all yours."

* * *

Perhaps I shouldn't be advising someone else on his career, I thought when I opened my e-mail. Mixed in with questions about sick leave, complaints about coworkers, and the inevitable ads for Viagra, there was a memo from Mr. Wills.

Re: news and publicity surrounding Wills Rubber Company

Dear Jane,

You have nothing but my utmost sympathy regarding the recent events concerning your relationship with your gentleman friend and his apparent deception and subsequent disappearance. All of us here at Wills Rubber Company recognize that this is a difficult time for you, and we will do our best to keep Human Resources running smoothly until you feel you can return to your job in a calm and professional manner.

In addition to my concern for you, however, is a concern for the impact this resulting media attention has had on all of us here in the Wills Rubber family. We have had numerous phone inquiries regarding both your personal and professional qualities as well as intrusive in-person interview attempts, all of which combine to create a distracting work environment. Furthermore, Wills Rubber Company has been described more than once in the media as "a rubber manufacturer," when, as you are aware, we prefer to be identified as "an industry leader in the creation and distribution of playground flooring constructed from 100% recycled automobile tires."

We would appreciate your effort to keep Wills Rubber from inclusion in any sensationalist media reports and in correcting the description when such exposure is unavoidable. In the meantime, all of us are hoping for a quick resolution to your current situation, and we look forward to having you back in Brea.

Best regards,

Bob Wills

I responded to all of my e-mails (*Dear Mr. Wills, I assure you that this incident will have no effect on my work performance,* blah, blah, blah) and was on the verge of searching news reports and blogs for any stories about Jimmy when I realized that only one thing would make me feel better now.

I headed for the kitchen.

Chapter 21

Trey Hollingsworth's kitchen was, not surprisingly, far better equipped than the kitchenette at the Maui Hi. Beyond that, it had even more nifty stuff than my own kitchen at home, and I've got Calphalon. Among other things, Trey had professional-quality pots and pans, a heavy steel countertop mixer, and a breathtaking assortment of pale green silicone baking pans, none of which appeared to have ever been used.

First I threw together a buttermilk lemon cake, which I baked in a pineapple-shaped silicone pan. A pineapple cake would have been more thematic, but my lemon cake is truly exceptional. While that was in the oven (or should I say "in one of the ovens"), I whipped up some mango and jalapeño salsa as well as a Kula-greens salad with goat cheese and macadamia nuts; I'd toss it with a simple vinaigrette at the last minute.

It felt good to be doing something productive, to be in control of something, no matter how small. It made me believe that my life could eventually go back to normal.

* * *

"I *love* your *hair*!" Tiara said when she came into the main room. Her own tresses looked sleeker than they had on the beach.

"Thanks," I said, patting my head with one slightly mango-y hand.

"Did you use product?"

"Just a little mousse," I said. "The big difference was in having a blow dryer. I didn't have one at the Maui Hi, remember."

"Ahhhh." Tiara nodded sagely, as if everything suddenly made sense. "I have a lot of product if you want to borrow anything. Volumizing spray, sculpting lotion. Gel, of course. Polishing milk. Mousse can weigh your hair down." She was wearing her black halter top again, with a black skirt this time.

"I'm okay with the mousse," I said, wishing I'd worn something more exciting than my Lands' End tank top, which now had a couple of lemon-batter splotches on it. Okay: wishing I owned something more exciting.

"All right. But you can always change your mind." She tucked a product-heavy strand of hair behind her ear. Her earrings were enormous dangling things, like two chandeliers made of translucent shells.

A car pulled into the driveway, making crunching sounds on the white shells. A moment later, Michael came through the front door, cell-phone earpiece in place. "They're here. I'll tell them." He stopped short and sniffed. I pointed to the cake, which was on a cooling rack on the counter.

Once he had said, "Okay—keep us posted," I announced, "I made a lemon cake for dessert."

He responded with, "The police know who Jimmy really is."

We were all silent for a moment. I was afraid of what I might learn, afraid that things could actually get worse.

"His name is James Studebaker," Michael said. "He's twenty-eight years old." (Younger than me but older than Tiara, I registered.)

"He was born in Texas," Michael continued. (Tiara straightened with pride: he had told her the truth.) "But he moved to Lancaster when he was twelve." (Yessss!) "Graduated high school, did a year of community college before dropping out. Since then, he's bounced around the beaches—Redondo, Long Beach, Laguna. Works as a waiter, mostly—guess we knew that—plus he has a history of, well . . ."

"Faking his death?" I ventured.

"Attaching himself to wealthy older women."

Maybe I just imagined Tiara looking at me when he said that. I was all set to say, *Thirty-two is not old!* when Michael clarified.

"Jimmy had hooked up with a string of divorcées in their fifties and even sixties," he said. "He's been known to 'borrow' credit cards before, though always from people he knew. He's had charges filed against him but never a conviction. Still, I guess it was enough for him to want to use another name."

"How did the police find this out?" I asked. "From his photo?" The idea of a genteel older woman recognizing Jimmy from Tiara's mid-orgasm shot was almost too gross to contemplate.

"Nope." Michael shook his head. "From Scott. He's Jimmy's brother. Police got the number off his cell phone. He probably wouldn't have spilled everything, but he thinks Jimmy's dead, and he's pretty upset. At any rate, the police have scheduled a press conference for noon tomorrow. They're going to reveal his true identity and also say that he's probably still alive. That should take the heat off the rest of us."

"What about your other card?" I asked. "The Amex that you didn't cancel. Has he tried to use that?"

He shook his head. "Nope. He must be lying pretty low." His phone purred. "Hello?" He wandered over to the French doors, chatting.

Something was bothering Tiara. "It seems wrong to let Jimmy's brother think he's dead. Though I guess it isn't that long till tomorrow."

Something else was bothering me. If Jimmy was really alive, why would he leave his phone behind when he knew it would lead the police to Scott?

Tiara leaned on the counter and chewed on her cushiony lip for a while before speaking. "Did Jimmy make many calls when you were together?"

I thought about it. "No."

"I always thought that was weird," she said. "That a guy with his own business would get so few calls. And he never checked his e-mail. It made me wonder if there was something a little, you know—not right."

Huh. There had been times when I'd been concerned that Jimmy wasn't working hard enough, but I'd never actually found his behavior strange. It was disconcerting to think that Tiara had picked up on something that I hadn't.

When Michael got off the phone, he retrieved a bottle of white wine from a special minifridge next to the trash compactor. After a bit of digging, he found a metal corkscrew and opened the bottle without mangling the cork too badly. He poured the amber liquid into three superthin glasses.

The wine was slippery and smooth, with the faintest hint of vanilla. "Thanks for letting me stay in your house," I said.

"It's not my house. But you're welcome. Thanks for making dinner."

"My pleasure." I pulled the fish out of the big refrigerator and put a cast-iron skillet on top of the Viking stove.

"Is there a TV in here?" Tiara asked. "'Cause I'd just like to flip through the channels, if that's okay."

There was a television over the fireplace, but I hadn't noticed it before, mainly because it didn't look like a television. When off, it seemed to be nothing more than a big, tasteful painting: a primitive scene of a woman in a muumuu lounging on a chaise, flowers in her hair. But when Michael pushed a secret button on the frame, *shazaam!* The painting became a flat-screen TV.

"Not to be crass, but where did your friend get all his money?" I asked Michael as Tiara flipped through the channels.

"Trey was born lucky," Michael said. "Or rich, anyway. His grandfather, great-grandfather, whatever, was a shipping magnate. Since then, the family has invested wisely—and reproduced only in moderation. Trey works in the family business, managing their money, mostly." He looked around the vast room. "Guess he's doing okay."

Tiara paused on a local weather report. ("Highs in the low eighties. Possible showers in the late afternoon.") "There's nothing about us!"

"Bummer," I said.

Michael's phone rang. He checked the display and stuck the phone back in his pocket.

"Customer?" I asked.

He shook his head. "My mother."

"Nice."

He crossed his arms. "She's just going to want to know about the birthday party. And I haven't checked my schedule yet."

"So go check your schedule. You have a BlackBerry?"

He shook his head.

"You should think about getting one," I suggested.

"I had one, and I lost it," he confessed, avoiding my eyes. He looked at me, and his shoulders drooped. "Okay, actually I've lost two."

"C'mon," I said. "We'll check your schedule right now, figure out how to make this work."

Five minutes later, I was on his computer, booking a flight from Orange County to La Guardia (the party was in Manhattan), and he was on the phone to his mother. "Of course I'll be there."

"There," I said when he hung up. "Doesn't it feel good to have that arranged?"

Before he had a chance to tell me how wonderful and helpful I was being (or, perhaps, how anal and intrusive), Tiara burst into the room.

"The television!" she said. "My pictures! You gotta see!"

The segment was on one of those gossip programs that specializes in stories about celebrity rehab, solid gold baby strollers, and lurid crimes. When we got to the main room, there were photos of Tiara and me plastered across the (way too big) screen. And there was a headline above the pictures: PLAIN JANE AND THE LUSCIOUS LATINO.

My photograph was the one from the Maui newspaper, taken outside the police station, my hair unwashed, my face drawn, my Lands' End clothes hopelessly rumpled. I really shouldn't wear yellow.

Tiara's photo was from the paparazzi session outside the Maui. She looked like she was pole dancing with a palm tree, her breasts spilling out of her halter top, her plump lips parted invitingly, her eyes half closed in delight.

The show's host, a generic Ken doll with gobs of brown makeup, said something about, "Stay tuned for more shocking details," before cutting to a commercial.

"That is so wrong!" Tiara howled. "I can't believe they'd say that!"

I nodded silently, touched by her outrage.

"I'm only a quarter Cuban! And I'm proud of that. But they're, like, totally ignoring the fact that I'm also German, Norwegian, and Filipino."

Apparently, it was okay to call me plain: truth in advertising and all that.

Michael didn't come out unscathed, either. Once the commercial break finished, the Ken-doll host cut to a shot of Jimmies' "corporate headquarters," which turned out to be sandwiched between a dry cleaners and a tutoring franchise.

"Is that in Laguna Beach?" I asked. (I didn't think Laguna Beach allowed crappy strip malls.)

"It's kind of over the line," he mumbled.

"It doesn't look like an office," Tiara said. She was right. It had a big plate-glass window over a low strip of beige stucco, and—were those yellow booths inside? It reminded me of something. What was it?

"It looks like a Subway sandwich shop," Tiara said.

"It's just a work space," Michael snarled. "And the booths work really well for desks."

"Was it once a Subway?" I had to know.

"Not for a whole bunch of years," he said.

*　*　*

Out on the deck, the three of us scanned the ocean for whales and ate the dinner I'd made: grilled mahimahi topped with mango salsa, Kula greens tossed with a citrus vinaigrette, steamed rice, and, of course, the pineapple-shaped lemon cake. The air was perfect: warm with just the right amount of moisture and a touch of a flower-scented breeze. Below us, waves playfully slapped the rocks.

"So this photographer at the condo was saying this exposure could totally open the window for me to do other things," Tiara said. "Reality shows, print ads, the sky's the limit." She gestured with her fork as she yapped, launching a tiny chunk of mango that just managed to miss my shoulder. It hit my hair instead.

"Open doors." I slid the mango off a strand.

"Huh?" Her fork stopped moving.

"The expression is 'open doors,' not 'open the window.'"

"When a door closes, a window opens," Michael added helpfully.

"But a door didn't close," I said.

Michael picked up the wine bottle to refill my glass. "Boyfriend disappears, she finds out he had another woman? I'd call that a closed door. Slammed, even." He picked up his wineglass by the stem, his brown eyes crinkling in amusement.

A cell phone rang. Michael made a Pavlovian grab for his pocket, but it wasn't his phone, it was Tiara's—which, I feel the need to point out, she'd encrusted in pink rhinestones.

"It's my mom!" she squealed, opening the phone and scampering back into the house—at least, as much as a person can scamper on heels. "Mommy! Did you see me on TV?" She shut the French doors behind her.

"The picture really didn't look like you," Michael said.

"Sure it did."

He sipped his wine, considering. "It looked like you on a really lousy day. You didn't look that bad, all things considered."

We drank our wine and gazed at the sky. The sun was so huge and orange that it hurt my eyes.

"So, how'd you start your company?" I asked.

He raised his eyebrows. "What did Jimmy tell you?"

I thought back. "He said he didn't want to work for anyone else, so he just got some money together and did it."

"That's not so far from the truth," Michael said. "In college—I went to UCLA—I got really into surfing."

"Your parents must have been thrilled."

"Oh—very." He grinned. "It was exactly what they'd pictured when I said I wanted to go to college on the West Coast. Anyway, I had this plain black wetsuit I'd bought used, and it seemed really boring. So one day when I was supposed to be in class, I bought some fabric paints and painted a school of fish on it."

"What class did you skip?"

"Business."

My mouth twitched.

He smiled. "Okay, so maybe I should have made it to that one. Anyway, the other surfers were all, 'Hey, dude! That suit? Is so. Totally. Awesome.'" For a guy who owned a wetsuit company, Michael did a lousy impression of a surfer boy. "Some of them asked me to paint their suits, too."

"And that was it? You just got into business?"

"Well, no. Fabric paint doesn't hold up so well in salt water. After a few times in the ocean, the suits looked like crap."

"Did people get mad?"

"Nah. Surfers don't get mad. They just get . . . less mellow. At any rate, after college, I had a couple of sales jobs and hated them. I started diving, and it became the thing I lived for, the only thing that kept me going during the week. I started playing around with wetsuits again and finally figured out how to make the designs last.

"People kept saying, 'You could sell those,' so about six years ago, I decided to give it a shot. My parents lent me a few thousand dollars to get started. I found a manufacturer, did some really basic designs, and started selling the suits out of the back of my van. Two years ago, I hired Ana—her designs blow mine out of the water."

"So to speak."

"Right." He sipped his wine, smiling over the glass.

Beyond us, the sun slipped down, down, and finally disappeared into the sea. "Another day in paradise," I quipped.

"There's no place I'd rather be," he said with complete sincerity.

Chapter 22

For the first time all week, I woke up the next morning feeling almost happy. The bed had a down-filled pillow top; it was like sleeping on a cloud. Instead of cars pulling into the Maui Hi parking lot, the rhythm of the waves had lulled me to sleep and kept me there.

In this mood, even the "Plain Jane" segment seemed laughable. At noon, the police would deliver a statement revealing Jimmy's identity and declaring me (and Tiara, yeah, sure, whatever) to be innocent victims. Soon the public would lose interest in all of us.

After brewing a pot of coffee (Folger's, which seemed so wrong in the land of Kona coffee), I took my mug out to my own personal lanai. The ocean was calm and silver blue, the air damp and salty. And Folger's coffee turned out to be far better than I would have guessed. For the first time in days, I felt like I could breathe.

It was two hours later in California, so I called the office.

"What are you wearing?" I asked Lena, a frequent recipient of my "appropriate office attire" spiel.

She laughed. "You perv!"

"Lena . . ." I tried to sound threatening, but a whale jumping in the distance made me grin.

"White blouse, black skirt, totally boring. I look like a waitress."

"How many buttons are undone?" I asked.

Lena sighed and then paused, presumably to button up her gaping shirt. "Only one button open. Though I'll tell you, this high neck is kind of cutting off my circulation."

"You'll live," I said.

"You sound better than the last time we talked," she said. "Back to your usual bossy self."

"Thanks—I think. I feel better."

"Is it because of that other guy—the one they showed on the news? Because he's kind of hot—all dark and mysterious."

"He's not mysterious," I said. "He just doesn't like to get his picture taken. Anyway, I just wanted to check in, see if anyone needed me."

"Things are pretty quiet here," she said. "But there's a woman who's been calling for you, says she knows you from high school."

Even though I went home for Christmas every December, it had been years since I'd looked up any of my old friends, most of whom had moved away years ago. "Really? What's her name?"

"Let me check . . . here it is. Katie Rothman."

"Katie!" I felt a surge of something vaguely resembling happiness.

"So you do know her?"

"Oh, yeah, we used to be—we were really close. Did she leave a number?"

* * *

My heart raced as I dialed the New Jersey phone number. I hadn't seen Katie since her wedding to Ron, and I hadn't given her my new contact information when I'd moved. Still, I thought about her every time I went home, and I found myself missing her at odd moments.

"Hello?"

"Katie, this is—"

"Jane!" she crowed. "I thought you'd fallen off the face of the earth!"

"Your parents moved," I said lamely. "I didn't have a number for you . . ."

"It doesn't matter," she said. "You've got it now. How've you been?"

"Good," I said reflexively. Then: "Well, not really."

"Thorry," she said. "Thtupid question." Katie's lisp always came out when she felt emotional—on her own behalf or someone else's.

"Are you back in New Jersey?" I asked before the conversation veered to my newfound fame. "You have a 201 area code."

"Yup—my days as a cool New Yorker are over. We bought a house here last year—just couldn't see raising kids in the city."

"You have kids?" I pictured pink-cheeked babies with lots of piercings.

"Two," she said. "Seymour is three and Maya just turned one."

"That's wonderful," I said, feeling immensely relieved. Everything worked out for the best. Katie was happy. I had made the right choice, not telling her about Ron.

"But that's not what I called to talk about," she said.

"You saw me on the news." I sighed.

"Well, yeah, that's how I was able to track down your work number. But I figure you probably don't want to talk about that right now. What I had to tell you is, I saw Joey Ardolino!"

"No!" I could picture him perfectly, leaning against my locker, batting his absurdly long eyelashes: the first man to break my heart.

"My garbage disposal broke a couple of months ago," Katie said. "Seymour shoved some plastic play food into it—so I called a plumber, and it turned out to be Joey!"

"Joey's a plumber?" I pictured him living in a neat, modest house, coming home every night to a houseful of kids and a casserole made with cream-of-mushroom soup. It sounded like a pretty nice life, actually.

"Yeah, but that's not all," Katie said. "He's gay!"

"Joey's a *gay plumber*? Get out!" I broke into laughter.

Her laugh was high-pitched and infectious, just like it had always been. "I know! I said to him, 'Can't they kick you out of the union for that?' And he said, all serious, 'There is no union.' Which for some reason I thought was really funny."

"Oh my God," I hooted. "All that he put us through—and he didn't even like girls?"

"See?" she said. "It really *was* him and not us."

But what about the other men who'd broken my heart? What was their excuse?

"Tell me more about your life," I said. "How's Ron doing?"

"*Ron?*" She paused. "Omigod, Jane, it really has been a long time since we talked! Ron and I split up eight months after our wedding."

"I'm so sorry." My stomach clenched.

"Actually, it worked out really well," she said. "See, if we divorced before six months were up, we'd have to return all of our wedding gifts, and there was no way I was gonna hand over my rice cooker." That had been from me.

"What happened?" I asked, knowing what the answer would be.

"He was screwing around," she said casually. "And I caught him."

"Wow," I said, guilt flooding through me: I should have told her about Ron. I could have stopped her from marrying him. "But—you found someone else." Another artist, I figured, or maybe a musician.

"Patrick worked with Ron," she said. "Six months after the divorce, he called me up—said he'd wanted to wait a respectable amount of time before asking me out, but that he'd always had a thing for me."

"So he's an investment banker?"

"Yup. And the nicest man in the world," she said matter-of-factly.

"I need to tell you something," I blurted. "The night of your rehearsal dinner, Ron made a pass at me. I should have told you, but you looked so happy, and I didn't want to ruin things for you." I blinked away tears. "I'm so sorry, Katie. I should have said something."

"Ugh—he was such a jerk," she said, sounding completely unsurprised. "It wouldn't have made any difference if you'd told me what happened. That wasn't the first time he put the moves on one of my friends."

"It wasn't?"

"There were two other times before that—that I know about, anyway. When I confronted him, he said he was just a flirt and it didn't mean anything. And I believed him. I guess there are some things you have to find out for yourself."

"True," I said. "But preferably not on national television."

* * *

After I got off the phone, I headed for the kitchen, where I whipped up a batch of banana muffins and set to work unloading the dishwasher. Michael and I had cleaned the kitchen together the night before. He had loaded the dishwasher while I wiped the counters and put away the food. We made a good team.

"Something smells good," he said, wandering in from his bedroom shortly after the muffins came out. He was wearing blue gym shorts and a white T-shirt that said DIVE CATALINA. He had a slight case of bed head, but it actually made him look cute and vaguely boyish.

"Banana muffins," I said, placing one on a little plate and sliding it across the counter. "Careful, they're still a little hot."

He took a bite and nodded with pleasure. "Delicious," he said after swallowing.

"There's coffee, too," I said. "Though it's a little old. I'll make another pot." I turned to face the complicated stainless-steel coffeemaker that had taken me about fifteen minutes to figure out.

"No, no, this is fine." He took another big bite of the muffin and crossed the kitchen to pour himself a mug of the old coffee. We were standing so close I could see his morning stubble, brown with flecks of red.

"First you make dinner, now breakfast," he said, sliding the coffeepot back into place.

"Well, it's the least I could do."

He shot me a sly grin. "I could get used to having you around."

I felt myself blushing as I poured my own cup of coffee (which turned out to be just as overcooked as I'd feared). I thought about saying something flirtatious in return, but I couldn't think of anything sufficiently coy.

Instead, I asked, "Have you seen Tiara today?"

"Oh, yeah," he said casually. "She's in my bedroom."

I just about spit my coffee out. When he saw my expression, he said, "That came out wrong. What I meant is, Tiara is on my laptop, which happens to be in my bedroom. She's posting an announcement on her MySpace page." He slid onto a counter stool.

"What kind of announcement?" I took a stool next to him.

"She starts off by thanking people for their support."

"What people? What support?" The coffee was really pretty stale, but I didn't want to leave my spot next to Michael.

He rolled his eyes. "It wasn't clear. Then she goes into some 'We are the World' thing about taking pride in your heritage and not labeling people. There was more, but I wasn't really paying attention, to be completely honest."

Oh, yes—he definitely likes me better.

Tiara's voice came from down the hall and grew louder. "It's in the 'My Documents' folder. Yeah. And the file's called 'Cars.'" She came into the room with her pink rhinestone phone pressed to her ear. She wore a red Los Angeles Angels T-shirt and baggy pajama pants patterned with hearts. Her hair was pulled back in a ponytail, and her face had been scrubbed. She almost looked like a normal person.

"Well, I think the file's called 'Cars,'" she said into her phone. "Or maybe just 'Car,' you know, without the *s*. And if you don't see that, try 'Toyota.'" She stopped in the middle of the room and looked at the ceiling, as if begging God for technical assistance.

"Can't you just do a search?" she said, sounding peeved. "But I can't remember the name of the file, I told you!" At last, her eyes lit up. "Yes! Anaheim Auto Show—that's it!"

"Oh my gosh, Jane," Tiara said when she got off the phone. "More cooking? That is so sweet! You're like a mom or something."

I really wish people would stop staying that.

Resisting my impulse to pop up and get her breakfast, I remained planted on my kitchen bar stool. "Busy morning?"

"Oh. My. God." She held her pink phone between both hands as if in prayer. "On MySpace? I had, like, seven hundred friend requests." She put her hand (and her phone) over her heart. Well, somewhere in the vicinity of her heart, anyway.

After the Geoffrey episode, I had deleted my MySpace profile. Something told me I wouldn't have had seven hundred friend requests even if it were still active.

"It is, like, so gratifying to get that kind of support," Tiara continued. "To know that people care. So I spent a whole bunch of time writing a statement because I felt like people needed to hear from me. And just now? I was talking to this kid who lives next door to me and my mother. He's like thirteen or something, kind of creepy but smart with computers, and he's going to put a video of me at the Anaheim Auto Show on YouTube."

"Mm," I said. And then, to change the subject: "There's coffee made."

She poured herself a cup of coffee, added lots of cream and sugar, and took a taste. She grimaced. "Old." She put the mug in the sink and bent over to peer at the big coffee machine without touching it. "This machine is really, like, complicated . . ." she said, still bent over.

"Yes, it is."

She tilted her head one way. And then the other. "I don't think I can figure it out . . ."

I sighed in defeat. "I'll do it."

"Anyone mind if I turn on the TV?" Tiara chirped, heading for the big framed picture over the fireplace, leaving me behind to make her coffee. She hit the secret button without waiting for a reply.

Television was the last thing I wanted to see, followed closely by newspapers and Internet blogs. Fortunately, there was nothing on about us, just some children's programming, a Hawaiian travelogue, some soap operas, and a soccer match.

"Maybe people are losing interest," I said as fresh coffee gurgled and began to drip.

Michael walked across the kitchen to put his empty mug in the sink. "If they haven't lost interest yet, they will as soon as the police make their report. There's really nothing left to say."

Finally, Tiara gave up channel surfing and turned off the set with a sigh.

There was a buzzing sound over the intercom; someone was at the outside gate. Michael pushed the inside intercom button. "Yeah?"

"Maui police," came the static-filled response.

The three of us looked at one another. "Maybe the sergeant just wants to review his statements for the press conference," Michael suggested.

Moments later, Sergeant Hosozawa stood in the doorway, looking grim. But then, that was his usual expression. Detective McGuinn appeared equally drawn.

Sergeant Hosozawa's voice was strained. "We found the body," he said.

Chapter 23

Tiara began to scream. "But he's alive! You said so!"

Then she began to sob, an awful choking sound. This was even worse than getting booted from the Hyatt. I, on the other hand, was quiet, too nauseous and dizzy to make a single sound. I clutched the kitchen counter until Michael helped me onto a stool.

They found him this morning, the sergeant told us. The body had washed up farther down the coastline—north of Kihei, just where you'd expect the currents to take him. There was rough surf and jagged rocks. He'd gotten caught in an indentation in the rocks—a cave, almost. He was almost impossible to spot. It took some daredevil on a waverunner riding too close to the rocks to find him. He saw something that looked like an arm, and then he'd gone for help.

The cause of death was inconclusive. The sharks had gotten to him, but he was probably dead first—from natural causes, most likely: heart attack, decompression sickness. Of course his body had been so roughed up that it was hard to tell. We'd have to wait for the coroner's report. And they'd track down dental records, just for confirmation.

* * *

I spent the next few hours in my beautiful room, curled into a fetal position on the bed. Jimmy was dead. He hadn't left me on purpose, after all. Maybe he had loved me, if only a little.

At least there'd be no more surprises after this. No expectation of seeing him around every corner. No fear that he and Tiara would run off together.

In the early afternoon, I found her down by the water, barefoot on the lava rocks. She was wearing a white eyelet dress that made her look oddly virginal. The wind whipped the dress around her legs and her hair around her face. She squinted into the wind, her mouth grim, and hugged herself.

"I keep picturing him," she said, her eyes still on the bright water. "Down there. Drowning. Scared. You know?"

"I know." I swallowed, but the lump in my throat wouldn't go away.

"I got a call from an agent," she said quietly. I could barely hear her above the wind. "A real agent, not someone you pay, this guy I've been begging to take me on for two years. He wants to represent me."

"Congratulations." I checked her face. She didn't look happy.

"Is it wrong, though?" she asked, finally looking at me. "To get something out of Jimmy's death?"

I thought about it. "Maybe if he were a different person. A better person. But he used us, remember. Maybe this makes it even." I touched her shoulder. "You should tell the agent yes."

"Oh, I already did," she said. "And I've got my first interview, on the local news tonight. I just—I thought it would make me happier. I mean, all of my dreams are finally coming true. Right?"

*   *   *

Three months earlier, on an ashy-hot Sunday in November, while the Santa Ana winds blew dry desert air and wildfires burned in three directions, Jimmy had told me the truth about his surfing accident.

He'd come up to my condo late the night before, following a dinner shift at the restaurant. We'd spent the morning in bed and then headed to a local park to feed the ducks (because that's the kind of thing you do in the early stages of courtship).

But after five minutes in the throat-scratching heat, we were ready to pack it in. Even the duck pond, rimmed by towering trees, looked soupy warm.

"We could go back to the condo and jump in the pool," I suggested, slumped on a bench. My complex had a small rectangular pool that was rarely used, even in the summer. The water was always cold, but maybe the recent string of scorching days had nudged it into the bearable range.

"Don't have a swimsuit," Jimmy said abruptly, chucking a piece of stale bread at an apathetic mallard.

"We can swing by Wal-Mart," I said. "They might have some cheap ones left over from summer. If not, you can buy a pair of athletic shorts. No one will care."

"I don't like pools," he said, fishing in the plastic bread bag for another crumb.

"It's not the ocean," I conceded. "But it's better than nothing."

He shook his head quickly and shot me a side glance. In his

eyes I saw something like fear. I put my arm around his shoulders. He leaned against me.

"What is it?" I asked.

"Something happened," he said finally. "When I was fifteen." He touched the scar on his chin.

"You said you got that in a surfing accident," I said.

"I did. Sort of. But remember—I grew up in the desert. We didn't have an ocean."

If not the ocean—then where? "You surfed in a pool?" I guessed.

He nodded. And then he told me his story.

"There was this kid on my street, Ricky Ruiz. His family had a pool. I practically lived there in the summer—it was too hot to do anything but swim. We'd do flips off the diving board, have chicken fights, race underwater—pretty much anything we could think of. The house was low and pretty close to the pool, so sometimes we'd climb on the roof and take turns jumping off."

"His parents let you?" I asked, alarmed.

He shrugged. "They both worked. Ricky's older brother, Frankie, was in charge, but he was just as crazy as we were, maybe worse. And my parents didn't care what I did. Anyway, that summer Frankie got a surfboard. We'd take turns running from the edge and jumping onto the board, see how long we could stay on, how far we could go. You know—surfing. Only problem was, after a couple of weeks it was too easy. So I had the brilliant idea—"

He stopped abruptly, a stricken look on his face, like he was watching a movie that he'd seen before, still hoping for a different ending.

He took a deep breath. "I thought it would be fun if we jumped onto the board . . . from the roof. Ricky said he'd do it if I went first."

"Oh my God." I touched his chin. "This?"

He nodded. "Five stitches. And a broken leg."

"Which one?"

"Left."

I touched the leg carefully, as if it still needed healing.

He sat up straighter, facing the pond, seeing something else. "Frankie—Ricky's brother—drove me to the emergency room. We were there for three hours. I was really bummed because I'd have the cast on my leg all summer, which meant I couldn't swim.

"When we got back it was late afternoon. Ricky's parents were still at work. It took me a while to get out of the car, to hobble into the house on my crutches. When I did, I called out: 'Ricky— yo, dude!' But he didn't answer. So I yelled louder: 'Hey, asshole, don't make me come and find you! I can barely walk!'"

He started to shake. I rubbed his arm.

"I'd just made it into the living room when I heard Frankie scream." A sob escaped from his lips.

"Ricky?" I whispered.

"He said he'd do it." His voice cracked. "He said he'd do it if I did." The tears were coursing down his face now, his blue eyes rimmed with red.

"His body was under the surfboard, just stuck there. He hadn't even been hurt that bad—but the board knocked him uncon- scious, so he drowned, just sucked up all that water till it filled his lungs."

He rubbed his tears away with his palms, only to have his eyes fill again. "So now—I don't swim in pools. Ever. I don't even like to go in the ocean without a tank of oxygen. As long as I have my air, I'll be okay."

I put my arms around him and he held on tight. It was the only time I ever saw him cry. When he started breathing normally and pulled away, I pulled a travel-size package of Kleenex out of my bag and held it to him.

He laughed through his tears. "You're always prepared, aren't you?"

"I know. I'm kind of a geek."

He shook his head and gazed at me with an expression that looked an awful lot like love. "There's something about you, Jane. You make me feel . . . safe. It's like, as long as I'm with you, nothing bad can happen."

*   *   *

I spent the afternoon in forced normalcy. I called the airline to confirm my flight the next day (I'd already had them switch it to a paid ticket). I called my sister, who said that "Tiara Cardenas" had appeared on Yahoo's list of most popular searches. I talked briefly to my mother, who was on her way to the mall to find something to wear for lunch with Adele Pritchard. After that, I turned off my phone because there was no one else I wanted to talk to. I made a long list of things to accomplish when I got back to work. If I stayed busy enough for the next month—or twenty—I wouldn't have to think at all.

I took a break to watch Sergeant Hosozawa's (mercifully brief) press conference on TV. He announced that the body of a man between the age of twenty and forty, fitting the description of the missing California tourist, had been recovered off the coast of Kihei. The death was "presumed accidental at this time." He also said that the man previously known as Michael "Jimmy" James, aged thirty-four, of Laguna Beach, California, was actually James Studebaker, aged twenty-eight, also of Laguna Beach. The real Michael James, a victim of credit-card fraud and identity theft, was still very much alive.

I was relieved when it was finally late enough in the afternoon to start dinner. Tiara had left for her interview by then, so I was all alone in the house. There were tiny cooked shrimp and flour tortillas in the freezer, goat cheese and mozzarella in the fridge. Shrimp quesadillas would be easy and good.

I ran the cooked shrimp under cold water to thaw. With a heavy chef's knife from the butcher-block holder, I set to work chopping green onions and cilantro.

Michael came in from the driveway, toting his laptop. "How are you holding up?"

I stopped chopping and shrugged. "I'll survive. It'll be a relief to get home, get back into my routine." As I said this, I felt a pang at the thought of leaving Michael. "I just hope the press doesn't start bugging us again."

"There were a bunch of photographers smoking cigarettes out by the gate when I pulled in. I think Tiara tipped them off."

"Wonderful," I grumbled. "Did you hear the news? She got an agent. She's already out doing an interview."

"Yeah, she told me. Mind if I turn on the tube?" he asked. "I just want to check some basketball scores."

"Sure. No problem."

Michael pushed the secret button on the painting/television set and settled onto a white chaise, remote in hand. He found the basketball game, but when it went, almost immediately, to a commercial, he started channel surfing, keeping the sound very low.

There was a bag of salad in the refrigerator's crisper drawer; I dumped it into a large bowl. I put a cast-iron skillet on the stove and turned the heat on medium.

Michael paused at an old *Star Trek* episode. Or maybe it was a new *Star Trek* episode. I never quite got them straight.

When the quesadilla was all hot and melty, I slipped it out of the pan and onto the cutting board. I'd just made my first slice when a catalog shot of Jimmies wetsuits appeared on the enormous television.

"At least you're getting some free advertising," I said.

Michael turned up the sound just as the newscaster said, "A small start-up with a limited customer base."

I was just about to say that there was nothing wrong with being small when my photograph flashed on the screen. I clutched the knife handle and held my breath.

The photo wasn't the plain Jane shot that had become my standard representation. Instead, it was taken a few years ago, on a company retreat in Mexico. I was smiling at the camera, a frozen margarita in my hand, a handsome young man at my side. My dress was strappy and low cut, my teeth bright white against my tan.

"Change the channel," I pleaded, my entire body starting to shake and sweat. If Michael and I didn't see this report, maybe no one would. Maybe it would be like it never happened.

He reached for the remote, but it was too late. They switched to the recent photograph of me taken outside the police station. There I was, looking drawn—and slightly crazed, some might say. Only this time, the tag over my picture didn't say PLAIN JANE.

Instead, it said: STALKER.

Chapter 24

Okay, so maybe I should have mentioned the stalker episode ear-lier. But it happened so long ago, it's like I was a different person. Besides, *stalker* is such a nasty word and not really accurate. I wasn't stalking anyone, really. I was just . . . preoccupied. And premenstrual. For about four months.

Did I mention that I spent a couple of years at another com-pany, a manufacturer of cement fiber roofing? And that I left be-cause Wills offered greater growth opportunities? Because that's really what happened—all that's important, anyway. The, um, *incident* at my old job didn't seem relevant. Except, all of a sud-den, all these years later, it was.

Did I mention I was lonely in those years? Because it's one thing to seize the moment: move across the country and stay there when your only friend leaves. It's another thing to build some kind of a life with no family, no real friends—nothing to call your own, really, except a beat-up Honda Civic and a closet full of knee-length skirts.

His name was Keith. He was in sales. Of course he was: where else could someone so handsome, so charming, so *glib* end up? When I say handsome, by the way, I'm not talking about the sculpted good looks of a Fruit of the Loom model. I'm talking smoldering: huge brown eyes fringed by girlie lashes, thick black hair (molded into place by an astonishing array of salon products), dimples. His nose was a little wide, and his muscles were overdeveloped for my taste—which is a nice way of saying that his boobs were bigger than mine.

Did I mention I was lonely? Oh, yes, I guess I did.

I didn't even like him at first. He seemed like he had attention deficit disorder—never sitting still, never focusing. Plus, he was so full of crap, you could practically smell it on him—or you could if he didn't douse himself in some citrus-y cologne every morning. He'd come skipping over to my desk—or gliding, or skimming or bounding; the man never just *walked*—and he'd spout something like, "Such beauty! It blinds me!" And then he'd cover his eyes. Or he'd put a hand on his chest and say, "Be still, my beating heart!"

And then he'd ask me to do something for him: approve a vacation day, expedite an expense reimbursement, whatever. I'd do it, of course—but I would have done it anyway because it was my job.

Just so we're clear, I wasn't desperate, at least not romantically. If he'd asked me out, I probably would have said no. Plain Jane headlines aside, I've always attracted some men: not all of them, but enough. I was really skinny in those years, too, if only because food didn't fit into my budget (and because depression can be a powerful appetite suppressant). Besides, I was a twenty-four-year-old female with no obvious deformities, and for some guys, that's enough.

It happened during a sales retreat in Mexico. I wasn't even supposed to be there, but my boss's toddler got sick at the last minute, so I stepped in to deliver a snooze-worthy presentation entitled "Protecting the Company's Bottom Line by Limiting Excessive Sales Expenditures." It was all about how the sales force should save the big-ticket items—fancy dinners, concert tickets, baseball seats—for customers and exercise frugality when it was "just us" out on the road.

According to my boss's presentation, which I read verbatim, *Many grocery stores, seeking to meet the demands of our fast-paced society, have started offering prepared meals in their deli cases such as gourmet salads, enchiladas and even sushi. Many hotels, in response to the needs of busy travelers, supply refrigerators, microwaves, etc., which are helpful in preparing in-room meals and eliminate the need for expensive restaurant food.*

The irony in the presentation—aside from its obvious futility—was that the "just us" retreat was held in a luxury beachfront resort. The sales manager said it was important to let "his people" know how important they were, and nothing says "important" like a really swank hotel. When choosing a topic, my boss should have stuck to more modest goals, perhaps writing a speech called "Why a Strip Club Does Not Qualify as a Business Expense."

But more on that later.

It began with a margarita. Actually, it began with about fifteen margaritas, if you put Keith's and mine together. (I had to file the expense report, which is why I know the exact number. He put away nine; I had six.) We drank them over the course of about ten hours—tequila facilitates team building—which is why we wound up merely hammered and not, say, dead. It could have been worse. The one teetotaler in the group drank Mexican tap water the whole day and spent the rest of the retreat on the toilet.

Keith and I wound up in my room. You don't need to know the details, which is just as well since I don't remember them. The next day, I almost welcomed my hangover because the knife jabs in my brain kept me from thinking too much about what an idiot I'd been. I avoided eye contact with Keith, drank lots of bottled water (no ice, thanks), and sucked down every kind of painkiller I could find: Aleve, Tylenol, ibuprofen, aspirin. Someone told me you can take them all at once because they act on different parts of the body. Later I found out that that's only true for Tylenol and ibuprofen, so I'm lucky I didn't blow out a kidney.

Then again, if I'd blown out a kidney, at least I wouldn't have let Keith spend the night again. I couldn't blame it on margaritas this time, so I blamed it on loneliness. And Mexico. Also, Keith had been really nice to the waiter at dinner, ordering in perfect Spanish (his mother was from Colombia) and saying *no problemo* when our food took so long to come out of the kitchen. (I was considerably less patient; time crawls when you're sober.) That made me think Keith was a nicer, finer, more openhearted person than I'd given him credit for being. It wasn't until I filed the expense report that I realized he'd had six Bloody Marys at that point. When he said I'd done a great job on my speech—all in the delivery, really—I thought it meant he respected my intelligence.

What the hell. I was in Mexico. I was on vacation, sort of. I was lonely.

I probably would have left things in Mexico, but when I say Keith spent the night, I'm not just speaking in euphemisms. He was there when I went to sleep and he was there when I woke up in the morning. Most crucially, he was by my side when we rushed into the breakfast meeting forty-five minutes late, only to have everyone stare at us in shock before they burst out laughing. Later, over margaritas (I leaped off the wagon as soon as my headache went away), people said stuff like, "I kept wondering when you two were going to get together." People must think we are well suited, I reasoned. It wasn't until later that I came up with an alternate interpretation: we were destined to get together because Keith had already worked his way through every other young female in the office, and I was fresh meat.

Back in California, we quickly became a couple, talking first thing every morning, going out to lunch (when he wasn't traveling for work), and spending a few nights a week together. My emotions snuck up on me. What started with *Hey, I'm just killing time,* quickly morphed into *I miss him when he's gone.* From there, it was a short leap to the always-deadly *Maybe he's the one.*

I never thought he was perfect. His faults were too obvious to ignore. Like Jimmy, he was always canceling plans at the last minute. And he talked too much, often when I most craved quiet: first thing in the morning, or when I was paying my bills, or trying to watch TV. When we went out to dinner, he'd start conversations with people at other tables. He couldn't sit still, didn't cuddle. He'd use up the last scoop of coffee, the last drop of milk. He put empty cartons back in the fridge.

Worst of all, he flirted with other women. And he went to strip clubs.

But it was all okay. The way I saw it (warning: defeatist female rationalization ahead), we balanced each other. I needed someone more sociable, more fun—a man to add color to my drab little life. I needed to loosen up. Besides, I was so hyper-responsible, I needed to take care of someone else (yeah, I know—blech). Besides, Keith's flirtations didn't mean anything, right? Anyone could see his feelings for me were real.

Ha! In a way I deserved what came next (as I didn't deserve, say, misplacing a boyfriend off the coast of Maui).

After we'd been going out for almost three months, he cheated on me. Of course he did. I confronted him about it, our exchange already scripted in my deluded little mind:

Me: How could you?
Him: I'm so sorry, kitten. Please forgive me.
Me: Get out!
Him (crying): I don't deserve you. Just give me another chance, and I swear I'll never hurt you again.

At that point I was going to say I never wanted to see him again, let him wallow in misery for a couple of weeks, and then decide whether to let him come crawling back.

Unfortunately, the encounter didn't go as scripted.

Me: How could you?
Him (shrug): It's not like we're married.
Me: Get out!
Him: We're in a restaurant. You get out.

Honestly, stalking him wasn't so reprehensible. The guy deserved to be castrated. To make things worse, he was fooling around with someone from our office, this tacky girl named Danielle who had just started in accounts receivable. Danielle had dry, bleached hair that she flatironed superstraight, a tiny mouth crowded with crooked teeth, and a closet full of supertight jeans and metallic stiletto heels.

The instant our breakup was official (meaning, as soon as he'd thrown some money on the table—only his half, the cheap bastard—and strode out of the restaurant, making it clear he was leaving because he wanted to, not because I'd told him to get out), he strolled back to the office and over to Danielle's cubicle, where he said, loud enough for everyone to hear, "Hey, Dani, you and me still on for tonight?"

She was on the phone at the time, but she put the customer on hold and said, "Well, yeah! You get rid of her?"

I did what any woman would do under the circumstances. I screamed, I cried—and then I hacked into his e-mail. It wasn't hard. I work in human resources, remember. Anyone who thinks that e-mails sent through a company's internal system are truly private is sadly mistaken. Really, Keith should have known better than to write something like this gem to Danielle, dated two weeks before our breakup:

> You make me so hot, god I love yr breasts and yr ass, just thinking
> about them makes me feel like Im gonna cum.

Seriously. If Keith had read his employee handbook—which clearly outlined the potentially public nature of all in-house correspondence—he definitely would have thought twice before writing a message like this:

> Dani, Dont worry about that bitch, she means nothing to me, I'm
> just waiting for the chance to get rid of her, but I don't want a big
> seen.

After reading that, it took every ounce of my strength not to shoot back a message saying, *It's* scene, *not* seen, *you moron.*

And—were you out sick on that day in fourth grade when they taught contractions?

Instead, I checked his in-box. There I discovered that Danielle was not Keith's first indiscretion. There were several messages from a girl called Lola (for God's sake):

Hey, lover,

miss u, c u soon?

Lo

And:

Loverboy,

U banged me so good last nite I can barely sit down 2day, haha, when will I c u nxt?

Lo

And the kicker:

I was just thinking about what u sd last nite, like did I take home a lot of costumers or is it just u, i gotta tell u baby its just u.

Little Lola

Costumers? Huh? Did Keith have some kind of a Halloween fetish? Then it hit me: Keith wasn't Lola's costumer; he was her customer. Which meant that Lola was—oh, shit! I thought AIDS, I thought hepatitis, I thought syphilis, but mostly I thought *whore*—meaning Keith more than Lola.

Staying late at work that night (such a busy bee), I cross-checked Lola's e-mail dates with Keith's travel and expense reports. He'd eaten at a place called Bernie's on the night of each encounter.

Maybe Lola was a waitress, I thought with relief. Yeah: that could be it. Responsible as always, I saw my doctor; after all, Keith was promiscuous even if he wasn't bedding prostitutes. Fortunately, I'd always been a slave to safe sex, and the doctor gave me a clean bill of health and only the smallest of smirks.

Bernie's was a couple of towns over—a little far to drive during rush hour, but I decided an hour in bumper-to-bumper traffic was worth the peace of mind. There was no restaurant at the address listed on the receipt, though; instead, there was a strip club called the Candy Cane. (Stripper pole = cane, get it?) This discovery wasn't shocking, really: Keith had told me he went to strip clubs (such an up-front guy). He simply hadn't mentioned what happened afterward.

At work the next morning, I told Danielle about Lola. I pretended—to both her and myself—that I was trying to protect her, but really, of course, I just wanted to watch her suffer.

Her response? "He was just stepping out on you because you're such an icy-cold bitch and fucking you was like fucking a table."

Nice.

* * *

Later, she sent an e-mail to Keith:

I feel really bad for Jane because I can tell she's still so totally in love with you.

Keith wrote back:

She's kinda pathedic, I feel sorry for her, but I cant help the way I feel.

I considered going to the CEO, telling him about the strip clubs, getting Keith fired. The thing was, my motives would have been so obvious. Plus, I'd known about the strip clubs all along (just not Lola), and I probably should have mentioned them earlier.

So I followed him (which sounds so much nicer than, "I stalked him"). I took my Civic, my camera, and a whole lot of Starbucks coffee, and I watched as Keith went to his gym, to the grocery store, to Danielle's. Always to Danielle's. He spent a lot more time at her place than he ever had at mine. And then he went back to the gym.

Being a sales guy, he was on the road a lot, so it's not like I was doing this every day. It's not like I was obsessed. Okay, I was obsessed, but not because I loved him. I hated him! That's better, right? Eventually, he would grow bored with Danielle and head back to the Candy Cane. I'd get a picture of him going inside—maybe even a shot of Lola. And when Danielle saw the photo? I'd win.

I didn't win. After about a month and a half of this (during which Keith was mostly gone—honestly), the CEO summoned me into his office. Keith and Danielle were there, as was the president and my boss, the HR manager. For a second, I thought management was on my side, that they were going to chastise Keith and Danielle for being so mean to me. But then I saw Danielle smile, and I knew I was screwed.

Stalking is a serious offense, they said.

Keith went to strip clubs, I blurted out. And paid for it with his company credit card. I'd just been watching out for the bottom line, doing my job, protecting company resources.

Fired, they said.

"Me? But what about him?"

I could tell by the CEO's expression that he'd known about the strip clubs all along. My boss, the HR manager, looked genuinely shocked, which made me almost sort of like her (but not really).

The CEO gave a fake warning to Keith and then mumbled something about him being "one of our top performers" and "what he does in his free time is his own business." And then he said that Keith was planning to file a restraining order against me.

"I'll call all of our customers," I announced (still talking in "we" terms—such a loyal employee). "And I'll tell them that the company pays for gentleman's clubs and sex with strippers. What does that say about our ethics, our corporate culture? Who would want to do business with us?" I'm not sure if I really had the balls to do this—and I'm not sure if it would have worked—but at this point, it was my only ammunition.

"I've never paid for sex," Keith said, less defensive than proud.

"Of course you haven't," I shot back. "The company reimbursed you."

"I propose a revision to the employee handbook," my boss interjected. "To clarify expectations regarding appropriate use of corporate funds." My boss was such a weenie.

"Your employment is terminated, effective now," the CEO said to me. "Assuming you stay away from Keith and Danielle, I see no need to file anything with the police."

"What about a recommendation?" I asked.

"What about it?"

I held his eyes and spoke slowly. "I'm competent, smart, well versed in human resources. I've outgrown my current position, but any company would be lucky to have me. Right?"

The CEO stared at me. I stared back. I was twenty-four years old, remember. And sweating quite profusely. When he didn't respond, I said, "Because I wouldn't want to upset the customers if it wasn't necessary."

The CEO turned to my boss. "Put together a recommendation and I'll sign it."

And that was that.

Except now, apparently, it wasn't.

Chapter 25

So, my past had come back to bite me in the butt. On the plus side—if you can call it that—I was already so miserable that an extra dose of humiliation, no matter how potent, didn't have that much of an impact. Besides, I got to see a picture of Danielle (she was the one who tipped off the press, naturally), and she'd gotten really fat. There were comments from Keith ("I was frightened for my life"—oh, please) but no recent pictures, which I decided meant that he got fat, as well.

The story finally over, Michael clicked off the TV. "Wow," he said.

I said something like "urg"; the chef's knife was still clenched in my sweaty hand, making me look like a major psycho.

"I'm sure it's all lies," Michael said.

"Not entirely," I admitted, my voice squeaking. "I really did follow him. But it wasn't because I was so in love with him like that bi—" I glared at the TV, which was back to being a painting.

"Like Danielle said. He'd treated me really badly, and I was furious. I really wanted to kill him but figured I'd just get him fired instead."

There was a long, long pause, after which Michael said, "You might not want to use those words when you're talking to the police."

I began to shake. "Oh my God." I dropped the knife on the counter.

"Don't worry about dinner." Michael sprang up from his chair. "Why don't you sit down, have a glass of wine, maybe, and I'll serve."

I shook my head. "Not hungry anymore." I stumbled out of the kitchen and onto the couch.

"At least you have a good job now," Michael said, trying to make me feel better. "That whole thing that happened—at least it didn't hurt your career."

I turned to face him. No. Oh, no.

*   *   *

I'd turned my phone off after talking to my mother. Now, checking my voice-mail messages, I saw that Lena had called just before five o'clock California time, three o'clock here. When had the stalker story hit the wires? Odds were, it popped up on the Internet hours before I saw it.

"Jane? Hi. I hope you're okay." Lena sounded nervous on the message. "Sorry. That's a stupid thing to say because I know you're not okay, but I just—well, you know what I mean." She took a deep, noisy breath. "The thing is? There's something I need to send you. An e-mail." And then, the truth: "Mr. Wills had me type up a memo."

After setting up his laptop on the little table in his bedroom, Michael left me to read in privacy. I sat down carefully on the straight-backed chair, my legs so wobbly I feared I might fall over.

Re: Recent Developments
Dear Ms. Shea:

As you are aware, it has been with utmost sympathy that I have followed your travails since last weekend. While I must admit to being anxious about potential associations between the events and Wills Rubber Company, please know that my primary concern has always been for you and your well-being. Over the years I have valued your contributions to the company and had expected you to continue and grow with us for quite some time.

However, it has come to my attention that during your interview process neither you nor your previous employer disclosed certain events that reflect poorly on your character. You, perhaps better than anyone, are aware of our company's policies regarding employment disclosure as well as sexual harassment. As such, it is with great sadness that I must terminate your employment, effective immediately.

Sincerely,
Robert Wills

Just when I thought I couldn't feel any worse, I felt worse. The place where I worked with Keith and Danielle had had a sheen of sleaziness: padded expenses, questionable tax write-offs, slippery negotiations. Mr. Wills was a big reason I joined the rubber company (most of the other reasons involved being able to afford food and rent). He wasn't a guy you'd do tequila shots with, but that was the point. He was such a Boy Scout, such a goody-goody. He would never cross a line or tolerate inappropriate behavior.

And now? I was the one who had behaved inappropriately, the one who needed to be banished for the greater good.

*   *   *

Michael appeared in the doorway, a glass of white wine in his hand. "We can watch Tiara's YouTube video if it'll cheer you up," he said.

I shook my head, afraid I'd cry if I said anything.

"Here." He set the wine down on the table next to me.

I left the glass sitting there. "I just got fired," I said, my lip quivering, my hair falling in my face.

"Oh, no," he said softly. "I'm so sorry." He put his hand on my back. I stood up and threw my arms around him. He held me tight and stroked my back while I cried into his black shirt. He smelled like laundry detergent mixed with Coppertone.

"I got your shirt wet," I said, finally pulling away. I wiped my eyes.

"It'll dry." He picked up my wineglass. "C'mon." He motioned with his head. "Let's go watch the sunset."

He had set the table on the deck for two people, lit a candle, and put out the tossed salad and a platter of cut quesadillas. The sun wouldn't fall behind the horizon for another half hour or so, but the breeze had died down and the water had calmed.

"I'm not really a stalker," I said, staring at the water even though it hurt my eyes.

"I know," he said simply, serving me salad.

I looked at him with skepticism.

He put some greens on his own plate and put the serving spoons back in the teak bowl. "Your boyfriend was two-timing you and pretending to be somebody else, and you had no idea. You obviously weren't stalking him." He shot me a wry grin. "Though maybe you should have been."

"I thought about following him," I admitted. "One night when he said he had to work late, I almost drove down to his office—well, your office—just to see if I could spot him. But I thought about that other . . . experience. How ashamed I'd been. And I decided that surrendering my self-respect is worse than being lied to."

"Do you still feel that way?"

I thought about it. "Yes. I do."

I took a small bite of the salad. He'd tossed it with just the right amount of dressing.

"When are you flying out tomorrow?" he asked, reaching for a quesadilla.

"Late. It's the red-eye."

"You need a ride to the aiport?"

I was about to say I had a rental car, when I realized that Mary and Albert had already returned it. It was the kind of detail that didn't usually slip by me, but this wasn't a usual week.

"I'd love one. If you really don't mind," I said.

"It would be my pleasure." We locked eyes for a moment before turning back to our meal.

Michael seemed different from when I'd first met him: warmer, less distracted. Not only was he not making phone calls every five minutes, he didn't even seem to have his phone with him. He looked at me differently now, too. It felt like he was seeing the real me—not just the plain Jane who was plastered across the television or the company mom who never forgot a birthday.

He took a long drink of his wine, put the glass back on the

table, and blurted, "There's something I've been thinking about since that very first night we spent time together. You know—at the luau."

My face grew warm. "Yes?"

"I don't know if it's the right time to bring this up—I mean, after all that's happened. It's just—we're here. And I don't want the moment to slip by. Though I completely understand if you're not . . . ready."

"I'm probably not." My heart was pounding. "But . . . it wouldn't hurt to talk about it." Katie had gotten her happy ending. Maybe I would, too.

He played with the stem of his wineglass, trying to find the right words. "You've been through an awful lot. I know you've been hurt."

I nodded eagerly.

"And if you need some time to yourself—weeks, months, whatever—that's okay. I'll wait for you."

Tears sprang into my eyes. "You won't have to wait very long," I promised.

It was like this moment was meant to be—like it was fate, or something. Jimmy, Tiara—this crazy path had led me to Michael James. The real Michael James.

The sun cast a golden glow on his skin. Jimmy had been good-looking, of course, but in a flashy, fleeting kind of way. Michael was so classically handsome, with his sharp cheekbones, straight nose, dark hair, and warm brown eyes. More than that, he was beautiful inside, honest and strong. It had taken me a long time to find him, but the wait had been worth it.

"I probably couldn't pay you as much as you've been getting," he said. "But we could find a way to make it work."

"Wait—you'd pay me?" I was still focused on his cheekbones.

"Well, yeah, of course. Plus we could talk about bonus opportunities, maybe even equity. I really think you'd be great."

The bottom dropped out of my stomach. "You want to hire me?"

He nodded enthusiastically. "What you said about Ana? How I shouldn't have my designer answering phones? You were dead-on. I mean, she could add a lot more value by getting involved with production, marketing—stuff directly related to the product."

"You want me to be your secretary." My voice quavered.

"Administrator," he corrected, smiling gently. "Answering the phones is only a very small part of the job. You'd also be responsible for payroll, customer service, accounts payable, *and* accounts receivable." He raised his eyebrows to accentuate that last one. I'd open the checks. Woo-hoo.

His phone rang. He had it with him, after all. Of course he did.

"It's Tiara," he chirped, checking the display.

"Hey," Michael said to Tiara. "We're just eating dinner." He shot me a fond look. "Oh—already?" He looked at his diver's watch. "Okay, I'll see what I can do.

"Tiara's on her way back from the studio," he told me, standing up. "Asked if we could tape her interview."

Tiara's television debut was on a local program, hosted by a skinny, earnest woman named Suzy Lee and a smiley, square-headed guy named Chuck Makuakane. Apparently, it was Suzy's job to ask the questions and Chuck's job to stare at Tiara's breasts.

Tiara was wearing her black halter top with the black skirt. Someone in the news station's hair department had tamed her country-singer hair so it tumbled sleekly around her shoulders. Her makeup was subtle and flattering. She looked like an L.A. weather girl or entertainment reporter.

When we tuned in (as Michael tried to figure out the VCR and I tried not to cry), Suzy was just finishing with a recap of the story-to-date, which, as far as I could tell, mercifully excluded my stalker incident.

SUZY *(brows knitted in concern):* Tiara Cardenas. You've been through a lot this week.

TIARA *(looking at camera):* I have. And to everyone who's been so supportive of me, I can't thank you enough.

SUZY *(touching Tiara on the knee):* Some of the things people have posted about you have not been kind. They have focused on certain aspects of your . . .

TIARA *(eyes widening):* Yes?

CHUCK *(looking at Tiara's face):* Sexuality *(eyes back to Tiara's breasts).*

TIARA *(casting eyes down modestly):* Until this week, I thought I was in a loving, monogamous relationship. And our physical expression was just part of it. I'm not ashamed of that.

SUZY: You really loved him, huh?

TIARA *(solemnly):* I did. *(Brightening)* Let's be clear—I don't mind being called hot! *(Cue laughter from cohosts and stagehands.)* But what really bothers me? *(What would she say next—"the media's attacks on pretty friend Jane's appearance"?)* . . . Is the implied racial slur in my portrayal.

SUZY: I can see why that would be upsetting.

TIARA *(straightening):* I mean, like, saying Luscious Latino? That is so, like, a stereotype. As if, like, just because I've got a Spanish last name, I'm some kind of *[word beeped out by censors].*

SUZY: Last week we did a segment on racial profiling that touched on many of the same concerns. *(To camera)* Interested viewers can watch the clip on our Web site.

TIARA *(continuing):* But what's really crazy? I'm only one-quarter Cuban! And I'm proud of that, I get that from my dad. But—hello? I am also Filipino, Norwegian, and German. I am all of those things, but I'm also none of those things. That's the new face of America, people, and you better get used to it. You Hawaiians understand, because people here have always mixed. But at home, everyone wants to, like, pigeon-toe you into some category.

"That was masterful," Michael said, once the segment had finished.

"It's pigeon*hole*," I muttered.

Back outside, I planted my sorry ass back into the teak chair and said, "Jimmy's death is working out pretty well for Tiara. This afternoon, she seemed genuinely upset. Now she's fully recovered and ready to launch a career as a, what? Professional victim? Or a spokesperson for multiculturalism?" I took a long drink of my wine.

Michael considered. "Well, Jimmy used her, now she's using him. You can't really blame her."

"There is no way she wrote those words herself," I said.

"I don't know. I think Tiara's a lot smarter than she seems." He held out the platter. "Quesadilla?"

I put one on my plate but didn't eat it. "Well, she seems like an idiot. So being smarter isn't necessarily saying much." I really shouldn't drink on an empty stomach. Especially on a day when my boyfriend has been found dead, my worst secret exposed, and my entire career derailed.

"I think Tiara understands her greatest assets," he continued. "And she uses them to get what she wants." He refilled our wineglasses. What I really needed was a big glass of water and a couple of sleeping pills. "She's not so different from you or me, really," he added.

I gawked at him. "I do *not* bounce around with my boobs hanging out, coming on to every man I meet!"

His eyes widened. "That's not what I meant. You're good at other things—arranging, organizing. Cooking, of course. And so that's where you focus."

"Because I don't *have* big boobs, you mean?" I threw my fork on my plate. It bounced off, hit the table, and grazed my thigh before falling on the ground, where I let it lie. "Why do guys always like bimbos?"

He stared at me, shocked, for a moment before replying, "Not all guys like bimbos." And then, after consideration, he added, "Though pretty much all guys like sex. So I guess bimbos can seem like the quickest means to an end."

"Men are so shallow," I hissed. (Again, in my defense: dead boyfriend/lost job/public humiliation. It had been *a really bad day*.)

His mouth dropped and he glared at me before saying, "Just men?"

I tilted up my chin. "When it comes to . . . romance? Yes." (I am such a freaking prude, I couldn't even bring myself to say "sex.")

"Then how do you explain your himbos?" he asked, his brown eyes suddenly looking less puppylike than before.

"My *what*?"

"Your himbos. Pretty-boy Jimmy and your ex-boyfriend, that guy they showed on TV. The one with the dimples."

"What about them?"

"Did you like them for their stimulating conversation? For their depth?"

"I thought Jimmy was a business owner," I said, trying to keep my voice steady. "I thought he was you."

"But he obviously wasn't."

"My last boyfriend before Jimmy was a doctor," I said (even though I never really thought an ophthalmologist counted). "And I didn't just like him for his looks. In fact, he wasn't even that cute."

"So you just liked him because he was a doctor," Michael said evenly.

"Yes," I answered without thinking. And then, "I mean no. I liked him because he was . . . intelligent."

"Sure you did." He went back to his salad. After a few bites, still hunched over his plate, he said, "So I take it you don't want the job."

"No."

"You seemed interested at first," he told his salad.

"I thought you were attracted to me," I blurted before the censors in my brain had the opportunity to stop me.

He fixed me with a look of such pure astonishment that I popped out of my seat before I could embarrass myself further. "Thanks for dinner," I said curtly.

"I didn't make it," he said. "You did."

"Well, thanks for serving it, then."

I put my plate and glass in the sink. The dirty frying pan was still on the stove, but I didn't care. Michael could do the damn dishes. I had a packing list to attend to.

Chapter 26

Tiara's room smelled. During the past two days, she had infused it with the aromas of jasmine, plumeria, lily of the valley, and lemon, along with the scents of several other lotions, shampoos, hair products, and colognes that I couldn't identify. It was like walking into Macy's perfume department.

It was Thursday morning. I hadn't seen her the night before, having chosen to hole up in my room packing, reading, and wallowing in self-pity. At ten o'clock, I took double the recommended dose of Benadryl and fell into a woozy sleep.

Tiara was sitting cross-legged on her unmade bed, wearing her heart-patterned jammie bottoms with the Angels T-shirt. Her hair was in a ponytail, her face clean and clear. She looked like the sorority girl every guy liked and every girl hated.

"I was just wondering if you had any interest in sharing a shuttle to the airport," I said. I couldn't imagine that Michael would still want to drive me. "My flight's not till late, but I wouldn't mind getting there early."

"Thanks, but I changed my flight to Saturday," she told me. That was the day Michael was leaving, too: so nice that they'd have a little alone time. "Because tomorrow?" she said. "My agent got me this gig opening this fun new restaurant in Kihei. It's called Cheese the Day."

"Seize the Day," I corrected.

"No, *Cheese* the Day. It's a fondue place. He said fondue is the next big thing." And then, after a beat: "I'm not stupid."

"I know you're not." I sighed.

"So, anyways," Tiara said, getting excited and doing her flayed-nails thing. "It's, like, *Hawaiian* fondue—isn't that wild? 'Cause they're going to have all these Hawaiian fruits for dipping. So it's, like, fusion, you know? And I'm sort of fusion, too—that's what my agent said, that's my angle—so he thought it was a good fit. And the restaurant thinks I'll bring in a lot of press."

"I'm sure you will," I admitted.

"And today?" she said. "I'm having lunch in Lahaina with some reporter. I think he's from the Honolulu paper. I should probably check."

She glanced at the digital clock on her nightstand. "I better start getting ready. Because outside the gates? If it's anything like last night, it'll be packed with photographers. So I gotta look my best." She straightened her legs and slid off the bed.

"Have you seen Michael this morning?" I asked. I'd been avoiding the main room, but I really wanted a cup of coffee and some breakfast.

She shook her head. "He said he had a bunch of appointments scheduled today. I think he'll be gone for a while."

My phone rang: the office. "I've got to get this," I told Tiara.

My first thought was that it might be Mr. Wills apologizing for his memo and begging me to come back to work. I pressed the answer button, contemplating whether to accept his apology, when I realized it was Lena.

"How you doing?" she asked.

"Pretty crappy." I paused before asking, "Does everybody know I've been fired?"

"Mr. Wills hasn't announced it yet," she said. "But . . . news travels through the grapevine." The Wills Rubber grapevine is otherwise known as *Lena*. "Everyone thinks it's really unfair," she assured me.

"Not entirely," I said. "I should have come clean when I first interviewed."

"But then you wouldn't have gotten the job."

"There's that." And now, I thought, it'll be hard to get *any* job.

"I just called to let you know we're all pulling for you."

"Thanks," I said. "That means a lot." I was surprised to realize how much it did.

Since I'd already spent at least an hour that morning on my own personal lanai, I took my coffee and breakfast (toast and a banana: my standards had really fallen) out to the teak table on the deck. I squinted at the water, looking for whales, but all I saw was a kayaker, paddling lazily by.

I'd felt so happy the day before, being in this beautiful house, like it was magic or something. It was exactly how I'd felt the day I'd first arrived in California. While my friend cried on the phone to her boyfriend, I'd run down to the nearest beach and made straight for Pacific, only stopping when the surf splashed the edge of my shorts. I remember the stinging on my legs, the sun on my face, the lightness in my chest. From now on, things were going to be *different*.

The kayaker reached the rock outcropping and pivoted.

I could have stayed in New Jersey all those years ago. It wouldn't have made any difference. Of course it wasn't too late: I could always go back. At least I'd have Katie and Beth to hang out with. And I could make dinner for my mother every Sunday. She'd praise my cooking and my independence in equal measures and assure me that I didn't need a man. Plus, she could get me a bitchin' discount on bathroom hardware.

But moving back to New Jersey wouldn't really change anything. I was leaving Jimmy behind in Hawaii, but I'd never find a way to unload myself.

Beyond the rocks, the water changed from silver to bright blue, and the usual clouds snuggled the top of Lanai. The kayaker was still out there, coming closer to shore now, bobbing in the waves. Something glinted in the sunlight: a camera lens.

Shit. Now I was stuck in the house.

*   *   *

I figured I should let Sergeant Hosozawa know I was leaving town. "You want my contact information in California?" I asked, sitting on my bed. Even though the kayaker had finally left, I felt safer inside.

"Not especially." Irritated sigh. "But I guess we should have it."

My cell phone rang just as I was organizing my carry-on bag: paperback, magazine, sweater, wallet, comb, lip balm, itinerary, mints, Jimmy's car keys, and, of course, my planner. At the airport, I'd buy one of those U-shaped neck pillows on the off chance that I managed to sleep on the plane.

I didn't recognize the number on my phone's display, and I almost didn't answer. But I figured, if someone in the press had gotten hold of my number, I'd rather find out now.

I hit the answer button. "Yes?"

"Janie?" It took me a second to recognize the voice.

"Dad?" I thought: *Wait—is it my birthday?*

"I've been worried about you," he said.

So strange: with all the news reports swirling around, I'd wondered how everyone who knew me would react. I'd thought about my mom and my sister, of course, plus people from work, condo neighbors, college friends, old roommates and boyfriends, MySpace Geoffrey, the checkers at Trader Joe's, the people I worked out with at L.A. Fitness, even my Korean dry cleaner who barely speaks English. But I had never once wondered how my father was taking the news.

"I'm fine," I said.

Never let him see you sweat. Or cry. Never let him think you need him or love him.

"This must be really tough on you," he said. "I didn't even know you were seeing someone."

"It doesn't matter. It's over now." I wasn't trying to be funny—just nonchalant. Strong. Independent. Unemotional.

"You'll find someone else," he said.

Just like Mom did?

"I really can't talk," I said. "I'm leaving for the airport in a couple of hours and I haven't started packing yet." If he knew me at all, he'd know I was lying.

"Have to get back to work, huh?"

I swallowed. "Right."

"You always were a hard worker . . . I remember when you

were in fifth grade and you did that report about the Revolutionary War. You got a big stack of books out of the library and made piles of notes on index cards."

I didn't have the vaguest idea what he was talking about, but the index cards sounded like me.

"I'm around if you ever want to talk," he said. "You have this number?"

"I do now."

"Say hello to your mother for me. And your sister."

"Sure."

"And Janie?"

"Yeah?"

"I love you."

For the umpteenth time that day, tears sprang into my eyes. Fortunately, no one was there to see them.

"Thanks for calling, Dad. But I really gotta go."

*　*　*

I ran into Michael while hauling my suitcase and Jimmy's duffel bag to the front door. I'd considered leaving the duffel behind, but I thought his brother, Scott, might want it.

"Hi," I said. "I didn't think you'd be here."

Michael grinned wryly. "Good to see you, too." He was wearing yet another black polo shirt, this one threaded with faint beige stripes.

I was too worn out to be embarrassed, so I just shrugged. "My airport shuttle's coming in a few hours."

I'd called Mary for the number. She'd wished me luck and told me to call her if I ever came to Maui again: "I'll show you what a real luau looks like." I was touched but couldn't imagine that I'd ever come back.

Michael shook his head. "I'm driving you, remember?"

"You don't have to," I said. "It's nice of you to offer, but—"

"I want to. Besides, there are still a couple of photographers out there. You don't need them swarming a shuttle."

That settled it. I nodded my acceptance.

"What time is the flight?" he asked.

"Nine-fifteen. But I want to get there early because of security and all. I was thinking of leaving at around six."

"That'll give you over two hours at the airport," he said.

"You think we should leave at five-thirty?"

He almost laughed—it was kind of a "huh" sound. "No, I think six is fine."

"You sure?" I said. "I mean, you never know what can go wrong."

* * *

By five o'clock, my stomach was raw with hunger.

Michael knocked on my door. "Good news coming over the Internet," he said.

I raised my eyebrows. "*People* magazine has named me one of their fifty most beautiful people?"

He leaned against the door frame. "Even better. A dog in St. Louis called 911 after his owner had a heart attack. And in Hollywood, some blond actress—or maybe she's a singer—just left her husband for her personal trainer."

"Really? Who?"

He shrugged. "I don't remember—I don't follow that crap. The point is, our story isn't the best one out there anymore. I'm thinking our fifteen minutes are up."

"Thank God," I said. My stomach grumbled noisily. On impulse, I said, "Have you had anything to eat? Because if we leave now, we could grab a quick bite on the way to the airport. I can personally vouch for the Taco Bell."

"I think we can do better than that."

Twenty minutes later, we were in an outdoor courtyard in downtown Lahaina, sitting in white plastic chairs and waiting for our dinners from a funky little kabob place. Around us, kiosks displayed shell necklaces, beach hats, and polyester leis, but I wasn't in the mood for shopping. I'd ordered a blackened mahi-mahi kabob because Michael said it was the best thing on the menu, even though he got a plain fish one for himself. He insisted on paying for the whole thing, and I let him because I didn't want to make a big deal out of it. And because—oh, yeah—I was un-employed.

"Was this your first trip to Maui?" Michael asked. "I never asked."

I nodded, sucking iced tea through a straw.

"How did you like it?"

I raised my eyebrows and put down my paper cup. "About as much as Mrs. Lincoln liked the play."

"Sorry. Stupid question."

I shook my head. "Actually, it's as beautiful as I expected. I just don't think I could ever come here without thinking about Jimmy. Not with him dead."

Next to us, an abandoned open-air nightclub cast long shadows over the courtyard. The only sign of life was a painted board that read PLEASE DO NOT FEED BIRDS OR CATS. The building was two stories high, with a peaked roof, railings, and balconies reminiscent of New Orleans or the Caribbean. I thought of all the people who had spent rum-soaked evenings there, laughing and joking, never worrying about tomorrow. The ghosts of lost happiness floated along the warped floorboards and over the rickety railings.

A white cat crawled out from under the building and slunk over to us.

"Look," I said.

"That building is full of stray cats," Michael told me. "There's another one." A gray-and-white tabby with a bent ear sauntered past to find some unclaimed humans.

I thought of our kabobs. "Is that why you ordered your fish plain?"

He bent down to scratch the white cat behind her ears. "I'm a sucker for a cute face."

At one end, the courtyard opened to a view of the ocean across the street. It was that vibrant blue color that it gets near the end of the day, when everything looks too gorgeous to be real, like you're looking at life through a tinted lens, and you know it can't last.

Michael had been right: my blackened fish kabob, which came with spiced rice and purple mashed potatoes, was amazing—as good as anything at a fancy restaurant on Maui (or, so I assumed: I didn't have much to compare it with). Michael gave at least half of his fish to the cats; the little tabby had scampered back once he saw there were handouts.

"I thought you weren't supposed to feed the cats," I said, nodding toward the sign.

He shrugged. "When I see something starving, I feed it."

"You're a nice person," I blurted.

He looked at me in surprise. I expected him to say something sarcastic. Instead, he half smiled and said, "Don't let that get out. It could really ruin my reputation."

* * *

Climbing back in the car after dinner, I said, "Day four of my itinerary."

"What?"

"Before I came here, I made an itinerary. Day four was for exploring downtown Lahaina. That was assuming the weather was good all week. If the early days were cloudy, I might have changed things around."

"Maui isn't about itineraries, anyway," he said, turning his key in the ignition. He had put the convertible's top up since my luggage was in the backseat. "You should leave schedules on the mainland. Maui's about living in the moment, taking things as they come."

I snorted. "Yeah, well—that hasn't been working out so well for me." I looked at his profile. "I don't exactly see you living in the moment, either."

He pulled out of the parking spot and drove up the street. At a stoplight, he kept his eyes on the road and said, "One of the reasons I wanted to own my own business was so that I'd be able to make my own schedule. Travel, go diving whenever I wanted. And here I am, on Maui, and I haven't been diving once."

"Snorkeling was fun, though," I said. "I'd even say it was the best part of my vacation."

He turned to face me. "Better than the police interrogation?"

"Just a little." We shared a smile. Then the light turned green, and we drove on.

*　*　*

It was weird saying good-bye at the airport. It felt like Michael and I had become friends in the last few hours, even though it seemed unlikely we'd ever see each other again.

"You want me to park the car?" he asked. "I can help you with your bags."

I shook my head. "I don't have that much. Plus, you can't come past security, anyway."

He pulled his car to the curb, hauled my bags from the backseat, and put them on the sidewalk.

"Good luck, Jane."

"You, too," I said.

*   *   *

I had a little time to kill before my plane left. Okay, I had almost three hours. Being there reminded me of Jimmy, of course, as if the spirits of our happy, carefree, hungover selves were still staggering around the baggage claim and thinking how terrible it would be if our suitcases had been mistakenly shipped to Oahu or Kauai.

I was anxious to get home, to hole up in my sterile little apartment with the blinds shut, but being there, too, would remind me of Jimmy. I'd be seeing him stretched out on my couch, facedown on my bed, singing in my shower. The crumbs from his last California breakfast, scattered under my coffee table, would be waiting for me. I tried to remember when he'd last spent the night and when I'd last done laundry. Would his scent still cling to my sheets? But, no: I'd changed my linens the night before I left so we'd have a clean bed to come back to.

If only he hadn't died. I'd still be sad, of course, plus angry, hurt, and humiliated. But it would have been so nice to hate him purely, to wish him a crappy life and a million heartbreaks. Dead, he was not the Jimmy on the last day of his life but all of the Jimmys he had ever been: the cute waiter who'd seduced me on the beach, the man who'd fed me breakfast in bed.

Opposite the check-in counter was a little gift shop selling hula dolls, T-shirts, ukuleles, magazines, gum, and expensive bottles of water that would be confiscated at security. A display of tropical-print neck pillows stood near the entrance. I hesitated outside the door, considering. It would be nice to check in, unload my stuff, get through security, and then hit a gift shop. But what if the shops on the other side of security didn't have neck pillows? Or what if they only had those nylon ones that smell funny? Of course I could always check my bag and come back here before going to my gate, but then I'd be backtracking.

Have I mentioned my tendency to overthink?

"Just buy the damn pillow," I finally muttered. I plucked a blue one with white hibiscus flowers and set it on the checkout counter. Then, in a moment of unprecedented spontaneity, I added a packet of tropical-fruit Life Savers. Yeah, I was really getting a handle on that whole live-in-the-moment thing.

The young woman behind the counter was slim with black hair and café au lait skin. She wore a green polo shirt. She did not say "aloha." California seemed closer already.

After she rang up my purchases (which came in under twenty dollars—not bad, really), I pulled out my credit card.

The girl squinted at her computerized register for a moment before shaking her head. "You got another card?" she asked. "This one's not going through."

"What do you mean it's not going through? Is the magnetic strip worn?" I took the plastic back and looked at the back. The strip looked fine.

The girl shook her head. "They turned it down." She shrugged.

"But—I . . ."

Oh, hell, I didn't have time for this right now. With shaking hands, I pulled a twenty-dollar bill from my wallet. Sergeant Hosozawa said I was no longer a suspect, but maybe my credit-card company hadn't gotten the memo. Could they really freeze my account? Was I in some legal trouble now that the stalker thing had come out?

My purchase finally complete, I pulled my suitcase out of the shop and parked it by a wall. The evening was muggy, but the sweat gathering under my armpits was cold.

I called Visa, punching in my account number as instructed by the calm automated voice on the system. After slogging through a few menus, I got to talk to a real person with a southern accent. She sounded awfully perky considering that back east it was, what? Midnight?

She asked for my account number, which kind of annoyed me since I'd already punched it into my phone. And then, instead of telling me to stay put because an FBI agent was on his way to arrest my stalking, murderous ass, she said, "How kin ah help yew?"

"I just tried to use my card," I said. "In the airport in Maui. And it got turned down."

"Maui? Lucky yew! Let me just see here . . ."

"I know I paid my bill on time."

"Mm-hmm, you did. But . . . it looks like you've exceeded yer limit."

I thought through my recent expenditures: plane, condo, car rental. It was an awful lot.

"What's my balance?" The credit-card company had recently upped my limit, but the number escaped me.

Over the phone, I heard some key tapping, and then: "Twenty-three thousand dollars."

"What! There's no way I've spent that kind of money!"

And then: *Of course!*

"Can you tell me when the last charge was made on this card? And what it was?"

"I kin do that, ma'am . . . let's see . . . the most recent charge was made this morning, from the pool bar at the Grand Wailea Hotel. Was it nice there?"

"I wouldn't know."

Michael answered on the first ring.

"Where are you?" I asked.

"Still in Kahului," he said. "I stopped off at Costco."

"Can you come back and get me?"

Chapter 27

When we entered the plush hotel room, Jimmy was lounging on a king-size bed, wearing a white Grand Wailea robe and drinking a beer. *Cops* was on TV. The irony didn't strike me until later. He had shut the sliding-glass door that led to his lanai (wouldn't want to let in that clean, seventy-four-degree air). Overhead, a ceiling fan spun at full speed, and the air-conditioning vents gushed chilly air.

He looked surprised to see us. For a second, I thought we had the wrong room because he'd traded his tousled, surfer-boy look for close-cropped hair and trimmed facial scruff, making him unrecognizable from the fuzzy pictures broadcast over TV (and not just because he was less, you know, aroused). He still looked good, I had to admit, kind of like David Beckham. Maybe he'd pretend to own a soccer-equipment company next.

Sergeant Hosozawa held up his badge. "James Studebaker, you

are under arrest for fraud, identity theft, and impeding a police investigation."

Jimmy's expression changed from surprise to dismay. He dropped his head. So much for a future in soccer equipment.

I'd called Sergeant Hosozawa as soon as I'd gotten off the phone with Michael. The sergeant had asked me to meet him at the Grand Wailea Hotel to confirm Jimmy's identity. In the lobby, next to a stupendous fountain filled with koi and mermaid statues, the sergeant filled me in on a few details.

Like: right before Slaughterhouse Beach, there is a little turn-off in the road and a rough, extremely steep trail down to the water. The day after Jimmy disappeared, police noticed that the hillside had been disturbed, as if someone had recently scrambled up it with some heavy items.

And: early on the morning of Jimmy's disappearance, a bicycle was reported stolen from a condo complex a few doors down from the Maui Hi. Two days later, the bicycle was recovered in a parking lot in Kihei. The police figure that Jimmy stashed it on the hillside on the morning of his disappearance in preparation for his getaway. Since then, police had been showing Jimmy's photo around local hotels and condos, hoping to get a lead. (No, not Tiara's sex picture—once Jimmy's real identity had been discovered, they'd tracked down his DMV photo.)

And: Jimmy withdrew three hundred dollars from an ATM in Lahaina the morning he disappeared.

Finally, the clincher: Jimmy *wasn't* the only man who'd gone missing recently. A young blond man from Kahana with a history of alcohol abuse and domestic violence had gone fishing with his wife but had never returned. The wife said he'd gone to visit friends on the other side of the island. The friends said otherwise. She was now being held at the Wailuku station, charged with murdering her husband and dumping his body into the ocean.

"Why did you tell us that Jimmy was dead, then?" I asked.

"I never said that. I just said a man matching his description had been found."

"So you never thought I'd killed him?" I asked, remembering the suspicious glares he'd cast my way.

"No." The sergeant snickered at the absurdity, which I thought was insensitive under the circumstances. "But I wasn't sure how you'd react if he contacted you. I thought you might cover for him."

"I'm stupid," I said. "But I'm not that stupid."

The police didn't have to break down Jimmy's hotel-room door, which was kind of disappointing, though I'm sure the folks at the Grand Wailea appreciate a tasteful arrest. Also, while the sergeant drew his gun before he stepped in the room, he quickly put it back in his holster when he saw that Jimmy couldn't possibly be packing anything in his girlie geisha robe. Besides, there was plenty of police backup. Detective McGuinn was there, along with two other officers from the Wailuku station, one of whom kept gawking at the room and saying, "Check it out! Three phones in the room! How much do you figure a place like this costs?"

"Eight hundred bucks a night," I said. "Plus a twenty-five-dollar resort fee."

"Sorry about that, Jane," Jimmy said. "I woulda gone for a garden-view room, but they were booked."

I forced myself to look at him and tried—not entirely successfully—to keep my voice steady. "I can't believe you stole my credit-card number. That was really low." That may seem to be a petty thing to seize on in light of the circumstances, but for some reason it was really pissing me off right then.

Jimmy blinked his long lashes at me. "Sorry, baby, I had no choice. It would have set off alarms if I'd used any more of that Michael dude's cards."

"That would be me." Michael stepped forward, arms crossed. "I'm that Michael dude."

Jimmy flashed Michael a grin, as if he thought his charm would earn him a "get out of jail free" card. "Sure—you look like your pictures on TV." That would be the grim driver's-license photo. "Plus, I saw you at Fisherman's Cove once. You know—in Laguna. You shouldn't leave all your stuff out like that when you go diving. You're practically begging someone to rip you off."

"How many times have you stolen people's account information at the beach?" Sergeant Hosozawa asked.

"Never!" Jimmy said. "Well, you know, except for that once. I was standing nearby, suiting up, and I hear him on the phone, and he keeps saying, 'Jimmies, Jimmies, Jimmies.' Like he was calling for me, or something. Like the stuff was supposed to be mine."

"There was no apostrophe," I said. (Everyone ignored me.)

"Did you use my information to get any new credit cards?" Michael asked. "Or to take out loans or anything?"

"No!" Jimmy said. "That would have been so, like, wrong. I just copied the numbers you already had, and had this guy I know made up duplicate cards. I hardly even used them at first, but then there was this whole big Maui trip coming up, and I wanted to do things up right, you know?"

"Where did you unload the scuba gear?" the detective asked Jimmy.

"Flemings Beach," Jimmy said helpfully. That was the next beach down from Slaughterhouse. "I'd hidden a plastic bag there with a change of clothes." (If only Jimmy had a packing list, I would have noticed a missing outfit.) "I left all my gear on the beach, figuring someone would steal it."

He looked at Michael again. "Seriously, dude, you cannot just leave your stuff out like that."

For someone who spent so much time watching police and detective shows, Jimmy wasn't holding much back. Was he not paying attention when Detective Hosozawa read him his Miranda rights?

Jimmy tilted his chin up. His lip quivered, just a little—going for the sympathy vote. "I just wanted to give you a nice vacation, Jane."

"Who was the ring for?" I asked.

Before he could answer, Tiara burst through the door, looking like she had just come from a two-hour hair-and-makeup session—which, come to think of it, she probably had. "Oh my God, Jimmy, you're alive!" Behind her was an entourage: Suzy Lee, the talk-show woman; a cameraman; and a couple of other people who looked vaguely news-y.

Tiara lunged for Jimmy; Sergeant Hosozawa blocked her way. "Stand back, please, Miss Cardenas." He snarled at the newspeople. "And the rest of you—out of here! Now!"

Suzy opened her mouth to protest, but Sergeant Hosozawa gave her one of his scary looks. She nodded and backed out of the room.

Sergeant Hosozawa took a step toward the cameraman. "If a video of this shows up on the Internet or on TV or even in your goddamn living room, I will throw your ass in jail."

Sergeant Hosozawa was my new favorite person.

Tiara didn't let the disruption ruin her moment. As soon as she had an opening, she fell to her knees and clasped her hands. "Jimmy. You have hurt me. You have lied to me. But these past few days, believing you were dead, I realized how much you meant to me. Without you, life is not worth living." She got back on her feet and blinked back tears. Or maybe dust. "Jimmy Studebaker," she said, "if loving you is wrong, I don't want to be right."

Beside me, Sergeant Hosozawa muttered something that sounded an awful lot like "what the fuck." (Days later, a tape of Tiara's speech showed up on YouTube. I think she had a recorder hidden in her bra.)

While Tiara delivered her speech, Jimmy spun around on the bed and put his feet on the floor, facing her. Once she'd dropped her head to let us all know that the monologue was over, he said, "I'll never leave you again, baby, you have my word."

"Actually, you will be leaving her," the sergeant said. "You're going to jail."

"So you're saying the ring *was* for Tiara," I said to Jimmy, still looking for clarification. When he didn't answer, I blurted, "I thought *I* was your baby. Couldn't you give her a different pet name, at least?"

Jimmy blinked at me before his face crumpled with an emotion that I would have labeled shame if he had anything resembling a conscience. "You're such a good person, Jane. I thought maybe some of that would rub off. Like, if I was with you, I could be different. Better. I wanted so bad to make it work." He shook his head. "But the truth is, I'm not good enough for you, Jane. I never was."

"No shit," I muttered.

* * *

Soon after that, Jimmy, with a police escort, went into the bathroom to put on clothes (linen khakis and a Tommy Bahama shirt—both purchased in the hotel and charged to the room).

The police snapped on the handcuffs, draped a jacket over them, and hauled Jimmy away.

Tiara, wailing, tried to follow, but Sergeant Hosozawa wouldn't let her. Instead she stood in the doorway, calling, "I love you, Jimmy! No matter who you are!"

When Jimmy disappeared around the corner, she came back into the room, her eyes suspiciously dry.

"I'd better go," she said, forcing a sniffle. "The newspeople will be waiting downstairs."

Suddenly it hit me.

"How long have you known?" I demanded.

Her eyes widened: surprise, confusion. She bit her lip: vulnerability. "I never knew about you, Jane. I swear."

"That's not what I meant. How long have you known that Jimmy was alive?"

Her jaw dropped: shock! "The police called me about an hour ago. I called Suzy, and we rushed right over."

"Cut the crap, Tiara. You knew he was alive all along, didn't you?"

Her eyebrows knitted (concern). "Is that really what you believe?"

I ran the last week through my mind. "I think you really believed he was gone at first. And maybe you thought the dead body was his. But I think he called you. I think you knew."

Her eyes narrowed with calculation before reverting to wide-eyed vulnerability. "I'm hurt that you'd believe something like that, Jane. Really, really hurt."

*   *   *

"Do you think she knew?" I asked Michael once she'd left.

"Hard to say." He was standing at the thermostat, turning off the air-conditioning. "For her, it was the role of a lifetime—whether he was dead or not." He looked at me. "But you might be right. Are you going to tell the police?"

I shrugged. "There's nothing to tell—no proof, no admission. And I don't think she helped him, so she's not really an accessory to the crime." I shook my head. "I just want to move past all of this." I rubbed my arm. It really was cold in here.

The air-conditioning off, Michael slid open the glass door. Immediately the smell of salt and the sound of waves filled the room. I followed him out to the lanai. The moon—and about a thousand tiki torches—lit a wonderland of tropical pools, a wide white-sand beach, and the Pacific beyond.

"So, what now?" Michael asked, leaning on the railing and gazing out.

I took a deep breath, enjoying the damp air in my lungs. "I'll go home, take a little time off. I've been meaning to paint my bathroom. I'll close out my job at Wills, if they want me to. After that, the usual—update my résumé and start making phone calls. With any luck, someone will be looking for an anal-retentive stalker."

Michael grinned and turned his head. He looked younger in the moonlight, softer, like a college kid who hasn't been toughened by life. "No. I mean, what about right now? Do you want to come back to Trey's? Or would you rather stay by the airport?"

That's right: I'd need a place to sleep tonight. Above us, airplane lights twinkled alongside the stars. One of those planes might be mine—it was supposed to leave right about now—and here I was, standing on a lanai. The air smelled so sweet.

I looked back into the room. It was large and restful, decorated in beige and grays and potted palms. The bed was enormous, covered with a fluffy white comforter and lots of pillows.

In the closet there was probably another white cotton robe like the one Jimmy had worn.

"I think I'll stay here," I said, surprising myself. "In this room. I'm paying for it, anyway. Getting to the airport tomorrow shouldn't be a big deal—they must have a shuttle."

"You're going to stay . . . in Jimmy's room?"

"It's not really Jimmy's room," I said. "He didn't pay for it." I gazed at the room, imagining myself in it. "Did you see that big Jacuzzi tub? I can't remember the last time I took a bath." My shoulders relaxed at the very thought of the warm jets.

"In the morning I'll order room service," I continued. "No matter what it costs. And I'll eat it out on the lanai." Below us, the hotel's multilevel pools shone like enormous sapphires. "And then, before checkout, I'll go swimming. I mean—look at that! It's like a water park!"

Michael squinted at me. For once in my life, I had managed to surprise someone. "Your credit-card company won't like that," he said. "They may not even reimburse you."

I nodded. He was right.

"You know what?" I said. "I really don't care."

Afterword

Jimmy got three years in prison. Since the prison is in Honolulu, I can't feel that bad for him.

Tiara got her own TV show. I found out about it while reading the paper one day:

"THE BACHELOR"—WITH BARS

Just when you thought all of the good reality-show ideas had been taken, here comes something new. "Ball and Chain," tentatively scheduled to debut this summer, will pair lonely women with even lonelier men—inmates at an as-yet-undisclosed maximum security prison.

Hosting the series is Tiara Cardenas, who recently drew national attention when her boyfriend, James Studebaker, faked his disappearance while scuba diving off the coast of Maui. Ms. Cardenas insists, "Everyone deserves a second chance. There are no bars around our hearts, and sometimes love appears where you least expect to find it. I just want to help other women find their soul mates."

Ball and Chain was canceled after one barely watched episode. Last I saw (while channel surfing late one night), Tiara has moved on to a cable news show, where she's the entertainment correspondent. Now when she flutters her fingers, a chunky diamond sparkles on her left hand; as soon as she realized that the prison-love angle wasn't going to get her anywhere, she ditched Jimmy for a Lakers player.

As for me, I really did spend the night at the Grand Wailea. Michael said good-bye and drove back to Trey's house, so you can stop thinking your dirty little thoughts. The next night, I flew the red-eye home. The airline didn't even penalize me for missing my original flight. The jury's still out on the hotel charge.

Once back in Brea, I painted my bathroom turquoise, cleaned out my personal filing cabinet (being careful to shred all outdated statements), and got rid of everything that reminded me of Jimmy (except the television . . . and the couch . . . and the bed . . . and . . . well, I threw out a couple of greeting cards, anyway).

Then I repainted my bathroom—tan this time—because the turquoise was way too bright.

Neither my Korean dry cleaner nor the checkers at Trader Joe's recognized me as the woman from Maui, thank God. My hairdresser treated me like a celebrity, introducing me to everyone who walked by (the shampoo girls, other clients, hairspray sales reps) as "Jane Shea. You know—Jane Shea? Plain Jane from Maui—her boyfriend disappeared?"

The next month, I went to a new, quieter hairdresser and told her to get rid of all of those annoying, hard-to-style layers.

I thought about Michael every once in a while. Okay, I thought about Michael a lot. I could have easily Googled him or checked his Web site, but once again I decided that self-respect mattered more than knowledge—especially since knowledge wouldn't get me anywhere.

* * *

And then I ran into him. It was the following November. My hair was unwashed, my face free of makeup (unless you count remnants from the previous day), my eyes tired and baggy. My clothes were no better: old black sweatpants and a pilled fleece pullover, a faded one-piece bathing suit underneath. Naturally, Michael recognized me immediately.

We were on a dock in Long Beach, waiting to board a dive boat bound for Catalina Island. It was so early in the morning, the sun had just started to peek over the horizon. I was stumbling across the dock with my bag and tank, trying to spot someone from my dive class, when I found myself looking up at Michael: tall, tan, and fully awake.

"You're a diver now?" he asked, grinning. He looked different somehow, more relaxed. He was wearing jeans and a black sweatshirt and carrying his dive gear as if it weighed nothing.

"This is my last dive for certification," I said, heart racing (from coffee, I told myself). Truthfully, I hadn't enrolled in the certification course out of any love for the sport. Rather, I was annoyed at myself for giving up so easily the first time, as if getting water up my nose was the worst thing that could happen.

Since coming back from Maui, I'd pushed myself to try other things, too: a cooking group, a book club, yoga. (I was bad at the yoga; when I was supposed to be concentrating on my breathing, I made to-do lists in my head.) Through a local charity group, I'd helped organize a clothing drive for a women's shelter; next month I'd be collecting toys for Christmas. My busy schedule left me no time for dating—which was fine with me.

"Do you like diving?" Michael asked.

I considered. "I don't like getting up so early. And the gear can be a headache. But when I'm down there, under the water, I'm just . . . *there*. In the moment. I'm not so good at that on land."

I remembered being out in the water with Michael, seeing the turtles, squealing into my snorkel. It seemed like something out of a dream.

"Nobody is," he said.

"What've you been up to?" I asked (getting out of the moment). "How's work?"

"I sold my business a few months ago," he said. (Aha! That's what was different: no phone!) "A Chinese sportswear company offered me more than it was worth. I couldn't really say no."

"So are you retired now?" What was he? Thirty-five?

He shook his head. "They didn't pay me *that* much. No, I'm just taking some time off, trying to figure out my next step."

"Did you ever make it to Australia?" I asked.

He raised his eyebrows. "You remember that? Yeah, I did, actually. Just got back a couple of weeks ago. It was awesome."

Had he gone alone? It was none of my business.

"Plus I've been spending a lot of time in Maui," he continued. "I bought a condo in Wailea—not big, but it's right on the beach."

"Nice."

"You should visit some time."

I was all set to blurt out, "I'd love to!" when I realized that was just something people say—like, "Stop by when you're in the neighborhood." As if I'd ever find myself in Wailea.

"It must be nice," I said instead. "Having all this free time."

He ran a hand through his hair, which was longer than it had been in Maui. "I hate it. If I don't start working soon, I'm going to lose my mind."

I nodded with understanding. "Yeah, I didn't really like my time off, either. It was only a couple of months, though. And I managed to do some traveling—went down to Florida."

I hadn't seen my father since my college graduation, over ten years earlier. It shocked me to see how much older he had gotten. In my mind, he always looked the way he did when I was fourteen. Elise, on the other hand, looked suspiciously frozen in time. I still didn't like her—couldn't imagine that I ever would—but I appreciated how well she took care of my father.

"I'm working as an event coordinator for a catering company," I told Michael.

"I know," he said simply. When he saw my confusion, he explained: "I Googled you."

My mouth dropped open. "You crazy stalker."

He grinned. "Do you like it?"

"You stalking me? It's okay." I liked it. "Oh! The job? Yeah, I do, actually. It's an offshoot of a Korean restaurant. They hired me to help expand their Anglo customer base. The money's not great, but it combines food and organizing, so it's a good fit. Plus, I get all the kimchi I can eat."

Michael and I said good-bye when my dive instructor—a six-foot-tall woman named Sonia who scared the crap out of me—ushered our class of eight to the gangway. Once on board the big, square-hulled boat, I stowed my gear on a bunk bed belowdecks and came back up to the galley for some breakfast: a cup of coffee, scrambled eggs, and a piece of toast. Tran, my dive buddy, motioned me over to his table. We smiled at each other and looked out the window. Tran was from Vietnam, but his limited English had never been an issue since we couldn't talk underwater, anyway.

A couple of other people from our class joined us. Others stayed in the bunks below, preferring to sleep through the two-hour ride to Catalina. If not for Michael, I probably would have done the same: the rolling of the waves made the boat feel like a big cradle. Instead, I kept my eyes on the galley door, swallowing with disappointment every time it opened and Michael didn't come in.

When the island loomed into view, I went out to the deck to get my wetsuit out of my new dive bag. It was a beautiful day, a sharp, clear blue. It was a nice temperature, too—about seventy degrees.

There were a lot of people out on the decks. Michael was near the front of the boat, leaning against the rail. I made my way over piles of bags until I reached him.

"Hey," I said.

He glanced at me briefly before returning his eyes to the horizon. "I saw you go into the galley. I was wondering when you'd come out."

Suddenly, my pleasure at seeing him turned to irritation. I was done playing games. "You were welcome to come in at any time," I snapped.

He shook his head, still not looking at me. "Can't."

"The breakfast is for everyone," I said. "Not just the students. There was coffee, bacon, eggs—"

"No!" he said. "Stop!"

"What?" He'd seemed so normal back on the dock.

"You're going to make me throw up."

"*Excuse me?*" And then I got it. "You're seasick!" I probably shouldn't have sounded so happy.

He nodded miserably.

"Does this happen every time?"

He nodded again. "Though usually not this bad. Some boats are steadier. And the waves aren't usually this big. As long as I stay outside and stare at the horizon, I'll be okay. And I'll be fine once I'm off the boat. Just, please. Don't talk about food."

I leaned my arms on the railing next to him. Farther back, I could see other ill-looking passengers. "Why do you do this, then—if it makes you sick?"

He shrugged. "Sometimes you have to suffer for what you love." He shot me a side glance. "And I do a lot of beach dives, even though they're usually not as good."

About twelve feet below us, the water foamed white where it met the hull. Soon, I'd be going overboard. "Where's the platform?" I asked.

"What platform?"

"Where you get off the boat?"

He motioned to a hinged spot in the railing a little way down from us. "There."

"We have to jump from all the way up here?" I said, panic creeping into my voice.

"You don't jump in," he said. "You just take a big step. Didn't you practice that in the pool?"

"Yeah, but that was a one-foot drop." I peered back down. Maybe it wasn't twelve feet. Maybe it was fifteen. Or twenty. It was a really long way down.

"You'll be fine," he said. "With the wetsuit on, there's no slapping or anything. It doesn't hurt at all."

The rest of my class appeared from the various corners of the boat. We dragged our bags to the open stern, where we sat on benches and wiggled into our wetsuits. Across the deck, Michael yanked on a suit with three different shades of blue for the arms, legs, and torso. I looked away before he could catch me staring.

The students were first in the water. Waddling over to my place in line (my tank was so heavy I couldn't stand up straight), I caught Michael's eye. "How come your clothes are all black but your wetsuits are colored? Isn't it usually the other way around?"

"That's the idea," he said, attaching his tank to his BCD and checking the valves. "When I first went into business, I figured that if I wore black when I went on sales calls, the wetsuits would pop even more. Eventually all I owned was black clothes. I guess I can buy colored stuff now, huh?"

"You don't have to. You look good in black." I pulled my mask up over my face so he couldn't see me blush.

He stood up and shrugged the BCD onto his back as if it weighed nothing. "Here." He put a hand under my tank, taking some of the weight.

"Thanks," I said, straightening.

"It's your turn," he said, looking toward the water.

And it was (so much for relief). Sonia, my dive instructor, stood at the railing, motioning me forward. The gate now open, there was only one small step between me and the icy Pacific.

"Fins on! Mouthpiece in! One hand over the mask, one hand over your chest!" Sonia barked.

I moved toward the edge, equally terrified of Sonia and the enormous drop. Michael held my elbow while I yanked on my flippers, and then he helped me up to the step. My flippers stuck out over the edge. My heart pounded. Without Michael holding it, the tank weighed heavily against my shoulders. I imagined losing my balance and tumbling face-first into the waves.

"One big step, and keep your tips up," Sonia said. "Just like we did in class."

I nodded shakily, mask and mouthpiece hiding my terror.

Michael stood at the railing right next to me. I gave him one last slightly desperate look. His mask hung around his neck, the copper ring around his brown eyes glinting in the early morning sun. Now that we were in a protected cove, the sea was calmer, and color had returned to his face.

"You were right, you know," he said, a little smile tugging at the corners of his mouth. It was a nice mouth: wide and well-defined, entirely masculine.

"Huh?" I asked through the mouthpiece, trying to read his expression and maintain my precarious balance at the same time.

"I was attracted to you. I still am."

At that, I lost my footing. The bottom dropped out and the ocean tumbled up until sea and sky met in a flash of blue and white. But my feet stayed down, and my head stayed up—and you know what?

It didn't hurt at all.